Batteries Required

A Samantha Shaw Mystery

Batteries Required

Jennifer Apodaca

KENSINGTON BOOKS
www.kensingtonbooks.com

KENSINGTON BOOKS are published by

Kensington Publishing Corp.
850 Third Avenue
New York, NY 10022

All Kensington titles, imprints and distributed lines are available at special quantity discounts for bulk purchases for sales promotion, premiums, fund-raising, educational or institutional use.

Special book excerpts or customized printing can also be created to fit specific needs. For details, write or phone the office of the Kensington Special Sales Manager: Kensington Publishing Corp., 850 Third Avenue, New York, NY 10022. Attn. Special Sales Department. Phone: 1-800-221-2647.

Kensington and the K logo Reg. U.S. Pat. & TM Off.

Library of Congress Card Catalogue Number: 2004110752
ISBN 0-7582-0451-5

First Printing: May 2005
10 9 8 7 6 5 4 3 2 1

Printed in the United States of America

Batteries Required

1

The slot machine tricked me. I dumped in my money, believing I'd win the big prize. The Daystar Indian Casino in Temecula, California, gleefully sucked up my last twenty-dollar bill and suggested, in that innocent way of machines, that I try again.

Probably I would have if I'd had any more cash on me. Since all I had remaining was my pride, I left the gambling area, swept past a long bar, and went into the Nova Room. I looked past the bathroom-size wooden dance floor in the center of the bar to see the band playing onstage, the Silky Men.

They were a group of men who cross-dressed and sang in a comic routine. One of them, Rick Mesa, was the head soccer coach for the Soccer Club of Lake Elsinore. I had found out about his secret life as a cross-dressing entertainer while working on a case earlier that year.

I'm not actually a private detective. I'm a romance expert. I own the Heart Mates Dating Service, which is what brought me to the Daystar Indian Casino that night. My best friend, Angel Crimson, had provided the lingerie for the Silky Men, and she promised to pass out flyers for the open house I was having for Heart Mates on Wednesday night.

We figured lonely people go to the casino looking for love and companionship, so maybe we could interest them in my dating service in Lake Elsinore. It was only about thirty miles or so from the casino. That's not too far to travel for love, now is it?

But Angel had forgotten to pick up the flyers I'd had made to take to the casino. That meant I had to bring them to her at the casino after work on a Friday night. I found Angel and joined her at one of the small tables ringing the dance floor. Her long red hair was shiny straight, and she wore a green satin top that matched her emerald-colored eyes. Underneath the table, her black micromini skirt showed off her long legs. Angel looked like she could model lingerie for Victoria's Secret, but she'd rather sell lingerie than model it.

She was there to get bookings for her Tempt-an-Angel Lingerie line, which she sold through home parties. Sort of like Tupperware, only a hell of a lot more fun. At some point during their set, the lead singer for the Silky Men, Rick, would mention that their lingerie was provided by Tempt-an-Angel Lingerie. I don't know how, given that the band were men dressed up as women, but several women usually booked parties off that sales pitch. Go figure.

After ordering a glass of water, I pulled the stack of brochures promoting my open house out of my purse and slid them across the table. Then I asked, "Are you coming back here tomorrow night? Don't forget, I'm coming over to your house Sunday morning to pick up the couch." Angel was giving me a brown leather couch for the waiting area in Heart Mates. That couch would be a big step up from the metal folding chairs that I currently used.

Angel glanced down at the brochures. "I decided to get a room and stay the night, instead of driving back and forth." Then she looked up. "Why don't you stay with me? It'll be fun!"

Tempting, but . . . "I'm going to paint Heart Mates tomorrow, so I have to get up early. I want to have it all ready for the open house Wednesday night."

Angel ran her fingers down the length of her Cosmopolitan glass. "Damn, we could have heated up the place and set off the sprinklers." She grinned. "There's a rumor that a promoter might be here tonight or Saturday night, so I might be really late getting home tomorrow night. Make it ten or so on Sunday morning to pick up the couch."

Leaning forward, I said, "A promoter? To see Rick's group? That's great for them! And who knows, maybe it'll be good for your lingerie line, too." I shook my head at the way things were turning out for us. "When we made our pact to find our careers, I didn't quite imagine this for you." Angel and I had had a little party one night a couple of years ago, fueled by margaritas, where we acknowledged that we'd both married losers and had no lives. We had vowed to change that. I had found my career in Heart Mates. Angel had taken a little longer, but now she was working hard to build her lingerie line.

"Good evening, ladies."

Angel and I both looked to my right to see a doppelgänger for Richard Gere. Thin silver streaks ran through his wavy dark hair. Shaped brows over brown eyes, elegant face, and nicely draped suit—this man should have been on a private European island. He carried an expensive-looking briefcase.

Angel recovered before me. "Hello," she held out her hand, "I'm Angel."

He reached for her hand, and I swear to God, I thought he was going to kiss it. But instead, he smiled, revealing a row of white teeth. "Ah, the very woman I was searching for. I have been hearing very good things about you and your business venture. My name is Mitch St. Claire."

Angel took her hand back. "Really? And where would you have heard about me?"

"In the high-stakes gaming room. It appears you have made quite an impression on several future clients."

When had I become invisible? "Ahem."

Angel glanced at me. "This is Sam." She picked up a flyer from the stack in front of her. "Sam owns the Heart Mates Dating Service. You might be interested in attending the open house Wednesday night. She'll be serving wines from the Temecula wineries."

He turned to fix the full weight of his gaze on me. "Sam? Short for Samantha? Quite a lovely name."

I held out my hand. "I usually go by Sam." I just have a need to be contrary.

He wrapped his fingers around my palm. "I believe I may have heard of you. Perhaps you've been in the newspaper?"

Every time I stumbled onto a dead body, I ended up in the newspaper. Usually it wasn't a flattering article. I decided not to mention that. "Perhaps you've heard of my dating service, Heart Mates?" I glanced down at the flyer Angel had slid over to him.

He let go of my hand. "Perhaps. May I join you ladies?"

"Sure," Angel said.

I stifled a yawn. It had been a long week, and I wanted to get home to have ice cream with my two sons, TJ and Joel. I'd had a fast dinner with them, but there was never enough time.

Mitch pulled over a chair from another table and sat between us. He set down his briefcase and fixed his gaze on Angel. "I wanted to meet with you, Angel, to discuss a business proposition."

Angel sipped her Cosmopolitan and said, "What would that be, Mitch?"

She was mildly flirting. I wondered if she was interested in Mitch the man, his business proposition, or both? It had been a while since Angel had had a boyfriend. Stalking her ex-husband tended to cut down on her time for a social life.

"I'm in distribution and thought you might be interested in offering some of my merchandise through your home parties."

Trent Shaw popped into my head. "My dead husband was in distribution. He sold condoms." He had also sold coke sealed up in those condoms.

Mitch cut his brown eyes toward me. "Condoms have their place, certainly. But these products are of a more . . . ah . . . personal nature."

"More personal than condoms?" He had my interest now. Highly curious, I leaned forward.

"Actually, a little more embarrassing for some people to buy." Mitch turned to look at Angel. "That's why you sell your lingerie through home parties, right? To make it a fun, nonjudgmental atmosphere. A woman might not be comfortable buying overtly sexy lingerie at the mall, but at a home party where she can make her selections privately, she's more comfortable."

Angel flashed her brilliant smile. "I see you've done your homework, Mitch."

He nodded. "So why not take it a step further? What are the chances of these women going to the mall to buy sex toys?"

I blinked and took a drink of my water. *Sex toys?* "You

mean like fur-lined handcuffs and vibrators?" That was the full extent of my knowledge of sex toys. And none of that was from personal experience. I'd read about the fur-lined handcuffs in a romance book I reviewed for *Romance Rocks Magazine.*

"Precisely. I can offer a very nice selection at wholesale prices. But today, what I'd like to do is give you a sample kit and a catalogue so that you can see for yourself what I have to offer."

I choked and had to slap my hand over my nose to keep water from spewing out. Tears filled my eyes. Mitch looked over at me. "Does this make you uncomfortable, Sam?"

His slightly condescending tone sparked my instant denial. Through my fingers, I said, "Of course not." *Liar!* If I had taken my hand off my nose, it would have grown two inches. Vibrators! Omigod! What would my boyfriend, Gabe, say about that?

Like I didn't know.

Angel looked as calm and cool as if she were discussing vacuum cleaners or stock prices. "So you have a sample kit of your merchandise? Is it with you or would you like to send it to me?"

"I have it with me." He lifted his leather briefcase off the floor.

Oh boy, he wasn't going to, like, pull a big vibrator out and set it on the table, was he?

"Sam, is that you?" A familiar voice called out.

I whipped my head around. Uh-oh. "Linda, hello. What brings you out here tonight?" Linda Simpkins! The president of the PTA. My arms started to itch with hot, burning hives. I could just see it all over the PTA: *Samantha Shaw Investigating Sex Toys at the Daystar Casino.* As if I didn't get talked about enough, what with having myself augmented to a perky C cup, buying a dating service, and dating a hot PI five years younger than I was.

Linda stopped at my right shoulder. "It's our anniversary. Archie and I are staying here for the weekend. Angel, we ran into your ex-husband in the bar. Didn't see his wife anywhere."

Angel drained her glass. "Any chance he was dead when you saw him?"

Linda's eyes widened. "No, of course not."

"Then I'm not interested." Angel signaled for another drink.

I watched her for a second. Something had happened between Angel and Hugh. I'd find out what that was later. I looked over at Linda to see her studying Mitch. Oh crap, the sex toys! But thankfully, Mitch had set his briefcase back on the floor. Quickly, I said, "Linda, this is Mitch St. Claire. He and Angel are discussing some business."

Linda turned and smiled. "You do find the most interesting company, Sam. Well, I'd better be going! Bye now."

My hives calmed as she walked away. That had been really close. About the only person that could show up who would be more embarrassing than Linda would be my mother. But she and Angel's mom were safely tucked away on a cruise ship.

"As I was saying, I have this sample kit," Mitch leaned down and opened his briefcase.

I looked at Angel.

She shrugged.

We both turned back to watch Mitch pull out what looked like an oversize cigar box. It was covered in a blue velvet material with a white satin bow on top.

I breathed a huge sigh. OK. I could deal with this just as long as he didn't open that box.

Mitch slid the box to Angel. "I have placed a catalogue

inside that has all my contact information printed on it. Once you've had a chance to examine the items, let me know if you are interested."

I stared at the blue velvet box with its creamy white ribbon. Now, when he said "examined," did he mean "look at?" "Touch?" "Test?" Oh boy, I was losing it.

Angel pulled her hand painted straw purse into her lap, opened it, and dug inside. She came up with a business card and handed it to Mitch. "You can contact me at that phone number if you require your sample kit back before I call you."

Mitch took the card, then smiled. The smile reached his eyes. "The sample kit is yours to keep." He slipped the card into his briefcase and stood up. "I look forward to hearing from you, Angel." Then he made a point of picking up the flyer for the open house and studying it before looking at me. "Sam, very nice to meet you. I'm quite intrigued by your dating service."

Hmm, did he think I'd sell sex toys at Heart Mates? I fought hard to work a controlled smile onto my face. "Nice to meet you, Mitch."

Angel and I waited until he was out of sight before we broke into laughter. Finally, I managed to say, "Sex toys? What do you think is in there?" I stared at the box.

Her green eyes sparkled. "One way to find out." She reached for the box.

"Don't open it here!"

She laughed and slid the box across the table. "I'm not going to. You're going to take it home and not open it. Bring it over on Sunday when you come to get the couch. Once the guys get the couch loaded up and leave, we'll open it.

I looked down at the box and noticed that there was a paper seal that would be broken once it was opened. Well,

I guess that was some kind of sanitary thing, like the paper they put over toilets in hotel rooms to assure the incoming patron the toilet had been cleaned. What the heck, it'd be fun. Reaching for the box, I said, "It's a date."

I wondered if painting was a fat-burning exercise. Because if it was, I must have burned off five pounds painting my office. What a way to spend a Saturday. I stepped back to the middle of the small reception area of Heart Mates to take a look. I had rag-painted a pale cinnamon color over the vanilla base that my two teenage sons and my assistant, Blaine, had rolled onto the walls.

It looked good. Painting over the blue-speckled cubical wall, which gave me the illusion of an office, had turned out better than I had thought. As long as I didn't look up to the water-stained ceiling tiles or down to the wafer-thin, worn shiny, steel gray carpet, the place was looking good. Professional even.

Looking back to the reception area, I thought of the empty suite on the other side of that wall. If only I could afford to lease that suite and remove the wall. That'd be progress! But Heart Mates wasn't that big yet. I could barely afford the lease on this small, run-down suite. Still, the paint was an improvement and the open house was going to help fill out my client list.

"Painting, huh?"

Startled, I whirled around. In the open doorway of Heart Mates stood a woman holding a large box of See's candy. I recognized the sleek black box—truffles. I loved truffles. I tore my gaze from the candy and headed toward her. "Uh, yes. Heart Mates is closed today." I fixed a professional smile on my paint-splattered face. My old shorts and tight black T-shirt probably didn't convey a real business-like impression.

She stepped into the office, meeting me halfway. "I can see you are busy, but I'll just take a moment. I wanted to give you these." She held out the box of truffles.

I felt my thighs thicken just from looking at the candy box. Trying to ignore the chocolates, I studied her face and thought there might be some Cuban ancestors swimming in her gene pool. Large brown eyes set deep into a strong face and lots of black hair. She wasn't pretty, exactly. My impression was, *forceful.* As much as I loved chocolate truffles, I couldn't think of a reason why a woman I didn't know was giving them to me. "I'm not sure I understand."

"I'm Zoë Cash. I read your reviews in *Romance Rocks Magazine* all the time. You mention chocolate truffles sometimes, so I guessed you liked them."

Surreal weirdness mixed with the paint fumes. It was true that I wrote reviews of romance novels for *Romance Rocks Magazine.* Occasionally I got mail, either telling me what a no-taste bonehead I was or agreeing with my reviews. But so far, no one had ever tracked me down and brought me chocolates. I dropped my gaze to the box she held out. What if . . . they were poisoned? What if she was a writer I wrote a less than glowing review for and she was trying to kill me?

Stop it, I told myself. My husband, Trent, had died of a peanut allergy from eating peanut-butter-laced chocolate candy his mistress had made for him. So I was a little skittish about unexplainable gifts of chocolate. But murder seemed unlikely. "Zoë, nice to meet you. That's very kind of you to bring me chocolates, but I'm not supposed to accept gifts like this for reviews that I write." That sounded good. Who knew if it was true; I'd never been in this situation before.

"Oh well, this isn't for a review you wrote." Zoë held the

box in one hand, and gestured with the other. "I just knew that you'd understand."

OK, that line never brought good news. It usually meant that someone was in trouble and thought I could help. Once in a while, I did a little private investigating under my PI boyfriend's license. But this woman felt a little . . . *off* . . . to me. "Maybe you should make an appointment for when we are open, Zoë."

She shook her head. "Don't you see? When I found out that you owned a dating service named Heart Mates, I knew you were destined to help me." She waved her hand back and forth. "Help me find my heart mate."

Relief sagged through me. She wasn't a nut. She was lonely and wanted to sign up for one of our dating packages. Paint fumes were making me paranoid. I gestured around the office, "I can't sign you up today, since everything is a mess, but I'd be happy to get you all signed up Monday morning. In fact," I started around my assistant's sheet-covered desk. He always had a set of sign-up sheets attached to clipboards tucked into a drawer. "I can give you the paperwork to take home and fill out." I leaned over to pull open the bottom drawer.

"But I already know who my heat mate is. I don't need your dating service, Samantha."

I shut the drawer to the desk and stood up empty-handed. "Zoë, I'm not sure I understand what it is you want from me." I was hoping it wasn't something that was going to end up with me bleeding. Uneasiness curled inside of me again. But my sons and Blaine would be back any second. They had gone to the liquor store to buy some sodas, then grab something out of my car for me.

She sighed and blew a thick strand of hair out of her face. "My heart mate is R.V. Logan."

Omigod. R. V. Logan was the pen name of a local homicide detective who kept his romance writing a secret. Hot little giggles danced up my throat and tugged at my mouth. I fought it down. "R.V. Logan? The romance writer? She's—"

Zoë wasn't having any of that. "I heard at a romance convention that R. V. Logan is a man!"

Oh Lord, Detective Vance was not going to like this. On the other hand, I loved it! Vance was so arrogant, so sure no one would find out he wrote romances under a pen name. And his comeuppance stood right here in my dating service. The trouble was, I had a complicated relationship with Vance. I couldn't afford to piss him off. I stalled for time. "I don't really see what that has to do with me."

Zoë sighed. "You review all his books, so you must know where he lives. I want you to give me his address. I'll do the rest."

Oh, boy. This woman had to be a nut to assume I knew R. V. Logan's address. It was time to get rid of her. "Zoë, I review lots of romance novels, but they are sent to me by the author's publisher. I don't know where any of the authors live." But I did know where R. V. Logan worked—a couple of miles away, at the Lake Elsinore Police and Sheriff's station. I thought I should keep that detail to myself.

Anger stiffened Zoë's shoulders. "I don't believe you. Why won't you help me? I brought you these truffles."

Cripes. "Listen, Zoë, I—"

"Mom! We got the pillows, but what's this? Is it a present? Can I open it?"

I looked past Zoë to see Joel bounce through the door holding . . .

Uh-oh. Joel held the blue velvet box tied with the creamy ribbon. What if he opened it? Joel was only thirteen! I didn't want him to see what was in that box! Sex toys. How would I explain that? I'd purposely kept that hidden in the trunk of my T-bird so the boys wouldn't stumble across it. I rushed over to him. "Joel! That's . . . uh, Angel's. Here, let me have it."

Joel's blue eyes widened in surprise when I snatched it from his hands.

TJ walked in behind his brother, carrying two blue throw pillows. "Where do you want these pillows, Mom?" His serious face tightened in teenage disgust as he glanced down at the embroidered pillows, then back up at me. "They are kind of lame."

Still caught in the sex-toy panic, it took me a second to focus on TJ. He was holding the pillows, which were embroidered with *Get Hitched With Heart Mates*, and *Get Hot With Heart Mates*. "Grandpa had those made, TJ. He was trying to help with my refurbishing." The velvet box felt like a big neon sign in my hands that read SEX TOYS. I had to hide it. "Set those pillows under the sheet on Blaine's desk."

I turned and headed through a door into the freshly painted interview room to a second door that led to the storage room. I flipped on the light switch and looked around. Where was a good place to hide this box? The small bathroom to the right? No. Hey, the filing cabinets. We were mostly computerized, thanks to my assistant. I rushed to a filing cabinet and stuffed the velvet-covered box deep into a middle drawer. Relieved, I turned around.

Zoë stood behind me. "I know he's my heart mate. You have to help me."

A low throb beat at my temples. "I can't help you, Zoë. I know you probably came a long way, plus there's the trouble you went to in finding me." Where had she come from? She wore black yoga pants, a white T-shirt, and a short zip-up black jacket. Taller than my five foot five in heels, she looked strong. Yoga-strong.

She smiled, crinkling her brown eyes. "It wasn't that hard. You seem to be in the newspapers a lot."

There was that. "Look, maybe this R. V. Logan isn't who you think. Maybe by searching R. V. Logan down, you are missing out on finding your real heart mate."

Zoë adjusted the zipper on her jacket and looked around the storage area. "That your bathroom? Mind if I use it?"

"Sure." Anything to change the subject from R. V. Logan/Detective Logan Vance.

Zoë disappeared into the bathroom and shut the door. "Boss?"

Blaine appeared in the doorway. For painting, he had shed his customary blue button-down work shirt to reveal a white undershirt. He still looked like the car mechanic he had been when I recruited him to come work for me. "I got you a Diet Coke, and there's some chips and onion dip." He gestured his thumb toward the bathroom door. "Who's that?"

I walked past Blaine and said, "She just showed up. She believes that R. V. Logan, the romance writer, is a man and her heart mate. She also believes that I know where R. V. Logan lives because I review all his books."

"No shit?" Blaine followed me out into the reception area. "What did you tell her?"

I shrugged. "Told her I didn't know where he lived. That his publisher sends me the books."

TJ and Joel had spread out the chips and dip on the sheet covering Blaine's desk. The box of truffles sat unopened next to the bag of chips. TJ said, "Mom, that lady said we could have this candy. But I thought we should check with you."

I smiled at TJ. "If they are sealed, go ahead and open them, TJ." Let's be logical. I doubted Zoë would poison us with truffles if she wanted information from me.

"Here, Mom," Joel handed me a can of Diet Coke.

"Thanks, Joel."

Zoë came out from the bathroom. "Samantha, take a day to think about it. I know R. V. Logan is my heart mate, and once you realize that, you'll see that giving me his real name and address is the right thing to do." She stared hard at me, as if willing me to do what she wanted.

Her eyes were a darker brown than mine were. "Zoë, I'd like to help you, I really would. But I just don't know where R. V. Logan lives. Maybe if it's meant to be, you should look for book signings that R. V. Logan will be appearing at or something like that."

She shook her head. "You know he doesn't do those. He only signs stock at the distribution centers. No, Samantha, you are going to have to help me." She fixed her stare on me for another ten seconds, then said, "I'll be in touch." She turned and walked out.

"Mom," TJ said, "she's whacked."

I looked at my oldest son. He was growing more and more to resemble his good-looking dad every day. Fortunately, his character was nothing like Trent's. "Whacked? That fits. Pass me those truffles." I figured I'd better taste-test them just to be on the safe side.

Joel handed me the box. "Mom, you should really think about going into private investigating full-time. This romance stuff is dumb."

2

Sunday morning brought a whole new batch of aches from all the painting at Heart Mates. But the thought of the sex-toy kit got me out of bed. After a long hot shower, I pulled on a pair of black shorts, a white T-shirt, and a short, lightweight zip-up jacket. Layered to take off as I spent the day cleaning and finishing up at Heart Mates.

But first, I would meet Gabe at Angel's house. We'd get the couch onto his truck and he'd take it to Heart Mates, where Blaine would help him unload it. Then Angel and I would have a few minutes to see just what went into a sex-toy kit.

After breakfast with the boys, I headed to Angel's house. I was early; it was about 9:30 when I turned down the tree-lined street that wove through the hills looking over the lake for which the city of Lake Elsinore was named. Bright sunshine had dissipated the last of the morning fog, making for another beautiful spring day.

I pulled into Angel's driveway and parked the car. Gabe wasn't there yet. Hey, maybe we would have time to look through the sex-toy kit first. I had it stored deep in the *Romance Rocks* tote bag that I was using as a purse that day.

Getting out of my car, I looked at Angel's closed garage door. She must have parked her car in there when she got in the night before. I headed up the flagstone path to the wrought-iron gate that led to the atrium. Lots of plants and flowers in brightly colored clay pots were set around a wrought-iron table and cushioned chairs. Angel had a green thumb.

I did great with silk plants myself.

Smiling, I headed to the front door and knocked.

After a full minute of listening to some birds chirping in the distance and wondering about the mysterious sex-toy kit, I knocked again. Finally, I dug my keys out of the tote bag. I'd known Angel since high school, and knew she was a very sound sleeper.

Once I had my keys, I selected Angel's silver house key and slid it into the dead bolt. I turned it left and used my left shoulder to push open the door. Walking in, I shouted, "Time to get up, Angel!"

I had the door half-closed when I got a good look at the living room. The wood floors were littered with glamour and lingerie magazines, couch cushions, books, and more. The big custom-built entertainment center's doors hung open, spilling out DVDs, CDs, and . . .

It was all too much for my brain to identify.

Cripes, had Angel's house been burglarized while she was at Daystar? Had she called the cops when she got home the night before? And how had she managed to get to sleep knowing this mess waited for her when she got up?

But if someone had broken in, why hadn't they taken her flat screen TV? I could see it in the middle of the entertainment center.

Something was really wrong here. Angel would have called me if her house had been broken into. But Angel wasn't a slob like this, either. Hugging my tote bag close to my body, I stepped over pillows and magazines to head toward the hallway, which opened on the right of the living room.

"Angel?" I called out, then jumped at a creak. *Stop it,* I thought. It was just the old house groaning. There was lots of beautiful wood molding around the floors and ceilings that probably contributed to creaks. I turned left down the hallway toward Angel's bedroom.

Aware that Angel wasn't answering me, I felt a tight band of uneasiness forming around my chest. I stopped dead in the doorway of her bedroom.

Her beautiful jade green comforter and matching sheets were torn off the bed and thrown into a pile on the floor. Her dresser and nightstand had gaping black holes where the drawers had been ripped out and thrown on the ground. The king-size mattress listed halfway off the box spring.

"Angel?" It came out a whisper. Where was she? She didn't appear to be in the bedroom. I backed up, my heart thumping. I couldn't breathe. Prickles of sharp dread skittered up my spine like dozens of spider legs and slammed into the base of my skull.

Where was Angel?

She wasn't in the bed. I looked back at the pile of sheets. What if . . . ?

Awful thoughts and horrible images pelted my brain, making my head swim. I forced my tennis-shoe-clad feet to move into the bedroom toward the sheets piled at the bottom of the bed. I felt like I was watching myself on video or something. I saw myself bend over and grab a handful of the sheets and the comforter.

Did I want to know what was under that pile?

I had to know. I lifted up the edges of the pile.

Relief felt like a balloon releasing all its air. My lungs

just let go. Nothing. I had dreaded finding Angel crumpled up under the pile of bedding. Maybe Angel wasn't there. Maybe she had never come home from Daystar. I started to drop the covers, thinking that I should call the police, when I spotted something else.

A purse. Angel's hand painted straw purse, which I had seen her with at Daystar on Friday night. I picked up the purse and stared at it in my hand. If the purse was there, then Angel had to have come home from Daystar. I couldn't reason it out. If she had been home, where was she now? I opened the purse and looked inside. Lipsticks, business cards, cell phone, hair spray, but no wallet. Where was Angel's wallet?

A creaky sound snapped through the house like a bullet. Fear rushed through my head, making it hard to think. *Stupid, stupid!* I just walked on through the house, never thinking about what I might be walking into. What if whoever had caused all this destruction was still there? I should have called 911 when I first saw the living room.

Another creak popped.

I had to get out of there and call the police. I turned toward the bedroom door and started walking, easing one foot in front of the other until I got to the hallway. I stopped to listen. Past the doorway to the living room, there was a bathroom and two more bedrooms.

Did I hear something? Leaning toward the living room opening, I strained to listen. I didn't hear anything, except my own fear pulsing in my ears. Crap. For lack of a better plan, I thought about darting into the living room and then running right out the front door.

But what if Angel was down the hallway in her office? Or in the kitchen? Or the garage? She could be hurt and need help.

I leaned my forehead against the cool wall and tried to

get my thoughts in order. Angel would not leave me if I were in danger. Angel was fearless.

I was going to have to be fearless, too. "Damn," I muttered under my breath. Lifting my head, I listened. I could feel a slight breeze from where I'd left the front door open.

That was probably the creaking I'd heard—the front door moving in the breeze.

Not any braver, but determined to make sure Angel wasn't in the house, I leaned around to look into the living room. I didn't see anyone.

Quickly, I ran lightly across the opening to the bathroom on the left. I looked in to see the full bath, which was done up in black and copper. With a shower curtain that was closed and probably hiding a cloned monster that was a cross between Hannibal Lector and Norman Bates.

God, I needed to get a grip. Easing into the bathroom, I walked over the mess of towels and packaged toothbrushes, soaps, shampoos, and other oddities that Angel kept in there. Someone had dumped everything in the bathroom onto the floor and pawed through it.

I was getting pissed. Who had been going through Angel's things? Anger overrode my fear, and I reached for the copper and black shower curtain. Holding my breath, I slid it back on the plastic holders.

An empty bathtub and shower.

Thank God. Quickly, I turned and headed down to the guest bedroom on the left. No Angel. But the messy bandits had been in there too, ripping the royal blue comforter off the double bed. Turning, I went to the last room at the front of the house, which Angel used as an office.

What had been an organized office now looked like a volcanic eruption of lingerie. All the carefully hung pieces had been torn off the freestanding rod and *dismembered.*

Bits of black silk, shreds of white lace, hunks of red satin, all tossed one way and another. The brown leather couch had a box of destroyed panties and bras dumped on it.

My stomach turned liquid. There was something—not sexual, but enraged—in the destruction. Intentionally ruined, torn, or—

I saw the knife. Angel's butcher knife, the black hilt sticking up out of the back of the brown leather couch. The couch I was supposed to pick up and take to Heart Mates.

But that wasn't what pulled me into the room. It was the kitchen towel lying on the couch that did it. A dish towel that had baby bunnies stealing carrots on it. Only one carrot wasn't orange. It was reddish rust.

Blood. Dried or drying blood.

My heart hammered. The room swayed. The walls creaked.

Time to get out of the house. Now. I spun around and raced out of the room, down the hall, and out to the living room. I didn't look left or right, I just headed for the front door.

The memory of the kitchen towel hit me hard. I skidded to a stop before I reached the front door, my lungs bursting with panic.

The dish towel was from the kitchen. I looked past Angel's brand new couch, now torn apart, to the swinging door that led to her kitchen.

Trapped in a nightmare, I had no choice but to go into that kitchen. The kitchen knife and the blood on the towel from the kitchen propelled me. Was Angel in the kitchen? Was it her blood? I picked my way around couch cushions, DVDs, books, and other stuff toward the white swinging doors trimmed in green.

I pushed through the doors and took a step into the

kitchen. My shoe slid on the wet wood floor. Windmilling my arms, I managed to get my footing and looked down.

Red liquid? My mind tried to push it away, to deny what I was seeing, when the broken bottle and the pungent smell registered. Not blood, but red wine.

It was only wine spilled on the floor. From Angel's wine rack. I looked around. The wide kitchen had a wine rack and a kitchen table on the right. Glass-fronted cabinets over a sink and a stove on the left. The fridge was behind me. Straight ahead at the end of the kitchen, the door to the backyard hung open. Had it been forced open?

I couldn't worry about that at that moment; I had to find Angel. She wasn't in the kitchen.

My feet felt like lead, but I went back out to the living room. I had one more place to check. The garage. If Angel's car was gone, then maybe she had left on her own, gotten away.

She could have been at the police station right then, filing a report about a break-in. The garage door was behind the half-open front door. I slipped up behind it and put my hand on the knob.

Turning it, I pushed open the door and flicked on the garage lights.

Angel's fire red Trans Am gleamed under the overhead light. I peered into the passenger window, desperately hoping to see Angel sitting in there, anything to make this whole nightmare OK.

Instead, I saw the reflection of a big man standing behind me, holding a gun in his hand. I leaped into the garage and slammed the door with all my strength.

The door bounced back, hit me in the ass, and knocked me over the hood of Angel's car. My tote bag hit the ground and dumped out its contents.

I shoved off the car and turned, thinking to get to the button that would open the big garage door. I came face-to-chest with Gabe Pulizzi.

Panting, I forced my gaze up his T-shirt-covered chest, past the hard-cut Italian face up to his dark eyes. "You scared the hell out of me."

He arched a single eyebrow. "You're damn lucky it's me and not whoever trashed the house."

"Angel's not here—" Something registered in my memory. I dropped my gaze to Gabe's right hand. He had his gun. Gabe had a license to carry his gun, along with his PI license. But he normally didn't walk around with it. In fact, he usually kept it locked in the glove box of his truck when he was out.

Which meant he'd gone back to his truck and gotten his gun.

It hit me hard, and I forced myself to say what we were both thinking. "Angel's been kidnapped."

It was pretty standard to separate witnesses.

In this case, I thought maybe it might be more a power play than from any real need to keep our information pure. Detective Logan Vance of Robbery/Homicide had me wait in the atrium while he walked through the house with Gabe. I understood the reasoning. After all, Gabe was the trained cop.

I was sure the whole scene of Vance kissing me in front of Gabe last January, and the fight that followed, had nothing to do with Vance's decision to separate us and leave me sitting outside worrying.

I sighed. What difference did it make? All I cared about was finding Angel. I'd do anything to find her safe. I didn't have a sister, but I imagined Angel and I had that same connection, that sharing of a life. Angel had the ability to make me a better person than I was. If I wanted to ignore a problem, she'd make me face it.

And I'd do the same for her, make her face her fears. But Angel had only one horrible fear—dying alone.

My eyes filled and burned. She'd clung to Hugh Crimson, her worthless ex-husband, in order to have a baby. Most people thought his betrayal of Angel by screwing her manicurist was what had sent Angel on her mission of revenge.

Most people were wrong. Mostly wrong, anyway. Angel had been royally pissed off about that. But the real reason, the deepest reason, was that Hugh Crimson had lied to Angel about his ability to father a child. One of his manipulations had been to have a lab report changed to show he had a normal sperm count, when he was shooting blanks.

He had led Angel on for years, saying that they would have a baby together.

Because he knew that Angel did not want to die childless and alone.

When Angel had found out about that, the gloves came off and she decided to pay Hugh back for the years of emotional torture.

Sure, a psychiatrist might say that Angel was stalking and tormenting Hugh to avoid her own pain. But they'd be wrong. Angel was working through it. She kept moving forward, building a life with her lingerie company. She had lots of friends, and she'd accepted that she might not have her own kids. But she'd always have my two sons. They loved her more than they would have loved an aunt. She didn't have to worry about dying alone.

God. What if she was—

A noise saved me from finishing that thought. Detective Vance came out the front door. The sun shone down on him, catching the highlights in his ruthlessly short blond hair. His brown eyes were flat and grim. No dimples showed in his hard, square face. His swimmer shoulders were tight under his gray jacket. He watched me for a minute before walking over and sitting in the wrought-iron chair.

"Shaw."

"Vance." Our uneasy history, and my own unstable emotions, kept me cautious. "What do you know about this? Where's Angel?"

He shook his head and sighed. "I don't know, Shaw. There's no note. No sign of a ransom demand. Her mother is out of town?"

"On a cruise with my mother. I don't know if I should call her. What would I say? She's in the middle of the ocean—what can she do?" I hated feeling so out of control.

"Let us get a handle on the situation before you scare her mother. There's nothing she can do from the ship to help us right now."

"Nothing she can do?" My blood pressure shot up. "Angel is her daughter!"

Vance remained deadpan. "How do you feel right now, Shaw? Sitting here, waiting and not knowing. Why would you do that to Angel's mom? Wait until you have something concrete to tell her."

Damn it, he was right. I struggled to get my blood pressure and emotions under control. Once, I had gone to a yoga class with Angel, and supposedly, breathing was the key. I breathed.

I still felt like smacking Vance, but that was a step up from wanting to grab his gun and shoot him. "Fine, now what? Did you see the knife, and the blood on that dish towel? Her purse is here and so is her car. Someone kidnapped Angel. Are you going to call the FBI?" Crap, I was forgetting to breathe.

Vance hauled his little notebook out of his shirt pocket.

"We don't know that she was kidnapped, Shaw. What you see in that house might have been due to a lovers' quarrel, and they went off to Palm Springs to make up."

I wanted to shoot him again. Taking in a breath to send calming oxygen to all those angry cells, I struggled to be reasonable. "She didn't walk out of that house on her own. What are you going to do about it?"

His jaw twitched, and then he uncapped his Bic pen. "Let's start with what you know. Tell me where you last saw Angel."

That gave me something constructive to focus on. "Angel went to Daystar Casino, where the Silky Men were performing." Vance wrote as I summed up what I knew about Angel's visit to Daystar.

Vance looked up when I stopped talking. "She took her car to Daystar?"

"Yes. And that purse in her bedroom. I saw her with it Friday night. That's when we made the plans to meet here this morning."

Vance grimaced. "That would be the purse you picked up and rifled through on your trek through all my evidence?"

I winced, knowing how particular cops were about evidence. "I was looking for her, Vance. What if she'd been in the house and hurt?" I looked down at the frosted beveled glass top of the wrought-iron table.

He ignored my question. "Angel was here after you saw her at Daystar. When did she say she would be coming home?"

"After the Silky Men's set last night. She would have checked out of her room earlier and left her stuff in the car. Then watched the performance and come home sometime late last night. Maybe even early this morning."

He nodded and wrote. "Did she say she ran into any problems at the casino?"

"No." Angel was a beautiful and outgoing woman. Who would want to hurt her? I ran my finger over the beveled glass, feeling each cold bump. "Stuff like this doesn't happen. She can't just disappear."

Vance sighed and leaned back in the cushioned chair. "Has she ever done anything like this before?"

I glared at him. "You mean trashed her own house, then hailed a taxi and hid away while everyone was worried sick about her?" I did not want to believe this. It was easier to be angry with Vance than to believe something had happened to Angel. Where was she? Was she scared right now? Tied up? Hurt . . . or dead? *Stop it*, I told myself. I would not fall apart. I had to hold it together and think.

His jaw twitched, then settled. "This could be two separate events. What I meant was, is it possible that Angel went somewhere with someone and didn't tell you? Then her house was broken into?"

I narrowed my gaze. "You mean like she blew me off for some hotbody she met at the casino and took off to Hawaii?"

His mouth thinned. "Yes."

I shrugged, the anger washing out. Angel was Angel. She could be unpredictable, but . . . "I don't think so. She takes her lingerie business too seriously to up and disappear. We had a plan to meet this morning so I could pick up the couch." The one with a butcher knife in it. A shudder rolled up my spine, but I went on, "And I know she had booked a party or two for her Tempt-an-Angel Lingerie. She'd have come home to get the details arranged. Or at the very least, have her cell phone with her to do her business. She has both her landline and cell number on her business cards."

Vance nodded. "OK, we'll move on. What about problems? Has she gotten on the wrong side of anyone?"

"Her ex-husband," I muttered. I hadn't remembered to

ask Angel about Hugh at Daystar. When Linda had mentioned Hugh was there, I'd seen the look of disgust on Angel's face. "Angel was mad at him about something Friday night but I don't know what."

Vance looked at his notes. "Hugh Crimson, correct? He's sworn out a complaint in the past about her stalking him."

"It came to nothing." Mainly because the police liked Angel and detested Hugh.

Vance fixed his brown gaze on me. "Nothing, huh? Angel has some very high tech tracking equipment in her house."

I shrugged. "She collects stuff. It's a hobby."

"Shaw, I'm trying to get a picture here. Could her ex-husband have had something to do with this?"

It wasn't the time to worry about defending Angel. She could be in real danger. I tried to picture Hugh having something to do with the state of Angel's house. "Maybe . . . he's not that bright. He might trash her house, and he used to live here when they were married, so he'd have that going for him. But doing something physically to Angel?" I shook my head, I just couldn't see it. "Hugh's a coward; I can't see him dragging her out of the house."

"I'll talk to him, and his wife," he looked down at his notes, "Brandi."

"What else?"

Vance shut his notebook, and leaned his arms on the table. "I'm going to investigate, Shaw. I'm going to find Angel. I already told you I'd talk to her ex-husband. I'll call Daystar to find out when she checked out of her room, and the last time anyone saw her. I'll find out if she filed any complaints while there. I'll talk to Rick Mesa from the Silky Men. I may need you for more information, but I'll find her."

I watched his face. "*We'll* find her."

The silence stretched. Noise filtered out from the house, the sounds of police work. Birds chirped from the trees on the street. A car drove by. "Look, Shaw, I know she's your friend and you are worried—"

I held up my hand. "Do you know that Angel's biggest fear is dying alone with no one caring? No? Well, I do, Vance, and I'm not going to leave her out there alone." I stood up and walked away. I had to get home to my sons. They loved Angel and would be devastated.

Then I was going to find my best friend.

I just hoped I found her alive.

3

Gabe stood against my T-bird, which was parked on Angel's driveway. A cop-on-the-street expression stamped down hard on his face, leaving his eyes watchful and his mouth tight. He had his arms crossed over his chest, waiting. Patient, but ready.

Like a street fighter. Used to danger he couldn't quite see but a sixth sense warned him was there.

I'd bet Heart Mates that right then, his sixth sense was sending out warnings. "Gabe, what do you think happened to Angel?"

He uncrossed his arms, reached out, and tugged me to him. "I wish I knew, babe. The house looks tossed and searched by someone who was getting progressively pissed off. If Angel did drugs, I'd think she screwed a dealer."

I stiffened and looked up at his face. "You sound just like Vance. Blaming Angel, and she's the victim!"

"I know Angel's clean. But she might have crossed the path of someone who isn't clean by accident. Wouldn't be the first time. I have some calls into Daystar. I should get a call back soon. We'll have more to go on if we know when she left the casino. I'm going to put out more calls to some other contacts."

I nodded dumbly. That made a certain amount of sense. I had lectured Vance about doing something, but I didn't know what to do. How was I going to find Angel? Who could Angel have gotten mixed up with who would be involved in shady—"Hugh! Gabe, I think Angel was pissed at Hugh for something when I saw her at the casino. I don't know what it was, though. But Linda Simpkins had seen Hugh at the casino Friday night." Maybe there was more of a connection than I had thought when I talked to Vance.

"That's a good place to start." He touched my face. "We'll go talk to him as soon as we can."

I knew Gabe's plan had been to move the couch for me, then work on one of his current cases. His private investigating business was growing fast. "What about your work? Is this going to cause you problems?"

"I made a call and cleared my schedule."

A call? That was vague. But he clearly was dropping everything to help me find Angel. Gabe and I were at an uneasy place. He'd asked me to work for him and train as a private investigator, but Heart Mates was my career. I liked working part-time for him when something came up or I had another bill to pay. Gabe didn't push it and we sort of skirted the issue.

Now wasn't the time to sort this out. Angel was missing. "OK, but I have to get home to the boys. Check in with them. They'll be devastated."

Gabe nodded. "Let's go."

Home was where my grandfather lived. The boys and I had moved in with him not long after Trent died. In the beginning, the move had allowed the boys and me to get back on our feet, both financially and emotionally.

Then I began to realize that Grandpa needed us as much as we needed him. We had blended into a family. Grandpa helped with the boys and gave me emotional support, and we all kept him company. In his seventies now, Grandpa was a retired magician with an active social life in the senior community and on the Internet. Gossip was his retirement hobby.

Gabe and I pulled up side by side in the dirt lot facing the front porch of the little three-bedroom house.

Grandpa came out on the porch and watched us get out of our cars. Going up the steps, I could see the tense line of his thin shoulders and the concern stamped on his craggy face. His blue eyes were shadowed with worry.

He knew. I hugged him.

"Sammy, I got word. Angel's missing?"

Letting go of him, I stepped back. "Looks like it. Have you told the boys?"

He shook his head. "I put them to work making brownies. I knew you'd get home as soon as you could."

My throat tightened. No one supported my mothering skills like Grandpa. We both loved TJ and Joel, and tried our best to raise them right. What would I have done without him? "Thanks. I'll go in to talk to them. Gabe can catch you up."

Taking a breath, I walked into the house. Rich chocolate coated the air, while punches of laughter and the sound of spraying water filled the house. An occasional bark meant Ali, our crack guard dog, was helping TJ and Joel with cleanup duty.

I walked through the small living room to the dining room, set my purse on the glass-topped table, then did a ninety-degree turn into the long kitchen.

TJ wiped the counters with a sponge, while Joel stuck a bowl in the dishwasher with one hand and flung drops of water from his other hand toward TJ. Ali had her elegant German shepherd nose on the yellowed linoleum, licking up spots of batter.

"Smells good." I walked into the kitchen.

Ali finished licking up the chocolate, then came over to let me pet her. She sat down and leaned against my leg. Ali had washed out from the police dog program for a little problem she had with beer drinking. We adored Ali. Looking up to the boys, I said, "I hope you didn't give her too much chocolate. It'll upset her stomach."

TJ threw the sponge toward the sink, but missed and hit his brother. "Nah, we know people food will make her sick. We just let her lick up the spills."

Joel threw the sponge back, hitting TJ on the side of the face. "Mom, the brownies are almost done. Grandpa made coffee. Know what?" Joel looked at me with his vivid blue eyes. "Grandpa got a phone call, then suddenly asked TJ and me to make brownies. I think Grandpa was keeping us busy until you got home. What's up?"

I glanced to my left to see the full coffeemaker on the counter. The boys were too smart. I went to TJ first, put one arm around his shoulders, then put my other arm around Joel. We stood with our backs to the sink, looking toward the stove. "I just came from Angel's house. It looks like there's been a break-in there."

TJ said, "Where's Angel? Is she all right?"

I looked at TJ. He was the more serious of the two boys. "That's the problem, TJ. We don't know where Angel is. Her car is there, and one of her purses." I left out the part about the butcher knife and the blood on the towel. "The police are looking, and we are going to look for her, too."

TJ's shoulders went back, his whole body stiffening, while Joel shrank a bit, leaning in closer to me. "Mom," Joel said, "do you think she was kidnapped?"

My throat hurt. Ached. But I made myself look at Joel's pale face. "I don't know, Joel. But I do know this: none of us will stop looking until we find her."

The buzzer on the stove went off. The brownies were done.

I squeezed the boys, then let them go. "Why don't you get some milk and we'll eat the brownies hot."

TJ headed toward the fridge, but Ali beat him to it. She stuck her nose in the seam and barked.

"No beer, Ali." I grabbed a potholder to take the brownies out. I set the hot pan on the top of the stove and closed the oven door.

Joel handed me a stack of paper plates. "Mom, is Gabe here?"

"On the porch with Grandpa. He had some calls to make." I opened a drawer and pulled out a knife.

Joel shifted back and forth on his feet. "Do you think I should take him some coffee? Or brownies?"

Finding the serrated cake knife, I shut the drawer and looked at Joel. I wanted to make the world right for my son. But what Joel needed right now was to check in with Gabe. Though I never had intended to bring another man into TJ and Joel's life, Gabe had just sort of merged in. The boys respected him, maybe even had a little hero worship going on. "Take him some coffee, Joel. He'd like that."

Joel went to the coffeemaker, got a cup down from the cupboard, and carefully poured in some coffee.

TJ set two glasses of milk on the kitchen table, then went to the coffeemaker. "I'll take Grandpa some coffee," he volunteered.

I watched my two sons walk out to gather strength from Gabe Pulizzi. Ali slid her head beneath my hand and looked up at me. I met her liquid brown-and-gold eyes. She was a female. She understood. Love meant letting them go just a little bit.

And trusting Gabe to be the man they needed him to be.

I rubbed Ali's ears, then decided I'd try to call Rick Mesa. My phone tree Rolodex was on the counter and I quickly looked up Rick's number. He might be the last person to have seen Angel at Daystar since she was there to watch his group play their set. The phone rang until the answering machine picked up.

Damn.

I hung up the phone and went to the sink and washed my hands. On autopilot, I went back to the stove, picked up the knife and cut some hot brownies. But my thoughts were rushing around, dredging up every possibility. Could Angel have surprised a burglar? Been doing some kind of housecleaning and cut herself? What? *Where are you, Angel?* My eyes stung with tears.

I heard the front door open. It sounded like they were all coming into the house. Blinking, I fought to steady myself. To be strong. The boys came in first. I turned and handed them each a plate of brownies. They took them to the table.

Then Grandpa came up, putting his hand on my shoulder. "How are you, Sammy?"

I looked up into his crafty blue eyes. Grandpa had been the father I never had. Father–daughter dances? Grandpa went and charmed everyone there into forgetting that he wasn't my father, but my grandfather. He made the absence of a biological dad bearable.

Hell, I'd have traded any father for Grandpa.

"I'm scared for her, Grandpa."

He put his arm around me. "Me, too, Sammy. Me, too. I'm gonna check in with all my friends and see if anyone's heard anything. Angel's not the type of woman to go unnoticed. Someone may have seen something and not realized Angel was in danger."

In spite of my utter terror for Angel, I smiled. It was true. Angel was stunning, with long red hair, green eyes, and killer legs. But the real core of Angel was her fearless determination. She was bright, resourceful, and not a woman who was easily controlled. That gave me hope for her.

Putting my arm around his waist, I said, "Thank you, Grandpa."

He kissed my head, picked up a plate with a warm crumbling brownie, and went to the table. I followed, carrying two more plates. I set one in front of Gabe, then took the seat next to him.

Gabe looked over at me. "Sam, can you put together a list of phone numbers of the guys in the the Silky Men's group and Angel's friends? Barney and the boys can call them to see if anyone knows where Angel is, or has heard from her."

I nodded and glanced at my sons. Both of them looked a little more hopeful and steady. Having a job made them feel like they were doing something. I reached behind me to Grandpa's desk and grabbed a yellow pad of paper. I started making the list.

Gabe went on, "OK, here's what I got from my source at the casino. Angel checked out Saturday morning around eleven, but stayed at the casino long enough to charge a dinner at about five-thirty in the afternoon and a couple of Diet Cokes at the last show of the evening. We presume she left after that show and came home, meaning she wouldn't have gotten home before eleven."

I stopped writing and looked at Gabe. "How did you get all that?"

"The head of security at Daystar is a friend of mine. Another ex-cop. I told him it was extremely urgent that we locate Angel. Also, Daystar has a reputation to worry about. They want us to find her."

It made sense, though I doubted any of this information flowed over official channels. "OK, here's the list." I slid it to Grandpa.

Gabe took a bite of the brownie, then washed it down with coffee. "The police will check the local hospitals and urgent-care facilities to see if"—he glanced at the boys— "anything significant turns up there."

Meaning, I knew, a knife wound. I appreciated Gabe's sparing the boys that information.

He looked at me. "In the meantime, Sam and I will go talk to Angel's ex-husband and take a look around. You up for it, Sam? Or would you rather stay here at the house?"

I looked around the table. The men I loved the most in the world sat around the table. But Angel was my best friend. She had seen me through some really tough times and celebrated my good times. I meant to be there for her during this bad time. Grandpa and Ali would take care of TJ and Joel. "I'm going with you. We're going to find her."

Since Angel had gotten the house in the divorce, Hugh Crimson and his wife, Brandi, lived in Brandi's duplex off Lincoln Street. Hugh's beat-up old Mercedes dripped oil on the asphalt driveway. But I didn't see any sign of cops.

Or Angel.

The weed-choked brown grass crunched beneath my shoes. We headed up to Hugh's half of the duplex. I rang the doorbell.

Hugh yanked open the door, his large forehead gleaming like a dead fish in the sunlight. His rat eyes darted around. "What the fuck do you want, Sam? I already told that cop you sent over here I don't know where Angel is."

Rage slapped hard against my breastbone. I wanted to slam my fist into Hugh's solar plexus. "When was the last time you saw Angel?" It was all I could do to control my fear and anger.

"Go to hell," Hugh moved back to slam the door.

Gabe stepped into the opening, threw his shoulder into the door, and knocked it from Hugh's hold. Then he grabbed Hugh by his preppy golf shirt and slammed him up against a mirrored wall. "Let's try it again. When was the last time you saw Angel?"

"Let go of me! I'll have you arrested for assault! My father is Grant Crimson, the best criminal defense lawyer in the Inland Empire."

In response, Gabe jerked Hugh forward, then slammed him back up against the wall. "You screamed lawyer faster than all the scum I ever arrested."

Hugh's eyes widened so that rims of white glowed his fear. "You're a cop? This is harassment!"

Gabe shifted lightly on his feet. "Not a cop anymore. I don't have to follow all those rules. Hell, if you trip and smash your nose in your own house, I can't be blamed for that, right, Sam?"

Huh? Rooted to the porch, I could almost see the barely controlled fury rising off Gabe's skin. OK, time to step up with the program. Gabe knew how to handle Hugh Crimson's bloated self-importance. "Hugh's known to be a klutz, Gabe. No one can blame you for that."

"You bitch!" Hugh's eyes bulged.

Whack. Gabe slammed Hugh's head back into the mirrored wall again. I clenched my teeth, wondering why the squares of mirrors didn't break, and how Hugh could be such a lumbering dumbass.

Gabe said, "One more time, Crimson. When was the last time you saw Angel?"

Hugh held up his hands. "OK! Friday! I went over there Friday morning."

Now we were getting somewhere. I stepped into the foyer. "You went to Angel's house? Why?"

He shifted his eyes to me. "She ruined my career! She told the FBI a bunch of lies! Now they won't clear me for a private patrol operator's license. How am I going to start my own private security company now?"

Gabe snorted.

Raw anger hot-flashed through my body. Suddenly it seemed possible that Hugh had done something to Angel. "Where is she, Hugh? What did you do to Angel? We know you followed her to Daystar Friday night." Rage had me leaping to conclusions.

He blinked his eyes rapidly, looking back and forth between me and Gabe, who had him pinned to the wall. "Nothing! I didn't do anything! Well, I told her I was going to file a lawsuit, but that's all!"

God, he was such a weasel. "Why were you at Daystar?"

The way his eyes kept darting to Gabe, then away, I knew he was scared. The veins in his neck stood out. "I didn't know she was going to be there! You have to believe me! I was planning my lawsuit against her for destroying my chances at the license, that's all!"

My fury deflated. Hugh was the type to hide behind his daddy's law practice, not stalk and kidnap someone. "You can't file the suit—you never passed your bar exam." I looked around the duplex, wondering where Brandi was. Empty beer cans and Frito bags littered the couch and coffee table. The TV blared a tough-guy movie. Looking back at Hugh, I said, "Where's Brandi?"

Gabe let go of Hugh and stepped back.

Hugh made a show of fixing his polo shirt but didn't meet my eyes. "She went on a trip with her mother."

I stared at Hugh's face. I could see the anger had colored his pasty complexion ruddy. "You better be telling the truth about Angel." I turned and stormed out of the house.

I was shaking. Hugh hadn't always been that big a loser. He'd been OK when he and Angel first married. He'd been in law school, struggling his way through. It was when life started making demands on him that his dad couldn't fix that he began sliding into becoming the loser he was today.

I stormed over the dead grass to the passenger side of the truck.

Gabe came up behind me. "You OK?" His voice was soft.

I leaned my back against the cold door. "I don't think Hugh did anything to Angel. He might trash the house, but he doesn't have the guts to face Angel."

"Not himself, I agree with that. There were no visible cuts on him so I doubt it's his blood on that dish towel in Angel's house. But Hugh strikes me as the type to hire someone. Or he could have gotten involved with the wrong person and they went after Angel for some reason."

"It could be Angel's blood." I hated even saying the words.

Gabe looked at me. "Possible, but we don't know. Do you buy that story about his wife being on a trip with her mother?"

I shook my head. "I don't know. She might have left him."

"Think, Sam. Let's say this latest career setback with being turned down for the private patrol license caused his wife to leave, and Hugh blames Angel for that. What would he do?"

I rubbed my forehead, trying to think. Hugh hated

looking bad. He blamed Angel when he couldn't pass the bar. He found a way to have the lab reports changed so he couldn't be blamed for not having children. And eventually, he proved his manhood by banging a dumb, young girl. "Nothing violent, I don't think." So what would he do? I dropped my hand and looked at Gabe. "But he would try to make Angel look bad. Blame her. Be able to say, 'See, she's a bitch or she's crazy.'"

Gabe nodded. "I'll see if I can find out what he was doing at Daystar. I'll probably have another face-to-face with Hugh after I have some information, so I can tell if he's lying or not."

I put my hands flat against the door of the truck behind my hips. "You scared him bad enough that I think he's telling more truth than lies."

"Maybe. It all depends what the stakes are for Hugh."

God, I was scared. "You mean he might be more afraid of someone or something else?"

Gabe shrugged.

My head throbbed behind my eyes. "What now?"

Gabe leaned over me, putting his hands on the truck over my head. "You have to hold it together, Sam. You know Angel the best. You have to think like her. Things like how would she react to Hugh being pissed about losing his chance at that license? If Hugh went over and yelled at Angel or threatened her, what would she do?"

Easy question. "Tell him to go to hell. That he got what he deserved. And threatening her with a lawsuit? She would have laughed in his face."

"Pissing him off more," Gabe pointed out.

"Maybe. Angel isn't afraid like that. But what do we do now?"

"Keep figuring out what happened. First, we'll go home and see if Barney and the boys had any luck getting ahold of Rick or anyone else in the Silky Men. Then we'll go back over to Angel's house and start talking to her neighbors. We're going to try and reconstruct her exact moves."

Monday mornings suck. This Monday morning sucked worse than usual. Dragging myself out of bed, I hit the shower and tried to convince myself that I'd had a nightmare and Angel wasn't really missing.

But by the time I got the boys off to school and into my car for the drive to work, I had to face it. Angel was missing.

While driving to the office, I went over everything. Grandpa and the boys hadn't gotten any answer at Rick's house, or from any of the other guys. Gabe and I had talked to Angel's neighbors, but they hadn't noticed anything unusual. We had gone to Rick's house and he still wasn't home. Then Gabe had spent a few hours doing surveillance on Hugh, but Hugh never left his house.

Today, Gabe and I were going to head out to Daystar and see what we could pick up of Angel's trail there.

But first, I was going to work while Gabe got a few hours' sleep. I needed to keep busy. I pulled into the row of parking spaces that faced Mission Trail Street. I walked with a heavy stride to the strip mall that housed Heart Mates. Going into work was better than sitting home and stewing. I unlocked the door and went in.

The smell of fresh paint hit me. Propping the door open, I looked around. Jeez, the place was a mess. Blaine wasn't there yet, so his desk in the reception area was still covered. I had planned on picking up the couch the day before, then spending the rest of the day cleaning. I had an open house in two days and I didn't care.

I would cancel it.

Almost against my will, I looked right to the little sitting area where the brown leather couch was meant to go. Empty. The couch, the open house, the empty suite that I had coveted on the other side of that wall, none of it mattered to me anymore. I just wanted Angel to turn up safe and sound.

Shaking my head, I knew I had to pull myself together. Make coffee, open up everything, and start cleaning. I hoped that the mindless activity would help me think of something, anything that might help us find Angel.

I also wanted to call Detective Vance to see what he knew.

"Hey, boss."

I jumped and realized I had been standing in the middle of the reception area, mindlessly staring at the sheet-covered desk. I turned my head to see Blaine come in carrying two paper cups and a white bag, all from Smash Coffee. Wearing his customary blue button-down work shirt and Levis, he settled his brown gaze on me. "I wasn't sure you'd be here, but I brought you coffee and a muffin. Chocolate chip. Any word on Angel?"

Small towns didn't have many secrets. I shook my head and took the coffee from him. It smelled like fresh-ground beans. "No. Thanks for the coffee."

He waved it off, set his coffee and the muffin bag on the floor. He stripped the paint-splattered sheet off his desk. "Anything I can do, Sam? You know, to help find Angel?"

"I don't know." I moved the two blue pillows with the cute sayings—the ones Grandpa had made for me—off Blaine's desk. I had put them under the sheet for safe-keeping. Now I didn't know what to do with them. Heart Mates and all my dreams had dropped like a lead ball down my priority list. "Gabe and I are going out to Daystar later to see what we can find out."

Blaine set the folded sheet on the ground and picked

up his coffee and the bag to put them on his desk. Then he frowned at the floor. "What's that?"

"What?" I turned to look at the floor by the door. There was a greeting-card-size, grayish lavender envelope on the carpet. It sort of blended into the steel-gray-colored carpet. I hadn't even noticed it. It must have been slid under the door.

Angel! My mouth dried, sealing my tongue to the roof. I went a few steps and bent over to pick it up. My hands shook and my palms were damp and tingling. Could it be a ransom note? A threat? In a greeting-card envelope? Did that make sense?

God, just let Angel be all right. Please. I prayed silently.

"Boss?" Blaine came around his desk. "Open it."

I lifted my eyes to Blaine's. He thought of Angel as a friend, too. Then I stuck my index finger under the fold and tore the envelope.

I pulled out a store-bought card. It had a picture of a colorful bouquet on the front, with the words "Love is in Bloom."

"Maybe it's from Gabe?" Blaine asked.

I shook my head. This wasn't Gabe's style. And we'd both been preoccupied with Angel. No, this was something else. My fingers felt thick and clumsy as I tried to open the card.

Finally the card opened. It took me a second to see the inside had been left blank by the card company, but someone had pasted on big chunks of printed words.

Huh? If this was a ransom demand, they had done it wrong. In all the movies, the kidnappers always cut the letters or words out of magazines, but these words didn't have a slick, glossy finish.

The words were about the size of the type in a mass-market paperback book.

"What does it say?" Blaine demanded.

Frowning, I scanned the words. "It's a scene from a book, a kidnapping—" I couldn't breathe. Fear raced through me. Hot prickles popped out on my back and arms. Was this a description of Angel's kidnapping?

I stared at the words pasted onto the greeting card. This couldn't be a description of Angel's kidnapping. That didn't even make sense. And how would they find a book that had the exact same kidnapping . . .

Unless the kidnapper had copied the actual kidnapping from a book. I shivered at the thought. It would take a true crazy person to do that.

Blaine's voice cut into my thoughts. "Boss, what is it?"

I looked up at Blaine's intense brown gaze. "I don't know. It's a scene from a book, I think." I looked down again, skimming the words. "Wait, this is familiar. I think I've read this somewhere . . ."

"How can you remember, with all the books you read?" Blaine asked. "Want me to call the police?"

But I knew this writing. I recognized it. I closed my eyes, trying to put the kidnapping scene in context, when it hit me. I opened my eyes and said, "Vance!"

Blaine reached for the phone. "I'll call him."

"No!"

Blaine held the phone in one of his blunt-fingered hands and looked at me. "Come again?"

"I didn't mean for you to call Vance, I meant this is *Vance's writing*. It's from one of the books that he wrote under his pen name. A romance where the hero/cop's love interest is kidnapped. That book was hot."

"So that card has nothing to do with Angel? Then who left it for you? Why?"

I turned the card over and looked at the back.

"Samantha, R. V. Logan is looking for me, his heart mate. He wants me to find him. Don't keep us apart. Zoë." I groaned out loud. "Cripes, it's from Zoë." Talk about crazy. The question became, was she crazy like Kathy Bates in the movie *Misery*–crazy?

Blaine set the phone down. "That chick that was here on Saturday?"

"Woman," I corrected. "And yeah, her. I hoped she had gone away."

Sighing, Blaine said, "You don't have that kind of luck, boss. Crazies home in on you, like you are their mother ship."

"Gee, thanks." I tossed the card down on my desk. "I don't have time for crazies. Angel is out there some-where." I thought of her, scared and afraid of dying alone. I couldn't let that happen. I wouldn't let that happen. "I just hope Gabe and I find out something at the casino that will help us find her." Now for the hard part. "Since she hasn't turned up, I think I'm going to try and call her mother on the ship." Both of us turned to look at the phone on the desk.

It rang.

Cripes! My heart jumped in my chest. But that was silly—it wasn't like Angel's mom was calling me from the ship. It was just a coincidence that the phone had rung when Blaine and I looked at it. Pulling myself together, I took a step and grabbed the phone. "Heart Mates, this is Samantha. How can I help you?" It was automatic, almost soothing to be doing something so normal.

"You can help me find the pricks who destroyed my house."

Omigod! I plunked my backside down on the edge of the desk. Dizziness spun around in my head. Was I hear-ing things? "Angel?"

4

I left Blaine at the office and drove to Angel's house. I couldn't believe it! She was alive, and apparently fine. The short version that I'd gotten on the phone with her was that she'd gone to Las Vegas with Rick Mesa and his group. That explained why we never had been able to get ahold of Rick. The promoter who had seen the Silky Men's show at Daystar had booked them a Sunday matinee as a test show at one of the hotels that had a cancellation. Angel had gone along with Rick, in his truck, to promote her lingerie. That explained why Angel had gone home, left her car in the garage, and changed purses.

Her cell phone's battery had died, and Angel had just left it home because Rick was waiting for her. She had tried me from the hotel once, but my landline had been busy and my cell phone had said "out of service." Some days, technology can be cruel.

I spotted Detective Vance's car parked in Angel's driveway when I arrived. I parked on the street in front of her house and walked up the driveway, through the flagstone atrium to the front door. I reached out to the doorknob when it swung open.

Vance glared down at me. "Christ, what now? Did you lose a kid this time?"

I almost stepped back at the onslaught of his fury, but held my ground. "It was a reasonable conclusion, Vance. Angel's car was here, her house was obviously broken into and there was blood!" My face heated.

"Shaw, next time you stumble onto a disaster—and there will be a next time—don't call me." He strode by me.

Damn, he pissed me off. I turned and said, "Fine, I won't call you. I'll just give your newest fan, who came looking for you at my office, your work address. She's convinced you are her heart mate and that I know where you live."

Vance slammed to a stop and turned around. From across the courtyard, I got the full view of Detective Vance. Charcoal gray suit, mint green shirt, dapper tie, all draped over that hard swimmer's body. The sun had cut through the fog to pick out the highlights in his short-cropped hair. I knew that dimples lived beneath the surface of his hard, square face, but right now, they were hiding. He took three long strides back to me. "Are you threatening me?"

Kind of. I lifted my chin to fix my I-mean-business-mom glare on him. "I'm just passing along information."

He took another step, forcing me to tilt my head back to keep my gaze on his eyes. "And what information is that? That you have another wacko client? Because that's not exactly a news flash, Shaw."

"Her name is Zoë Cash. She came into Heart Mates Saturday and brought me chocolate truffles. She was convinced that since I write reviews for all your books in *Romance Rocks Magazine,* I know where you live."

His face tightened from warm, breathing male to wooden

statue. I could see the effort it took to move his jaw and say, "What did you tell her?"

"That I don't know where you live. That your publisher sends me the review copies. I left out the part about the stick up your ass." *Shut up!* Jeez, my mouth just spewed before my brain could filter it. Vance was not a man to piss off. But he just rubbed me the wrong way, sparking my temper.

Vance rocked back on his polished shoes. "You know, Shaw, I did you a favor by investigating your friend's disappearance. Normally, we wait a day or two because adults have a funny way of deciding to take a quick trip and not check in with Mommy. But given your worry and the state of the house, I put myself on the line. Then guess what? Ms. Crimson shows up and I look like a fool at the station for calling a simple breaking and entering a kidnapping. And now you are threatening me?"

Crap. "I'm not threatening you." Not anymore, since he rightly pointed out that he had helped me when I needed it. "You just irritate me." Mouth before brain again. Scrunching up my face, I said, "Look, Vance, I didn't get any sleep and I haven't had enough coffee. I'm in a bad mood, OK? I know you don't want the cops you work with to find out you write romances. I won't tell Zoë that you live here in Elsinore. In fact, I already got rid of her."

He leaned down, and I got a whiff of the coconut scent that always clung to him. "You know what, Shaw? I don't believe you. There's no romance fan looking for me, just as there was no kidnapping of Ms. Crimson. These are just your way of getting my attention. Obviously, you're tiring of Pulizzi and want the real thing."

Stunned, I took a breath and said, "The real thing? Is that something out of your books, Vance? I'd rewrite that if I were you. It sounds like some kind of reality show where the viewer has to tell the difference between a penis and a hot dog. Not your best work." OK, maybe I should have shut up. But damn it, Vance looked down at me one moment, then tried to seduce me the next. Men!

His dimples broke over his face in a stunning smile. "Try me, Shaw. When you want to be a grown-up woman, you let me know. One night with me and you'll know the meaning of bliss. You'll never go back to your wallbangers with wannabes like Pulizzi." He turned and walked away.

God, he was so damned arrogant. "Vance!"

He opened the gate, then stopped and looked back at me.

So damned good-looking. That smirk had to go. I summoned up my best smile. "You know the saying. Those who can, do. Those who can't, write. And Vance, you write some hot sex."

The gate slammed closed.

"That was fun. And hotter than a forest fire."

I turned to look at my best friend in the world. She was gorgeous, wearing cropped black pants and a printed long-sleeved shirt that teased the waistline of her pants. Her long red hair fell straight to her waist. Today she wore very chic glasses over her green eyes, her only concession to being tired. "Angel, if I weren't so happy to see you, I'd kick your butt." I went up and hugged her. "I haven't been that scared since . . . I don't know when. I thought something horrible had happened to you."

Freeing herself from my hug, Angel grinned. "I'm fine, but that prick Hugh is going to pay."

I followed Angel into the house, through the messy living room to the kitchen. The wine had been cleaned up, but the wood floor was still sticky. "You really think Hugh did this?"

"Who else would do it? Hugh or that bimbo he married.

I'm not going to let him get away with it." Angel got down two unbroken mugs and poured in coffee. "But enough of that. I've already called my housecleaners and they will be here to do the worst of the cleanup." She sat down.

I took a seat at the kitchen table and shook my head. "Gabe and I had a chat with Hugh. He was pissed at you, but he swore he had nothing to do with your house or your disappearance. Of course, he was right about the disappearance. Oh, and Brandi isn't there right now. She's on a trip with her mother."

Angel set down two mugs of coffee, her eyes sparkling. "Sounds like the slut left him."

"Sluts are like that," I agreed and picked up my coffee. My brain was on overload after the past weekend.

Angel sat in the chair across from me. "Hey, where's the sample kit? I thought about that all weekend. It's an intriguing idea to add something like that to my lingerie line."

My mind blanked. "Sample . . . oh!" The velvet box of sex toys. "In all the confusion, I'd sort of forgotten about it. I hid it in my bedroom. The boys accidentally found it in my car."

Angel leaned forward. "Did they open it?"

I shook my head. "Nope, I got it away from them and stuck it in a filing cabinet. Zoë followed me in there." I told Angel the story about Zoë, Vance's stalker-fan, and ended with the card she left at Heart Mates. "I don't think she's going to give up."

"So that was the truth when you told Vance that. I thought you made it up to irritate him."

"Nope, Zoë's a real, bona fide stalker-fan." I set my coffee cup down. Relief that Angel had turned up OK was settling into tiredness. But now that the Angel crisis was solved, I had a business to run. "I'll swing by home and pick up that sample kit. I need to get a change of clothes anyway. Then I have to clean the office from all the painting. My open house is only two days away. Can you make it by work this afternoon? We can investigate the sample kit then."

"I have some work to do, too." She stopped talking, looking at the sticky wood floor. "I probably won't get much work done, but I can get the cleaners started and inventory what was destroyed of my lingerie, call my insurance agent." Angel picked up her coffee, took a long drink, and sighed. "I'll need the break this afternoon."

When I got home, I rushed inside and picked up the cordless phone from the base in the kitchen. I'd already left a message for Gabe that Angel was safe. I had hoped Grandpa would be home so I could tell him in person about Angel, but since he wasn't home, I was going to call his cell phone.

Ali greeted me from the other side of the sliding glass door. She barked and fixed her big German shepherd eyes on me in a pleading stare.

"Can't play right now, Ali," I told her while dialing the phone and heading down the hallway to my bedroom. I told myself I'd make it up to Ali tonight when I got home.

"Hello?"

"Grandpa," I said as I turned into my bedroom. "Great news! Angel's OK. I just saw her." I summed up Angel's story for Grandpa and turned to the closet on my left. I pulled the door open but my attention was on Grandpa.

"That girl sure scared us, Sammy. I'm going to tell her so, too, when I see her. Right after I hug her."

I smiled. "You do that, Grandpa. I'd better run now. I'm picking up some clothes and going back to work." I hung up and tossed the phone on my bed, then I turned back to my closet. No way was I going to tell Grandpa that I had come home to retrieve a sex-toy kit for Angel and me to look at! My face heated just thinking about it as I reached up and shuffled through shoeboxes on the top shelf until I found the one I wanted. I fished the sample kit out of there and stuck it deep into my big black leather purse with the letter *S* stamped on it in hot pink. I never used this purse unless I needed to hide something.

Jeez, I was too old to be embarrassed!

I replaced the shoebox, reached back into my closet, and chose a black filmy skirt and a white top to change into after I cleaned the office. I shut the closet door.

And came face to face with a man. "Omigod!" I slammed myself back against the closet door. My purse hit the wall and slid off my shoulder to the floor. The clothes fell from my nerveless fingers. Finally, my brain registered the man's identity. "Gabe! What are you doing here?"

Dressed in black jeans and a teal blue shirt that set off his olive skin, he rested against the wall on his left shoulder with his arms crossed over his chest. He lifted an eyebrow. "Got your message that Angel's home, and safe. Called you at the office. Blaine said you were stopping by the house before going back to work."

My pulse pounded in my ears. First, it had been shock and fear, but now . . . well hell, it was Gabe. Dangerous, sexy . . . Gabe. "Uh, yeah, guess it was all a mistake with Angel."

Gabe lifted a single brow. "Her house was tossed. That wasn't a mistake."

"Angel thinks Hugh did that."

"Did you see a cut on Hugh, Sam?"

The bloodstains on the kitchen towel. "No, but . . ."

Gabe pushed his shoulder off the wall. "I didn't come here to talk about Angel." He stepped in front of me, bracing his hands on the wall behind my head. Pitching his voice to a sexy growl, he said, "I can't get the picture of you bent over Angel's car in your shorts out of my head."

He smelled fresh from the shower with an Irish Spring tang. The heat coming from him was all-male. The tired nerves in my body sprang to life with a heated sizzle. "I didn't bend over the car; the garage door smacked into me and knocked me over the hood of Angel's car." OK, maybe I didn't need to remind him of that.

Gabe smiled, leaning his body flush into mine. "You made it look sexy."

He made me feel sexy. All my worries and time pressures slid away on a wave of lust. "You sure it was me and not the red car?" I was shameless, fishing for more compliments.

"The red car was a hot background, but it was your ass in those tight shorts that had my attention." He took his hands off the wall and slid them behind me to cup my butt through my jeans and pull me into his hips. "You always get my attention."

Oh yeah, I could feel his attention in his jeans pressed against me. Smiling, I said, "So then what did you come here for?"

"To see you. Touch you." He lowered his mouth to mine. "Taste you."

I kissed him back, wrapping my arms around his waist.

Gabe's cell phone rang.

He groaned out, "Damn." Breaking the kiss, he let go of my butt to yank the phone off his belt. After looking at the screen, he put it to his ear. "Pulizzi."

I leaned my head against the wall and watched Gabe. I wanted to possess this man, but I knew that wasn't going to happen. One day, when his old wounds healed, Gabe was going to want a family. A wife, babies . . . the whole romantic package. Not a woman like me, who was five years older, had ready-made teenage children and an aging grandfather, and was done with childbearing.

Gabe said into the phone, "No, it's better if we arrive at the motel together. I'll pick you up in ten."

I snapped out of my thoughts. *Motel? Together?* "Who was that?"

He closed his phone, slid it back in his belt, and settled his gaze on me. "My new assistant, Dee."

"A woman? You hired a woman full-time? Does she work out of her house? Or your house?"

"Dee answers phones for me and is beginning her training to get a PI license."

What was that feeling in my stomach? Oh yeah—hot, pissed-off, irrational jealousy. "And the two of you are going to a motel?"

"To work on a domestic case that I put on hold when we thought Angel was missing."

"You're chasing a cheater?"

"Yep."

"With Dee?" Did I think this was going to get any better with clarification?

"Need a woman to make the cover work. A man who sees me show up at the motel with a woman will assume I'm cheating just like him."

"OK." *Not OK!* This woman was in my place. I was the one who helped Gabe. Well, truthfully, usually Gabe helped me, but still. I wanted this Dee to explode into fiery hellish flames and die. Cripes, it felt like my stomach was on fire.

Gabe slid up a single eyebrow. "You look upset. If I remember correctly, you didn't want to commit to getting a PI license."

I narrowed my eyes. "Are you trying to make me jealous? It's bad enough I had to deal with Vance and his bold suggestions. What is it with you men?"

Gabe took a step, bringing his hard body up against mine. "What did Vance say to you?"

Satisfaction cooled the fire in my belly. "This morning at Angel's house, he assured me that a night with him would teach me bliss and I'd forget all about wallbangers with wannabes. I think wannabes refers to you." Yeah, like I'd ever forget Gabe's hot and hard body.

Gabe's eyes glittered hard hate and his breathing roughened. "I'm going to kill him."

I smiled. "No time for murder, Gabe. You have to go chase down a cheater with Dee." He wouldn't be thinking about Dee now.

Gabe's expression eased. He slid his hand behind my head. "There's always time for murder and sex." His kiss seared right through my jealousy.

Wallbanger sounded good to me. I kissed him back and went to work on the buttons of his shirt. A fast rush of pure lust wiped out my fatigue. I needed Gabe. The pool of sizzling heat spread deep in my belly, and lower, increasing my urgency. I spread his shirt open, touching his hard, warm chest.

And felt the pounding of his heart beneath my fingers.

He broke the kiss to pull my T-shirt off. Sweeping aside a bra cup, he freed my breast and played his thumb over my nipple. I reached for his pants, undoing the buttons and pulling him free. Wrapping my hand around his penis, I felt the hard throb of his need. I softened my touch, running a finger along the heavy underside and looked up into Gabe's face.

His eyes darkened and his nostrils flared as he thrust deeper into my hand.

The phone rang. This time it was my phone.

Gabe spanned his hands around my waist. "Ignore it. I want you naked. No distractions."

Sharp regret cut through my lust. "I have to answer it. It might be the school about the boys."

Gabe groaned and stepped back. I took a last look at him—his shirt hung open, revealing a hard chest covered in warm olive skin. His pants lay open, revealing a throbbing erection.

But I was a mother, too.

I went to the phone on my nightstand. "Hello."

"Sam? You sound breathless."

"Linda?" Cripes, what timing! I wished I hadn't answered the stupid phone! And just what did the PTA president want? My volunteering days were over. I immediately started making a mental list of excuses, then jumped a foot when I felt Gabe slide his arms around my naked waist.

In my ear, Linda said, "I just wondered what was going on with Angel? I heard she was missing, then she's back. And she looked sort of mad at the casino over the weekend. Is she all right?"

What? Did she say something about Angel? It was hard to concentrate. Gabe undid the snap of my jeans. I heard the hiss of the zipper sliding down. Then he tugged the jeans down my hips.

"Sam?"

Linda! On the phone. About Angel. "Angel's fine, Linda." The cool air hit my naked butt. I started babbling. "She was just away on business. And you know how it is, since Angel and Hugh are divorced, they don't like talking about each other." My jeans and panties were pooled at my ankles. Gabe leaned around me. I could feel his heated skin, and his engorged penis pressing into me. He was naked. He slid one hand into the cup of my bra and the other hand between my legs. "Linda, I have to—"

She cut me off. "I'm glad Angel's all right. Uh, Sam, you

know the Harvest Festival is coming up at the school. What booth can I put you down for?"

"Harvest Festival?" I didn't even know what I was saying. My entire being focused in on the feel of Gabe's body behind me. The touch of his lips on the back of my neck. My breasts pulling tight as he teased my nipples. And lower, where he parted me and stroked me, making me wet and ready to beg. He brought me to the edge. He slid a finger inside of me, lifted his mouth off my neck to whisper into my ear, "Hang up."

I said into the phone, "What? Linda, you are breaking up. I can't h—" I hung up and tried to turn.

He held me in place. "I want you like this. Now. Like I saw you over the car."

I should have felt awkward, but I didn't. Not with Gabe. He took his hands from pleasuring me to take hold of my hands and put them on the nightstand.

He slid into me, filling up the ache he created.

The phone rang.

I didn't care. I rocked back against Gabe, ripping a groan from him. He reacted by grabbing my hips and thrusting into me. The thing between us, the heat, the needs, grew and stoked the flames into a firestorm. I lost track of everything but the two of us. "Gabe . . ."

He leaned over me, surrounding me, and slid his hand down my belly to touch me into an orgasm. "Mine, Sam." His words were as deep and consuming as the orgasm that followed them.

5

I came out of the bathroom to find Gabe on his cell phone. "I'm on my way, Dee." He ended the call.

Die, Dee, Die. I was more raw than usual where Gabe was concerned. Sex with Gabe forced up the feelings I struggled to control. There were a couple of reasons I hadn't committed to Gabe about getting my PI license. First, I loved Heart Mates. I wasn't giving up my dating service.

The incredible thing was that Gabe understood that. Even more incredible, he believed I could do it all, have Heart Mates and get my PI license. He knew that getting my license would represent a kind of power that I'd never had in my life—the power to try to find out who my biological dad was, for instance.

The second reason I couldn't commit was that the lines between our lives keep blurring, and that scared the hell out of me. I had worked so hard to grow into a strong woman; what if I relied on him too much?

What if he left me?

If Gabe left me that day, I'd be OK. It would hurt, but I'd survive it. But—

Stop it. He had accepted my nonanswer about working

with him, and moved on. Hadn't I just heard him planning to meet Dee to chase a cheater? He wasn't worrying over his feelings for me.

It was just sex.

Shutting down my thoughts, I went to my purse and the clothes that I had dropped on the floor and gathered them up. "I have to go, too. See you whenever you're done." I stood and walked purposefully out my bedroom door. I had a life, too, and it was time to get on with it.

I got halfway down the hallway when Gabe caught one of my shoulders, turning me to face him. He fixed his dark eyes on me. "When I'm done with this case, I'm going to find you and drag you to my house, into my room, and handcuff you to my bed. No more hit-and-run sex, babe."

My mouth went dry. Sure, people say stuff like that. Gabe meant it. "You can't—"

"Yes, I can. And in between making you scream, we're going to talk." He let go of me and reached into his front pocket. He came out with a silver key. "Here's my house key."

I blinked, trying to get the image of being at Gabe's sexual mercy out of my head. "What am I supposed to do with this? Handcuff myself to your bed?"

"I could work with that." He flashed a wicked grin. "But I was thinking that Angel might be in more trouble than you realize. If she needs a safe place while I'm gone, she can use my house. You know the alarm codes." He kissed me and left.

I stood in the hallway with his house key in my hand. *Handcuffs.* He couldn't be serious, but Gabe was . . . well . . . Gabe.

Thinking of handcuffs reminded me I had a sex-toy kit tucked away in my oversize purse.

Wonder what Gabe would do if he knew that.

* * *

Blaine and I worked for two solid hours moving furniture and cleaning at Heart Mates. Paint fumes aside, the place looked better. The pale cinnamon rag-painted design warmed up the office and hopefully would keep the customers' eyes off the aforementioned wafer-thin steel gray carpet beneath their feet and the yellowed, water-stained ceiling tiles overhead.

It felt good to make some solid progress. Things were looking up. Angel was home safe. Heart Mates had a small but growing client list, and the open house would help spread our name.

Best of all, I had an interview with a potential client in one hour.

"Boss, I'll go pick up some lunch." Blaine finished putting the old folding chairs back in the reception area since Angel's brown leather sofa was ruined. He looked up at me. "You might want to clean up and change before the new client comes in."

I didn't have to look at my dirt-stained T-shirt or jeans to agree. Even more depressing was how tight my jeans felt. "I brought a change of clothes. Can you bring me a salad or something like that?" This time I did look down. "These jeans are kind of tight."

Blaine headed around his desk to pick up the blue work shirt he'd left draped over his chair. Putting that on over his undershirt, he eyed me. "All your clothes are tight. I thought that was your intention."

"Ha ha." That probably came out a little sarcastic. "I don't see *you* losing any weight."

Blaine walked past me to the door and said, "Don't have to. With all the money you are paying me, I can get all the women I want." At the door he turned around. "OK if I take your T-bird?"

I went into my office and got my purse out of my desk. Walking back out to the reception area, I dug my keys out and tossed them to Blaine, along with the comment, "What's the matter—that early 90s, primer-painted Hyundai not quite the chick magnet you thought it was?"

He snatched them out of the air. "I just didn't want to spill anything in my car," he said, and left.

I watched Blaine walk out the door and to my car. The truth was that Blaine took care of my fully restored classic T-bird. He could drive it anytime he wanted to. As a highly skilled mechanic, Blaine could work anywhere. He chose to stay with Heart Mates and me. We were a good team.

I hurried to the door of my office to get the clothes that I had hung there. I headed through the newly cleaned interview room, into the storage area that led to the alley. Turning on the overhead light, I spotted all the paint cans and supplies. I had to get rid of that stuff. Ignoring it for the moment, I turned right, into the cramped little bathroom.

A single glance in the mirror revealed bags under my eyes and dust on my face. Quickly, I stripped out of my jeans and T-shirt. I used a washcloth to get rid of most of the dust and grime before stepping into my short black skirt with the sheer flowered overlay. After that, I put on my white camisole, then the sheer white, sleeveless romantic shirt.

So far, so good.

I put my purse on the closed toilet, moved aside the velvet box holding the sample sex-toy kit, and found my makeup bag. Lots of concealer, then a little color, to make me look alive. Not much I could do with my frizzy hair. But hey, that natural wave added to the romance of my outfit.

And the shoes! Cool shoes always made me feel better.

These were ultracool knockoffs, with wedge platforms and romantic lace straps that tied around my ankles.

I didn't have a full-length mirror, so I put my purse on the ground and stepped up on the closed lid of the toilet. An act of supreme balance in four-inch wedge heels!

The woman in the medicine cabinet mirror wasn't bad. Maybe a little thick in the thighs, but the wedge shoes helped.

Not bad for a dating expert and mother of two!

"Hello? Anyone here?" A deep voice called out.

Startled, I jerked and lost my balance. Teetering on top of the toilet, I grabbed the shelf over the toilet with my right hand.

For a second, everything sort of stopped. I thought I was OK.

Then the shelf pulled out of the wall.

I overbalanced and the shelf flew out of my hand.

"Oh!" I fell and slammed my left thigh into the counter. "Ouch! Shit!"

The shelf clattered to the floor, spilling toilet paper rolls, a can of air freshener, and a bottle of hand soap.

I managed to grab the edges of the counter and slide my butt onto the two-inch space between the edge of the counter and the sink. My heart pounded from that panicked falling feeling. I was OK, even though it felt like a sledgehammer had hit my left thigh.

I took a second to catch my breath and—

The bathroom door burst open.

I screamed.

"It's OK, ma'am, I'm a fireman."

Huh? A fireman? I swung my legs around to see who was breaking into my bathroom. My legs stopped, but one shoe flew off my foot and slammed into the intruder's forehead. All I saw was a pair of shocked green eyes before a large man sank to the ground.

The remaining shoe hung by the strap tied around my ankle. Guess I hadn't tied the one that flew off my foot tight enough. I reached down, untied the shoe and tossed it to the ground. Then I slid off the counter and tested my weight on my legs. Yep, the left thigh hurt, but I could stand. So I stood there, staring down at the heap of man in my bathroom doorway.

Who was he? Why had he crashed into my bathroom? Should I call 911 while he was out on the floor? I wasn't expecting anyone—

Cripes! The new client.

I definitely had a headache coming on.

"Boss? What the hell happened?" Blaine stood behind the unconscious man, holding a fast-food bag. He looked up at me.

"You know the appointment that was coming in today—did he say what his job happened to be?"

Blaine looked down at the unconscious man, who groaned and moved his hand to his forehead. Then Blaine answered, "Fireman."

"Damn. I just knocked out our potential client. Guess I'd better call 911."

I took a careful step over the body.

A hand grabbed my right calf. "Ma'am, don't call 911. I'm OK."

Those green eyes were looking up at me. "Good, you're awake." Really, I didn't quite know what to say. My left thigh throbbed. I could almost feel the bruise forming. I glanced over at the bathroom door. It appeared fine. I figured he had just opened it with the knob rather than breaking it down. Looking back at the man on the floor, I had to admit that he had a nice set of shoulders to force open a door with.

Jeez. How did these things happen to me? *Focus!* I told

myself. I had an injured almost-was-a-client on the floor of my bathroom. "Are you sure? How many fingers am I holding up?" I made a fist and stuck out my first two fingers.

He squinted, then grinned. "I think two. And I believe your panties are black lace."

He was looking up my skirt! I yanked my calf from his hand, and then yelped as my left thigh reminded me of how I had hit the counter. I caught hold of Blaine's thick arm and looked up into his face.

He was laughing!

"I can't believe you are laughing!"

Blaine leaned over the prone fireman and set the food bag on the counter just inside the bathroom. Then he took hold of my arm. "You can't blame the guy, boss. You were standing over him like Marilyn Monroe over a vent. A guy's gonna look."

At least I had clean panties on. They were from Angel's lingerie line. Sort of like modified boxer shorts, very chic. But still, I hadn't planned to model them for a potential client. Fixing my mom-stare on my face, I glared at the man on the floor. "Get up."

He rolled up to his feet, then shook his head like a big shaggy dog. "What hit me?"

"My shoe." The answer came out automatically, while I sized up this guy. He stood about five to seven inches taller than my five foot five, OK, maybe five foot four in bare feet. Still, the guy was tall, broad through the shoulders in his white-with-green-palm trees button-down shirt. The short sleeves revealed tanned muscular arms.

A closer look at his eyes revealed just enough yellowish brown to make their color hazel. His curly brown hair was tamed by a good cut and styling products.

What did this guy need a dating service for? I couldn't

believe my good luck. I could sell tickets for this guy's dates!

Unless he took offense to me knocking him out cold with my shoe and refused to sign up. OK, time to turn on my businesswoman charm.

I stuck out my hand. "I'm Samantha Shaw. I'm so sorry about this little incident."

His hand enveloped mine in strong warmth. "A pleasure, Samantha. I'm Bob Lovett. Usually I get a lady's name before I look up her skirt."

His grin crinkled his eyes and made him appear like he didn't take himself too seriously. "Do you always barge in to bathrooms like that?"

His smile widened, making his eyes crinkle. "Only when I hear a scream and swearing." He let go of my hand, leaned over and picked up my big purse, and—

Uh-oh.

"Here's your purse, and uh . . . makeup kit?" He looked doubtfully at the blue velvet box in his hand.

Oh boy! My purse must have been knocked over and spilled out the sample sex-toy kit. Thank God it hadn't broken open. While not exactly a makeup kit, it sure brought color to my cheeks. "Thanks." I snatched the velvet box first, then took my purse. "Blaine, can you get Bob settled filling out the forms? I'll be right back!" Without looking, I dashed into the interview room, hoping to make a clean break for my office and get rid of the sample sex-toy kit.

"Samantha!"

Damn. I turned and looked back at Bob. Now what?

He grinned. "Your shoes." He held up my platform shoes.

Bob and I finished the interview in half an hour. He was new in town and worked a lot of hours as a fireman, so it was hard for him to find time to date. He had seen the flyer for the open house that I'd left at Smash Coffee and thought it would be fun to join the dating service. He signed the forms for Gabe to do a background check.

Blaine was taking some still shots for our albums while I ate my salad in my office. I'd had exactly two bites, when Angel walked in. She'd kept her black pants on but had changed her long-sleeved shirt for a light green see-through shirt over a darker green lacy camisole that came from her lingerie collection. "Where's Blaine?"

I put down my fork. "He's taking pictures of my newest client. A fireman!" I was so excited about Fireman Bob. "And you know what? He seems normal."

Angel dropped into the chair across from my desk. "Cute?"

I reached down into my desk drawer and used two hands to heft out my purse. "Why?" Bob was going to be my most popular single male, as long as there really wasn't anything wrong with him. I wondered if Gabe would dig up something horrible when he did the background check.

"Because if he's cute, he'll attract a lot of women to Heart Mates."

A flash of shame fluttered over me. Angel was looking out for me, not trying to steal my fireman. "That's what I'm counting on. Of course, he did look up my skirt, so maybe he's not quite as normal as I thought."

Angel's green eyes glittered in the overhead lighting and she leaned forward. "How did that happen?"

I reached into my purse and got out the blue velvet sex-toy kit while telling her about the bathroom incident. Then I set my purse in my drawer and held up the sex-toy kit. "Then he picked this up off the floor and handed it to me. He thought it was a makeup kit or something. Can you imagine—what if he had opened it! What would he have thought I was doing in the bathroom?"

Angel burst out laughing. She leaned over my desk and snatched a couple of mandarin oranges from my salad and said, "Speaking of the sex-toy kit, guess who has left me three messages?"

I set the sex-toy kit down and picked up my Diet Coke. "Who?" I took a drink of my soda.

"Mitch St. Claire."

Putting the can down, I grinned. "Ah, the boy with the toys."

Angel grinned back. "He wants to take me to dinner to talk about those toys. He said that he's very impressed with my business skills. He's planning on calling me later today to find out a good time to pick me up for dinner."

"Rather confident, isn't he?" I watched her. "Are you interested in Mitch?" Though Mitch was older than Angel and I, he had that smooth Richard Gere thing going for him. Confidence, the look of money, a certain . . . I couldn't quite put my finger on it. It was the way he seemed to know that I was shocked when he pitched his sex-toy kit idea to Angel. The way he managed to turn it back on me so that my uneasiness seemed silly. So did that mean he was good at putting people at ease? I didn't know him well enough to be sure.

Angel reached over to snag another mandarin orange from my salad. "I'm more interested in Tempt-an-Angel. I might be willing to go to dinner to discuss business."

Uh-huh. It had been a while since Angel dated. "What about sex?" Was that what Mitch was thinking? Maybe his ability to put people at ease was a way to manipulate a woman into sex. He'd be in for a rude awakening if he tried that kind of thing on Angel. She was not a woman easily manipulated.

"Hmm." Angel swallowed the orange slice. "Well, I do like to see a preview before I make a commitment." She reached for the sex-toy kit, pulled it toward her and grinned. "Like the sex toys; I'm viewing those before buying. You think he'll get naked and let me take a look?"

I laughed, trying to picture Mitch-the-smooth-guy handling that request. Then the searing image of a very naked Gabe handling me rose in my brain. Which then made me wonder what he was doing with his new assistant. I shoved it away. "You just be careful."

"Yes, Mom." She untied the white satin ribbon on the blue velvet box.

I rolled my eyes. "Let me put it another way. Did he leave a phone number for you to return his calls?"

She looked up at me. "Suspicious, aren't you? Nope, all that is supposed to be in here," she looked down at the sex-toy kit, then back up at me, "remember?"

Damn, she had me. I knew what was the matter with me. "You're right. It's just that you really scared me, Angel. I thought you'd been kidnapped." My stomach clenched around the few bites of salad that I had eaten. It wasn't Mitch that made me uneasy, it was leftover fear of something bad happening to Angel. In the hours we thought she'd been kidnapped, I had been devastated. "You are my best friend."

Angel pulled off the ribbon and unconsciously wrapped it around one hand. Forgetting the sex-toy kit for a minute, she said, "I never meant to scare you like that. Hell, you wouldn't have been that scared if dumbass Hugh hadn't trashed my place."

I watched her wrap and unwrap the creamy ribbon around her hand. "Are you sure it was Hugh?" Gabe didn't seem convinced, but I didn't tell Angel that.

She nodded yes. "It was Hugh. It's the way he is. Everything that goes wrong in his life is my fault. I told him it was his fault. He's the one that got that lab technician to change the results on his sperm test. The only reason I found out was that she botched the job and was fired. All I did was tell the FBI agent doing the background check the truth."

She was right. Hugh might do something like trash her house. But still . . . "That knife in the couch, did that seem like Hugh?"

Angel dropped her shoulders, releasing some of her tension. "That is just like Hugh. Remember there was some blood on a dish towel, right? Hugh probably got a knife from my kitchen, went into my office and started slicing up my lingerie merchandise and cut himself. In anger, he jammed the knife into the couch."

"I can see that." I took a drink of my soda, thinking. "But I didn't see any cuts on Hugh."

She yanked the ribbon tight around her hand. "Good, maybe he cut off his own dick."

I laughed. "He was walking fine, at least when Gabe wasn't slamming him into the walls."

"Now there's something I'm sorry I missed seeing."

I studied Angel. I remembered how pissed she seemed to be at Hugh at the casino on Friday night. "Angel, is there something more going on between you and Hugh?"

She raised her eyebrows. "He trashed my house and destroyed most of my lingerie."

True, but I felt like I was missing something. "But, Angel, you were upset Friday night at the casino, before he trashed your house." When Linda had mentioned seeing Hugh to Angel at the casino, Angel got upset.

"Because he's an ass." She unwound the ribbon from around her hand and tossed it into the trash can at the end of my desk. "Right now, I need to focus on Tempt-an-Angel. Recoup some losses from Hugh's stunt. So let's take a look at that sex-toy kit. That might be a good money-maker." She reached over to the velvet box in front of her. Something wasn't right there. I'd never known Angel to worry about money. She had invested well in the stock market after her divorce from Hugh. I started to say something about it when a scream erupted from the reception area.

Angel and I both jumped up and ran out of my office.

Zoë stood in the doorway of Heart Mates and pointed at Bob. "You must be R. V. Logan! I knew it! I knew Samantha knew him!"

Bob stood by Blaine's desk, his hazel eyes open wide and his mouth gaping at Zoë. "Do you mean me?" He thumped himself in the chest.

Zoë fast-walked in the door to Blaine's desk. She was toting a shopping bag with her. "Of course, you. You look exactly like I knew you would. Very masculine."

I glanced up at Blaine, who was behind his desk holding the clipboard of forms that Bob had filled out and the digital camera he had used to take pictures. Meeting my gaze, his thick lips twitched and he shrugged his big shoulders up into what little neck he had.

Message received—female criers and lunatics were my department. Zoë didn't strike me as the type to cry, but she had real lunatic possibilities.

I rushed from my door to get between Zoë and Bob. "Zoë, this gentleman here is one of our newest clients. He's a fireman, not a writer."

"A writer?" Bob looked at Zoë and laughed. "What kind of writer did you think I was?"

Zoë turned her dark brown eyes on Bob. "A romance writer, of course." She tugged down her white men's shirt over her deep purple yoga pants, and shifted the handle of the shopping bag from her right hand to her left.

"Zoë," I said, looking down at the fairly large shopping bag. I noticed that the yoga pants ended just below Zoë's knees, showing about two inches of rock-solid bare calf. She had on thick white socks and slip-on leather sandals. I almost lost my train of thought. Oh, right . . . saving Bob from Zoë. I looked back up at her face. "Is there something I can help you with?"

She ignored me and zeroed in on Bob. "How do I know you're not R. V. Logan?"

"Want me to throw Samantha over my shoulder to prove I'm a fireman?" He grinned, looked around the reception area, and spotted Angel. His grin froze. "Or how about that gorgeous redhead?"

For a second, the room went silent.

Then Angel started walking toward Bob. "Cool." She flashed her bright grin. "I'm Angel. Go ahead, fireman, throw me over your shoulder." She stopped in front of him.

Fireman Bob glanced past Angel to me, and shrugged.

Then he leaned down, scooping Angel up over his shoulder. He anchored her there with a hand on the back of her thigh. "Any particular place you'd like me to carry you, Angel?"

I glared at Bob. "Put her down!" Damn it, I could feel the sparks between the two of them. Bob was supposed to be my ringer for Heart Mates. A cute, personable guy. OK, maybe throwing women over his shoulder was a little forward, but Angel had practically dared him.

Bob grinned and set Angel back to her feet.

Angel turned and looked at Zoë. "Yep, he's a fireman."

Maybe Gabe was right. I should work for him. It had to be better than dealing with lunatics.

And the sex really rocked.

6

"You people are strange," Zoë announced. She apparently believed Angel that Bob was a fireman.

Like Angel would know that just from the way Bob picked her up and tossed her over his shoulder. My office was full of strange people.

Zoë turned to me and held out the bag she was carrying. "This is for you."

I reached for the blue bag. "What's this?" I opened it and looked inside. It was filled with tissue paper and . . . "Rose petals?" I reached in and started to pull items out of the rose petals and tissue paper. The first was a bottle of Zinfandel wine. I set that on Blaine's desk. Next came out a plastic tray with a see-through cover. Inside I could see a half dozen chocolate-covered strawberries. I added that to the wine. Fishing around in the bag, I found the latest R. V. Logan novel and a scented candle. "Zoë, what's all this?"

She shrugged, and her thick dark hair danced around her shoulders. "Thought you'd enjoy the book with a little wine, strawberries, and a candle. I have the same thing for R. V. Logan." She shifted her weight, but her gaze stayed riveted on me. "He can sign the copy of his book for me. I need his address, Samantha."

Bob crossed his arms over his chest. "All this for a man who writes romances?"

Zoë looked at him. "Samantha won't give me his address and phone number. He's my heart mate."

Both his eyebrows hit his hairline. "So you are bribing her?"

Zoë pursed her lips. "I am simply demonstrating how important romance is. How important it is that I find R. V. Logan." Zoë turned her attention back to me. "Samantha, didn't you read that card I left for you? The hero in R. V. Logan's book never gave up looking for the kidnapped heroine. I know R. V. wouldn't want me to give up looking for him."

Omigod, the woman was a bona fide wacko job. I had to end this. "Angel, can you take Zoë into my office?" I turned and looked at my newest client. "Bob, did Blaine get all your still shots? Is there anything else we can do for you today?"

He laughed. "This has been the most fun I've had since I moved here. I'll be back for your open house. I wouldn't miss it. See ya." He sauntered out the door.

I turned to Blaine. "If you laugh, I will hit you over the head with this bottle of wine." I picked up the Zinfandel to prove my point.

He forced an innocent look over his face. "Who, me?"

I slammed the bottle down and turned away to stalk into my office. Zoë sat in the chair Angel had been in earlier. "So what's in that box?" She pointed to the blue velvet box on my desk. "That's the second time I've seen it."

Angel stood at the end of my desk and grinned. "It's my secret box, Zoë. Sam was holding it for me while I was away on my secret mission."

I bit back a groan. I really had to get Angel a boyfriend

to spend some of her mischievous energy on. "She's teasing you, Zoë. That box is a gift for Angel from a business associate." I leaned past Zoë and snatched up the sex-toy kit. Then I gave Angel a warning look as I passed her to sit in my chair, where I quickly leaned down and stuck the box in my bottom drawer. With the sex-toy kit safely stored away, I sat up and prepared to deal with the stalker-fan who wouldn't go away. "Zoë, I thought I made it clear to you that I don't know where R. V. Logan lives. The publisher sends me the books to review."

She shook her head. "You know where he lives. You couldn't write such intimate reviews if you didn't know R. V. Logan. I left that card here for you to make you understand how R. V. Logan must be looking for me. When his hero's lady was kidnapped, he never let the hero give up looking for her."

"Makes perfect sense to me, Sam," Angel said.

I glanced up at her. "You told a man to throw you over his shoulder; you don't get a vote." I turned to Zoë. "I'd like to help you, Zoë." I decided to try to play into her fantasy to get rid of her. Make her think I was on her side. Anything to make her go away. "The problem is that I really don't know where R. V. Logan lives. In fact, until you told me, I didn't know R. V. Logan was a man." *Liar.* I knew. Detective Vance had swept into town and caught the case of a murder of a friend of mine. Vance's attitude toward me had been so hostile that I was suspicious. But it was Grandpa who'd figured it out with his Internet sleuthing. He'd somehow tracked down that R. V. Logan was really Detective Logan Reed Vance. Fortunately for Vance, few people had Grandpa's Internet skills, or vast connections through his Triple M Magicians group. Bringing myself back to the current problem, I said, "Zoë, why don't you try writing R. V. Logan a letter?"

"A letter? I didn't bring you truffles, wine, chocolate-covered strawberries, and a candle to get advice on writing a letter!"

A phone rang. Unfortunately, it wasn't mine. It was Angel's cell phone. She pulled it out of her purse and left my office to take the call.

I unfolded my hands and lifted them in a helpless gesture. "I don't know what else to tell you." Other than maybe to get some therapy. Sheesh.

"Sam," Angel stuck her head in the door. "That was the cleaners at my house. They are almost done and want me to take a look. And I have a delivery of new merchandise coming. I have to run. We'll reschedule our *meeting* later."

I nodded and Angel left. I turned back to Zoë.

She stood up and reached into a pocket of her pants. She pulled out a framed photo of some kind. She set that down on my desk. "You show R. V. Logan that picture. He'll know I'm his heart mate then." She walked out.

I stared at the photo. It was a five-by-seven in a heavy crystal frame with hand painted red hearts. The picture was of Zoë, and she—

"Oh boy."

Zoë had on a tight, bright yellow bodysuit, and she was in a yoga position with her legs behind her head.

"Who's that?"

I jumped and dropped the picture. "Grandpa!" I put my hand over my heart to keep it from bursting out of my chest.

Grandpa crinkled up his faded blue eyes and laughed. "I still got it, Sammy."

"Yes, you do." I knew Grandpa meant his ability to move around unnoticed. Magicians needed to know how and when to command attention and when to deflect attention from themselves. I leaned back in my chair. "What are you doing here? Are the boys OK?"

"The boys are fine. I was out this way and thought I'd stop by to let you know I'll pick the boys up from school." He lifted up a blue bag. "Blaine said this is yours?"

Blaine must have put all that stuff Zoë brought me back in the bag. "R. V. Logan has a very determined, possibly lunatic, fan. She's trying to bribe me into telling her his address."

Grandpa's craggy face widened in a grin. "I doubt Vance took that news very well."

I laughed. "Vance doesn't take any news from me well. And he doesn't exactly trust me to keep his secret."

He glanced into the bag. "You sure this fan isn't trying to seduce you?"

"Grandpa!" I tried to look stern, but it was kind of funny.

"Hey, I saw Angel in the parking lot. She said you two are getting together tonight to look at something you got from the casino. What's up?"

Ah. His love of gossip surfaced. I turned to reach into my drawer and pulled out the velvet box. "Actually, Angel and I haven't seen it yet, either. Every time we try, something gets in the way. Could you take this home for me? Maybe stick it in the cupboard in my bathroom with that stuff in the bag?" I figured the boys wouldn't be looking around in there.

Grandpa held the bag open so I could slide it in. "What's in there, Sam?"

I looked up at him. "Something that Angel is considering adding to her lingerie line. I think it's some kind of lotions or something." OK, I lied. But he was my grandpa! No way was I going to say "sex toys" to my grandpa! I didn't want him to know what was in that velvet box. And that made me consider the fact that he was also a magician and a damn good one. I narrowed my gaze to what I hoped looked like a stern warning. "There's a seal on that box, Grandpa. Angel and I will know if you open it."

He closed the bag with his blue-veined fingers. "Now you're hurting my feelings, Sammy. I wouldn't snoop around your stuff." He leaned down and kissed my cheek. "See you at home."

I couldn't help but laugh. "Hey, Grandpa."

He stopped at my cubicle door and looked back at me. He used his free hand to hike up his polyester pants, which were sliding down his bony hips. "What?"

"If you don't snoop, what do you call all that sneaking around the Internet you do? Breaking into hospital records to find out what procedures your friends are having done? Hmm?" Grandpa held fast to his magician's secrets, but gossip was a huge commodity in the senior-citizen community. He did his part by snooping around on the Internet and finding out all kinds of titillating information. He also helped me crack a few cases when I worked under Gabe's PI license.

He gave up on his sagging pants to fix his stare on me. His aging, milky blue eyes sharpened into a piercing and commanding blue. "Research, Sammy. I call it research." Then he melted out of my office.

"Research, ha!" I yelled out over the cubicle wall. "Don't you do any research on Angel's box, Grandpa!"

Crap. I couldn't believe I'd just given my grandpa a sample sex-toy kit, then practically dared him to open it.

I spent the rest of the workday dodging phone calls from Linda Simpkins about volunteering for the Harvest Festival and getting ready for the Heart Mates open house in two days. Blaine was putting together a videotape presentation, while I worked with the winery and caterer we planned to use.

I was proud of the deal I'd cut with a Temecula winery. They were giving me a deep discount on their wines for adding them in on my Temecula Wine Tasting Date Package, and for promoting them on the night of the open house.

I was developing some real business savvy! Feeling pretty good, I locked up Heart Mates for the evening and waved good-bye to Blaine as he folded himself into his old Hyundai. Then I slid into my T-bird.

It took me about fifteen minutes to drive across town, past the lake, and get home. By the time I turned onto the dirt road that led up to our house, my lack of sleep the night before and worry about Angel caught up to me. I was dead tired.

Sex with Gabe might have sapped some of my energy, too.

I got out of the car and went into the house.

TJ was stretched out on the couch reading a book. Good Lord, he looked so big. Joel lay on his stomach playing a video game. "Hey, guys. Do you have your homework done?"

"Mine's done except for this reading." TJ didn't even look up from his paperback book.

Joel barely glanced up at me. "I didn't have any homework. What's for dinner?"

I tried to remember the last time I had gone to the grocery store. "Let me change clothes and I'll see what we have."

Both boys groaned. I looked around, "Where's Grandpa?"

"In his room. He's been on the phone." This time, TJ looked up from his book. "Can we go to the skate park tonight? A bunch of us from school are going."

I fell back on the automatic questions from the official mom list that are designed to trip up any nefarious plots hatched by kids. "Who else from school is going?"

TJ pulled a piece of paper out of the back of the book he was reading and held it out. "There's going to be a skateboard pro there tonight doing tricks. Lots of kids will be there."

Walking over, I took the paper and read it. "That's right, I saw this in the newspaper." I doubted the boys had gotten the newspaper in on any plots. This was probably OK.

Joel turned off the video game. "Can we go?"

"All right. I'll drop you off on my way to Angel's house and pick you up when I'm done." Which meant I had a half hour to get some dinner on. "Set the table and feed Ali," I said, and hurried down the hallway to my bedroom.

Grandpa's door was closed. I wasn't sure if he was on the phone or his old laptop. The computer in the dining room was newer and much better, but sometimes he used his laptop for privacy.

In my bedroom, I opened my closet and thought about Gabe. His warning about Angel made me anxious.

Or was it Gabe out at a motel with his new assistant that made me anxious? Annoyed at myself, I slid off my skirt and discovered a whopper of a bruise on my left thigh. Just looking at it hurt. I'd hit the edge of the counter in the bathroom at Heart Mates toward the top of my thigh. Or more specifically, just below the area of my saddlebag pouch of fat.

I had to start exercising more! And stop hurting myself. I pulled out a pair of jeans and winced as I dragged them over my bruised thigh. For lack of time, I left the white sheer top on and slid my bare feet into a pair of white sandals.

Heading out of my bedroom toward the kitchen, I thought about dinner. I was supposed to meet Angel at her house around seven. She had to run a few errands and pick up groceries.

Ali met me at the fridge. As soon as I opened the door to the side by side, she stuck her nose into the shelf where I kept the beer and barked.

Petting her head, I said, "Tell you what, Ali, I'll split it with you. You and me, we gotta stick together. We're the only females in the house, right?" I took the bottle of beer out, twisted off the cap, and headed for her water dish by the sliding glass door.

Ali barked her agreement and followed me.

Joel was already at her food dish, scooping some dry chunks out of the bag with the empty coffee can we used. When he finished, he went back to store Ali's food in the pantry.

TJ looked up from setting the table. "Mom, do you know what's for dinner yet?"

Ali sat down and waited patiently for me to pour out half my beer in her empty water dish. I thought frantically about dinner. I knew I had a bag of Tater Tots in the freezer, and some ground meat. . . . I finished pouring the beer and looked at TJ. "Sloppy Joes and Tater Tots."

"Table's set. Can I have my buns toasted?"

Buns? Crap, did I have buns? I sipped some beer and rushed over to preheat the oven, then went to the freezer. I got out the bag of Tater Tots and breathed a big sigh of relief when I saw the buns. Sure, they were hot dog buns, instead of hamburger buns, but I could make this work. "Sure, TJ."

"Can I do the Tater Tots?" Joel asked.

The three of us cooked dinner while Ali drank her beer and watched from her blanket.

At dinner, Grandpa said, "I'm having some friends over tonight for cards."

I looked up from my half-eaten Sloppy Joe on a toasted hot dog bun. "No cheating, Grandpa."

He laughed. "We're just playing some gin rummy. How could I cheat?" He stood up. "Clear up, boys. I'll do the dishes so your mom can take you to the skate park."

Taking my dish to the sink, I said, "Thanks, Grandpa."

"Mom!" Joel yelled as he passed by the kitchen. "We're going to be late! We'll wait for you outside!"

Shaking my head, I rushed down the hall to brush my teeth and grab my purse, then I hurried back through the kitchen to kiss Grandpa. "OK if I take your Jeep? I'll pick the boys up at nine, and we'll be home after that."

"Sure, Sammy, you go have fun."

It wasn't until after I dropped the boys off at the skate park that I realized I had forgotten to get the sex-toy kit. The skate park was only two minutes from home, so I whipped the Jeep back out onto Grand, then pulled onto the dirt road to the house.

Wow! Several people had already showed up for Grandpa's card game. I took the keys out and rushed into the house. There were six aging heads bent over the kitchen table. "Don't mind me; I just forgot something."

I hurried into my bedroom, then into the small adjoining bathroom. Bending down, I grabbed the shopping bag from under the sink. As I headed back out of my bedroom, I opened up the bag.

No velvet box. There was the wine, the strawberries—ugh, those should probably have gone in the fridge, the book . . .

Grandpa. I knew he was up to something.

I went storming down the hallway and took a fast right into the long kitchen, which ended in the dining room. Ali hurried over to see what was wrong.

I marched down the length of the kitchen. There they were—six respected senior citizens. Male senior citizens, all gathered around the table, doing nothing.

Probably because they were waiting for me to leave so they could look at the sample sex-toy kit.

"Grandpa, where's the cards?" I stopped next to his chair. I looked around at the men. Some had coffee, some had water. There was a big bowl of potato chips in the center of the table.

But no cards.

Grandpa looked up at me. "We haven't started playing yet. Hank here was telling us about his prostate problem."

I glanced at Hank, who flushed a bright red over his bald head. That only made me more suspicious. Hank talked about his bowels without embarrassment. No, that wasn't an embarrassment blush, it was guilt.

"The game is up, Grandpa. Hand it over." I held out my hand. I could not believe it! There wasn't a man at this table under sixty-five, and they had gathered like a bunch of teenage boys to read their dads' *Playboy* magazines. Sheesh!

"Hand what over?" Grandpa lifted his coffee cup and took a sip.

I nearly grinned. He was cool. "Hand over the velvet box that belongs to Angel, or I am going to call her right now and tell her what you are up to. Then Angel and I are going to go to your morning coffee at Jack in the Box and tell all the ladies there how you men were acting like horny teenagers."

"Humph!"

"Better give it to her."

"Young lady, such language!"

I ignored the muttering of the other men and stared at Grandpa. He reached down under a stack of newspapers on the floor and brought out the velvet box. "Is this what you are looking for, Sam? Why didn't you say so?" He handed it to me.

I took the box and studied it. "Did you open it?"

"No."

It didn't look like he had opened it, since the white strip of paper sealing the box shut was still attached. I stuck it into the shopping bag full of bribes that Zoë had given me.

The phone rang.

I glanced at my watch and figured it was Angel calling to see where I was. I answered it. "Hello."

"Sam! I've been trying to reach you all day!"

I closed my eyes and leaned my forehead against the wall. Linda Simpkins. "Hi, Linda. It's been a killer day. One emergency after another. I haven't had time to call you back. Can I call you tomorrow? I have to leave right now to take the boys somewhere." Lord, I was getting to be a chronic liar.

"Sam, we could do this really fast. I just need to know which night you can work the Harvest Festival."

The night after never. To create my cover, I pulled the phone away and yelled, "I'm coming, Joel!" Then I put the phone back against my head and said, "Linda, I have to run. Let me look at my calendar and I'll get back to you. Bye." I hung up.

Lifting my forehead off the wall, I turned to see all the men were staring at me. Heat flushed my face and neck. "I'm late. You guys have fun." Clutching my bag and my purse, I hurried out the door.

Driving down Lake Street, I still couldn't get over Grandpa and his cronies. What had tipped him off that there was something . . . *interesting* . . . in that box? He must not have bought my story that there were lotions in there. Or had it simply been that I told him not to open it?

OK, it was kind of funny. Grandpa! He was in his seventies!

I made a left turn into the hills overlooking the lake. I bumped along in Grandpa's Jeep until I turned onto Angel's tree-lined street. Even with no streetlights, I easily found her driveway. Years of traveling the same route made it automatic.

I parked next to Angel's blood red car.

Was Gabe staking out his cheater or bending his new partner over . . .

I turned off the ignition, grabbed my purse and my shopping bag, then got out of the Jeep. I fast-walked up the driveway to escape the direction of my thoughts. Angel and I would break open the wine and eat the chocolate-covered strawberries while we explored the sample sex-toy kit.

And talk. Girlfriend talk. I'd tell her about Gabe and his new partner, she'd tell me what was bothering her about Hugh and whatever else was going on in her life. I'd help her solve her latest problem with Hugh, and she'd probably insist on gathering up some of her high tech spy gear and tracking down the motel Gabe was working at.

Going through the gate into the flagstone atrium, I shifted the bag containing the wine, the strawberries, and the sex-toy kit from my right hand to my left.

Did I want to spy on Gabe?

A loud thud came from inside Angel's house. I forgot about spying on Gabe and froze at her front door. The hairs on the back of my neck spiked up. What was that? Angel's car was in the driveway. She might easily have just returned from the grocery store and dropped something.

I didn't believe that. Terror washed up my spine, tightening my shoulder blades and neck. Being a natural born coward, I was really starting to resent finding myself in these situations that required action.

Brave action.

Crap. My hand was on the cool door handle. I pressed my ear up to the wood and listened.

Angel's voice bled through. "What do you want? Get out!"

Could it be Hugh in there? Or someone else? I hadn't brought my stun gun or Ali. God. But I had my cell phone! I set down the shopping bag, then reached into my purse and pulled out my cell phone. I dialed 911, but my finger hovered over the send button.

Vance had been really pissed off over the last false emergency. Accusing me of trying to get close to him. On the other hand, Vance didn't answer 911. But he'd said the entire police station knew that Vance had handled the last call as a kidnapping and Angel had turned up fine. Would they believe me now?

There was shuffling noise coming from inside the house.

Make a decision! I shouted in my head. I looked around for a weapon and spotted the bottle of Zinfandel inside the shopping bag on the ground. I hooked my cell phone onto my jeans, then got the bottle of wine out. All I would have to do was push "send" and the phone would dial through to 911.

I was going into the house.

With the decision made, I refused to consider it anymore. *Just move.* I put my hand on the doorknob and turned it as quietly as I could. Once I'd turned it as far as it would go, I took a breath, steadied the wine bottle in my right hand, and pushed the door open.

The first thing I saw was a man's back as he stood over

Angel, who was sprawled on the couch. He was waving a gun in her face.

A bag of groceries had spilled out eggs, Diet Coke, and a few other items onto the hardwood floor. Somewhere in my brain, facts were being catalogued: Angel had gone shopping, maybe surprised the intruder. And it didn't appear that the intruder had heard me come in.

Angel must have realized though, because her gaze shifted past the man toward me.

The man screamed at Angel, "Where is it?"

Angel looked back at the man as I hit the send button on my cell phone hooked to my jeans.

The man added, "I want my—"

I lunged forward, swinging the wine bottle toward his head.

The man whirled around and brought his right arm up. The wine bottle missed his head, but slammed into his right arm, knocking the gun from his hand and then breaking. He yelped and brought his arm into his body.

Angel saw her chance, stood up, and launched her body into the intruder, slamming him into the hardwood floor. "Sam! Get the gun!"

I wrenched my cell phone off my jeans and got it to my ear while rushing to get the gun, which had dropped to the floor. It was only a few feet from the man's reach. In my ear, a seriously annoyed phone operator said, "Hello? Anybody there? 911, do you have an emergency? What's the address?"

"Yes! A man with a gun!" I rattled off the address, dropped the phone and reached down to get the gun.

The man's large, strong hand clamped around my wrist. He yanked hard and I fell over him and Angel into a big dog pile.

"Let go of my hair, you prick!" Angel bellowed.

I scrambled off the mound and got to my knees. The gun was on the other side of Angel and the intruder. He had a handful of Angel's long red hair.

Blood ran down his arm. The wine bottle must have broken the skin.

I grabbed the first weapon I could find, a six-pack of cans of Diet Coke. The man hung on to Angel's hair while getting to his knees. I swung the six-pack into the back of his head.

"Ooof!" He flew forward, letting go of Angel's hair to land on top of the gun. He didn't move.

Dead?

Angel leaped up and ran toward her bedroom. I stood there holding a single can of Diet Coke. It had slipped the plastic ring, so that the remaining cans hit the man in the head and fell to the ground. One can had exploded, spraying us with cola. The man appeared stunned but he was stirring.

Not dead.

I heard the distant sound of sirens.

The sound snapped me out of my fog. My heart thudded against my chest. Shit! The man started getting to his knees. He shook his head once, and then he was on his knees and reaching for his gun. I had to do something! But before I could figure out what, he grabbed his gun and stood up, pointing the gun right at my face.

I held up the can of Diet Coke, like some kind of shield. My brain registered the sirens, which were growing louder. "The police are here!"

"Freeze! I have a gun!" Angel's voice boomed.

"I'll blow off her face!" The man retorted without looking Angel's way. To me, he said, "Start backing up, toward the kitchen."

My vision tunneled and all I saw was the little hole at the

end of the gun. Fear turned my stomach to a rancid, burning liquid. My skin heated and terror roared in my ears. I backed up, carefully, once step at a time.

I didn't want my face blown off!

But the gun was getting closer, that tiny hole growing bigger. With every step I took backward, the intruder with the gun took two steps forward, bringing him closer and closer to me. By the time I got to the swinging doors that led to the kitchen, the gun was pressed up to the center of my forehead.

TJ and Joel swam up behind my eyes. Who would pick them up from the skate park if I were dead? Memory snapshots of TJ and Joel riding their skateboards surfaced, then other pictures: TJ and Grandpa with their heads bent together over the computer. Joel and Ali playing on the trampoline. Mother's Day, when they cooked breakfast for me.

The memories vanished when the intruder moved the gun and shoved me hard. I went over sideways, dropping the can of soda and landing on the hardwood floor. The can exploded more soda all over me.

The intruder ran through the kitchen and out the back door.

Angel dashed past me, screaming that she would shoot.

"Angel, no!" I yelled as I scrambled to my feet, stumbling once when my thigh screamed a painful reminder of my bruise. I ignored the pain and hurried after Angel. I didn't want her to get shot! I raced through the swinging doors into the kitchen, but she had stopped at the back door, her gun hanging in her hand at her side. "He's gone."

My legs started to shake. It took all my willpower to get across the kitchen to Angel. I put my arm around her shoulder, to steady myself and offer her comfort. "He might have killed you. What did he want?"

She turned and looked at me with blazing green eyes. "I'm not sure what he wanted, but I know who he is."

7

Loud sirens blared down the street as Angel and I stood together looking out the back door of her house. We were both on adrenaline overload from being terrorized by the man with the gun.

"Who?" I had my arm around Angel, and I turned to look at her face. "You know who that was?" I felt a shiver start deep in my chest.

She dragged her gaze from the darkened night to me. "Zack Quinn. A poker dealer from Daystar. What the hell did he want?"

It took the police an hour or so to determine that the alleged suspect was gone. Alleged! The fact that there was no forced entry appeared to make the uniformed cops doubtful of our story. They took a report and uttered useless suggestions. We had just shut the front door after the police left, when someone knocked.

Angel hurried to the kitchen to retrieve the gun she had hidden in her Tupperware cupboard. While she did that, I looked through the peephole.

"It's Vance," I whispered when Angel returned with the

gun. She turned and opened a door to the entertainment center. Frowning at her, I said, "You have a permit for that thing, don't you?"

Angel pushed her red hair back off her face. "Yes, but it's less explaining if the police don't see it. I'm not about to let them confiscate it while they check on the permit. You saw how the cops didn't quite believe us when they couldn't find a broken window or a forced door that showed evidence of a break-in."

Watching Angel tuck the gun into the entertainment center, then shut the door, I thought about the times I'd seen Gabe unlock doors using some handy little tools he had, so I knew it could be done. But the cops had to know that was possible, too. Maybe they were so busy that they looked for reasons not to believe there was a crime.

With the gun hidden, I opened the front door.

Vance glared at me. "You. Of course." He sighed and walked in without an invitation. "I heard the report of an armed intruder."

The faint smell of coconut followed him. I took a look at Vance. Tan pants, expensive-looking black shirt, nice shoes. "You aren't working; how did you hear?"

He made a face at me. "I'm a robbery–homicide detective, Shaw. Besides, the guys at the station thought I might have a personal interest in this case since it involved my kidnap victim." His gaze slid past me to Angel. "They called me away from a date."

Uh-oh. His fellow cops were harassing Vance. Did he come here to take that out on us? He wasn't exactly thrilled to see me here. Wait—he'd been on a date?

Angel used a fabric-covered rubber band to pull her hair back in a ponytail and walked up to stand beside me. "The police took a report. We told them that the intruder was Zack Quinn, a dealer from Daystar, but they don't seem to believe us."

Vance looked around Angel's living room, taking in the groceries on the floor, then he focused on the two of us. "Tell me what happened."

Angel stepped over the remainder of the mess and sat down on the couch. I followed her to take a seat on the arm while Vance chose a square chair placed at an angle to the couch. He reached into the pocket of his black shirt, then frowned.

"Missing something, Vance?" He always carried a small notebook and pen to write notes when investigating. Guess he didn't take that notebook with him on dates.

He ignored me and sat forward, resting his arms on his legs. "Ms. Crimson, please tell me what happened."

Angel shifted, pulling her green shirt and lacy green bodice away from her chest. She'd caught some of the Diet Coke and Zinfandel spray. "I unlocked and came in through the front door carrying a bag of groceries. After shutting the door, I was halfway across the living room to my kitchen when a man jumped out of the swinging doors to the kitchen and came after me. I dropped the bag of groceries and tried to run back to the front door, but he caught my arm and stuck his gun in my face."

Hearing the story, even for the second time, since she had already told the uniforms, sent shivers up my spine. God, Angel could have been shot—why?

"Did you recognize him then?" Vance asked.

Ah, Vance had been paying attention to what Angel and I had said so far. But I wasn't really surprised.

Angel nodded. "Yes. I said, 'Zack, what are you doing here?'" He jerked me to the couch and pushed me down. That's when he said, 'Where is it?' right about the time Sam burst in the front door."

Vance turned his head to look at me. His gaze slow-traveled down my stained white shirt, jeans, and sandals, then back up to my face.

I knew how I looked. "I hit him with the wine bottle I brought with me. It broke, the gun flew out of his hand, and I saw his arm bleeding. The gun landed on the ground. Angel tackled Zack, and they fell on the wood floor not far from the gun. I picked up the six-pack of Diet Coke and hit Zack with that. A couple of cans of the soda exploded."

Vance stared at me. "Looks like you are wearing most of the soda. Smells like some of the wine hit you, too."

The light went on. "Maybe that's why the cops seemed not to believe us. The smell of alcohol."

"It didn't help," Vance said. "So how did this Zack escape if you knocked him out?"

"He wasn't knocked out, at least not all the way. He managed to get up and grab his gun. He pointed it at me. Angel had run to the back of the house to get—" I remembered then that she didn't want me to mention her gun. "Uh, to find a weapon and came running back out screaming that she would shoot. Zack shoved me out of his way and ran out the back door. It had been standing open."

Vance shifted his gaze right, to Angel. "Shoot him? You had a gun?"

Angel pulled the length of her red hair over her shoulder. "Pepper spray, but I didn't tell him that."

I swallowed a groan. Lying to Vance wasn't really going to help us here. On the other hand, why complicate things? Angel hadn't fired the gun, and I doubted Zack had even seen it.

Vance narrowed his gaze. "Do you have a gun, Ms. Crimson?"

Angel stared back at him. "Is that relevant to finding

Zack Quinn? The man broke into my house and threatened me with a gun."

That a girl, Angel.

"What is your relationship with Zack Quinn? You recognized him, so you must have spent some time with him. Did you go to the casino this past weekend to meet with him?"

Angel's voice was calm. "No. I only talked to him two times at the casino when I was at his table playing poker. He flirted with me but that was it."

"Did you flirt back?"

Angel lifted her chin. "Define flirt."

I grinned at Vance in spite of the seriousness of the situation.

Vance wasn't laughing. "Did you act in such a way as to make Zack think you were interested in him?"

"No, I told him I wasn't interested in dating him."

I glanced over at Angel. She hadn't told me about that. But then, a lot of men hit on Angel. She was used to it.

"Did he give you anything to hold for him? Do you know what he was referring to when he said, 'Where is it?'"

She shook her head. "No, and I don't know what he was talking about. It just doesn't make any sense."

Vance leaned back in his chair. He was tall and well-built, with long legs and those shoulders of a swimmer. I knew that his good looks had forced him to prove himself in the cop world, where strength and loyalty were what counted. No one got by on looks. Looks didn't keep cops alive out on the streets.

"The way I see it, you might have picked up a stalker, Ms. Crimson. Or you aren't being straight with me and you are in some serious trouble here. Do you think it was Zack who broke in to your house over the weekend?"

I turned to look at Angel, too. She'd been so convinced that it had been Hugh who had done that.

Angel answered, "There was no real forced entry that time, either." She turned to look at me. "You found the back door open then, too, right?"

I thought back to the scene and nodded. The back door had been open. "How is Zack opening the back door?"

Vance stood. "Let's go take a look."

Angel rose, too. "The cops looked and took some pictures. The door wasn't forced open."

Vance started toward the kitchen. "Do you leave it unlocked?"

Angel followed. "No. There's an alley behind my fence. That would be stupid."

I was behind Angel and Vance. By the time I passed the table, I saw Vance had the door open and was looking at it. "It's not forced. Someone with good skills could have picked it."

I was tired. All the fear and adrenaline had drained out of me. My shirt was stiff with dried wine and soda. Great, more clothes ruined, and no one seemed to know what the hell was going on. "Vance, what are you going to do? Angel could have been killed!"

He shut the door. When he looked at me, his brown eyes narrowed on my ruined shirt. "You could have been killed, too, Shaw. What have you two gotten into?"

I took a breath, inhaling the sharp wine smell that drenched my shirt. But it was Vance's flat expression that scared me. "You don't believe us."

He shrugged and headed for the door. "I'll see what I can find out about Zack Quinn."

I followed Vance to the door, feeling helpless. What was going on? What did Zack Quinn want? My thoughts spun as Vance opened the door, then stopped. Suddenly, he bent over and picked up a shopping bag. "This must be yours. I saw it when I came in."

Uh-oh. I remembered the sex-toy kit I had confiscated from Grandpa. I grabbed for it. I did not want to explain that sample sex-toy kit to Detective Stick-Up-His-Butt.

The bag tore open, spilling out the container of chocolate-covered strawberries, a romance novel, a candle, and a tumble of loose red rose petals.

But no sex-toy kit. I stared down at the mess. At first, I had the sick thought that Vance already had seen the sex-toy kit. Then I realized—

Grandpa.

He must have pickpocketed it back from the bag when I was on the phone. After everything else that had happened that night, that didn't seem important.

Vance bent over and picked up the novel.

I fought a groan. It was the latest romance by R. V. Logan, aka Logan Vance. Cripes! I stood frozen to the spot, desperately trying to think of an explanation. No matter what I said, Vance was going to think I lusted after him.

He handed me the book and leaned in close with his coconut and male scent. "I can give you the real thing." Then he straightened up and left.

I watched him stride across the flagstone atrium and out the gate. The book felt like a steamy rock in my hand.

Once the gate clanged shut, I bent over to pick up the container of strawberries and the candle. I left the rose petals scattered on the stones and headed into the house.

On her knees, Angel scooped up the rest of the eggs, coke cans, and assorted foodstuffs and tossed it all in the trash can she had brought out from the kitchen. Then she picked up a spray bottle and started cleaning the wood floor. Glancing up at me, she said, "Maybe if you slept with him, he'd believe us."

"Ha ha." I tossed the book and the other stuff onto the couch and crouched down to help. My bruised thigh complained, but I ignored that. I grabbed another rag and helped Angel get the spills off the floor.

Angel scrubbed at some dried egg. "We're going to have to investigate on our own."

I looked up. "I'll call Gabe. Maybe he's done with his job. He'll—"

A phone rang. It sounded like my cell phone. Where was my cell phone?

Both Angel and I looked around. I remembered yelling at the 911 operator, then dropping the phone. I scrambled around on my hands and knees, following the sound of the ring.

I found it under the couch. It must have been kicked under there during the fight with Zack. Grabbing it, I said a breathless, "Hello!"

"Sam? I almost hung up."

"Grandpa! Sorry, we've had a problem here."

"Before I forget, I wanted to let you know that the boys are home. They said the skate-boarding pro didn't show, so another mom brought them home."

The sex-toy kit surfaced back in my head. "Grandpa, did they catch you with that blue velvet box?" That stupid sex-toy kit was turning out to be a pain in the ass.

Offended, he answered, "Of course not! My hands are quicker than that, Sammy."

Relief poured through me. "Thanks Grandpa. Uh, did you open it?" Too much had happened for me to be mad at Grandpa.

"No, the boys came home too soon."

I smiled at his petulant voice. "Hide it in my room, OK? I'm not sure when we'll be home." I explained about Zack from the casino.

"Hey, I'll see what I can find on Zack Quinn. Might be able to get some information from Daystar on him."

"Grandpa, don't do anything illegal." I had enough to worry about as it was. "Besides, Vance is looking for Zack. Just put that blue box away."

"Never hurts to just look," he said, then hung up.

I groaned and turned off my phone.

Angel took the trash and the rags to the kitchen, then returned and asked, "What's that about the blue velvet box? Do you mean the sex-toy kit Mitch St. Claire gave me?"

"Yep. I caught Grandpa and his friends getting ready to break it open. I put it in my bag to come over here but—" I shrugged my shoulders and noticed that my neck was tight.

"Barney pick pocketed it back from you," Angel finished for me.

I nodded, then rolled my neck and shoulders. Nothing like a struggle with a man who has a gun to tighten up my muscles. I was beginning to think that Gabe was right: I should get some serious training.

Or was that jealousy because he was training another woman?

Damn right.

I picked up my phone and started dialing. "I'll call Gabe and the three of us will figure out what to do next." After hitting send, I put the phone to my ear.

A female voice said, "Pulizzi Investigations. How can I help you?"

Huh? I had dialed Gabe's cell; why was a woman answering? I finally managed, "I'd like to speak to Gabe."

"Mr. Pulizzi is in the field right now. If you'll leave a message, I'll see that he gets it."

Swear to God, I could feel steam coming out of my ears,

just like in cartoons. "What are you doing answering Gabe's cell phone? Does he know you are answering? Just put him on the phone!"

"I'm sorry, but Mr. Pulizzi is in the field. You'll need to leave a message."

Breathe. Yoga breathe, then kill the bitch. "This is Samantha Shaw, Mr. Pulizzi's—" What? Girlfriend? And what if the bitch on the phone happened to be naked with Mr. Pulizzi? Calling myself his girlfriend would be humiliating. God.

"I know who you are. I will tell Mr. Pulizzi that you called." Click.

"Die, bitch." I slammed the phone down on the couch and leaned my head back against the headrest.

"Sam?" Angel sank down next to me.

"Is your gun still in the entertainment center?" Nothing was going right. But Gabe was not doing the naked Italian dance with his assistant. I trusted him.

I just didn't trust his assistant.

Angel reached over to touch my arm. "Tell me what's going on."

I looked over at her and felt a wave of guilt. Angel had been attacked in her own house and here I was thinking about myself. "Gabe's new assistant is screening his calls. I don't think he can help us right now." Pushing away the sick feeling that that produced, I looked over at Angel. "It's not safe here. You have to stay at my house."

Angel didn't move. "What new assistant?"

"The one he just hired. They are supposed to be chasing a cheater at some motel." I fought to keep away visions of Gabe naked in front of another woman. What did she look like? Who was she? Why was she still alive when I wanted her dead?

"What motel?"

I closed my eyes. "I don't think Gabe told me." What with all the sex, who had time for questions? My stomach burned.

"What did he tell you?"

"Her name is Dee. She's answering phones, doing paperwork, and training to get her PI license."

Angel lifted her eyebrows. "To replace you?"

"Only if she wants to die." I would not slip back into being the woman I'd been for most of my marriage. I'd told myself the story of my life that I wanted to believe, instead of facing the truth about my husband, my marriage, and myself.

Those days were over.

"Besides," I added, "Gabe gave me the key to his house." That had to mean something, right?

Angel perked up. "Why?"

"He said in case you needed a place to stay. I don't think he ever bought the theory that Hugh trashed your house." Which meant Gabe was right. Again.

"So we could take a run over to Gabe's house and see if we can find out which motel Gabe and the skank are doing their cheater chasing at?"

"Angel!" Laughing, I knew I was in trouble now. I handled stress by ruining clothes. Which was better than in the old days, when I used to bake something chocolate and eat it—although if the stress got bad enough, I still did that. Angel, however, handled stress by stalking. Usually, it was Hugh she spied on. But I'd just offered her a fresh victim—and a challenging one at that.

Stupid!

"Too risky. Gabe might show up at any time. He . . . uh . . . kind of suggested that he had plans to handcuff me to his bed." Probably he didn't think I'd share that detail with my best friend. Men were really naive.

"Cool. Hey, when I add sex toys to my line, you and Gabe can be my first customers."

I laughed, glad that I'd distracted her from the idea of snooping around Gabe's house. "The first thing we are going to do is get you out of here. It's not safe. Then we will figure out what's going on. Like you said, investigate."

Some of the sparkle slid back into her gaze. "And maybe show a certain PI that you are good at investigating? Prove his new assistant unnecessary?"

I lifted my chin, trying for a confident look. "I've already proved myself to Gabe." Just as long as he didn't see me right now, all splattered in soda and wine.

Angel stood up. "All right, I'll pack some clothes and we'll get out of here. I think I'll take Gabe up on his offer to stay at his house."

I had to follow Angel to Gabe's house to show her the alarm code and setup.

That was my story. The truth was that I was going to Gabe's to snoop. Gabe hadn't called me back. Why had Dee answered Gabe's cell phone? He always took his phone with him when he went "into the field." Sure, he set it to vibrate or left it in his truck if he didn't want the ring to give him away. And what was that comment, "I know who you are?" How did she know? What had Gabe said? What the hell were he and his assistant doing? Maybe I'd get a clue from his office which motel they had gone to. But then, if I found the name of the motel, what was I going to do?

We pulled up to Gabe's house. Angel parked on the street and I parked in the driveway.

Going up to his house, I took out the key Gabe had given me and stood under the pool of amber from the porch light. Stalling, I said, "I should have gone home and changed first." My shirt was stiff and stinky.

Angel stood right behind me. "You just called his house phone from your cell and there was no answer."

"Right. Here goes." I stuck the key into the dead bolt lock and turned.

The bolt slid back. OK. Then I reached down, pushed the thumb thingie on the doorknob, and leaned into the door.

It opened.

"We're in!" Angel announced.

I stepped into the tiled entryway. Gabe's house felt empty and ominous. I hit a wall switch by the door that turned on an overhead light. Then I went to the alarm panel set into the wall behind the door. It blinked a red warning light. All I had to do was hit the correct number sequence and the alarm would deactivate.

I reached out to the keypad to put in the code and went blank. "Oh God! I can't remember! It's seven, no five—" I banged my head against the wall.

"Sam!" Angel hissed.

Lifting my head off the wall, I stared at little red light blinking the warning. I had only seconds left! I knew the code. Gabe had given it to me a while back. *Come on, don't think, just do it!*

I reached out and hit seven—suddenly the code came back to me. I punched it in.

The nasty blinking red light died. The alarm was deactivated. I turned around, leaned against the wall, crossed my arms over my stomach, and tried not to throw up.

Guilt. And disgust. A grown woman does not snoop on her boyfriend. I saw that on Oprah—it was supposed to be a sign of an unhealthy relationship or something.

Angel asked, "What would have happened if you hadn't coded the alarm in time?"

I straightened up. "I don't know; I never asked. Chances

are that Gabe would know, though. Somehow. And he'd rush back here and shoot me, then ask questions."

"Cool."

"Not cool! Almost getting shot once is enough for me tonight. Maybe we should leave. You can stay at my house."

Angel looked around. "I'm staying here." Her mood improved with each illegal/stalking/snooping step we took. "Let's get started looking to see if we can get any information on Mr. Pulizzi's new assistant."

"This is a bad idea." I said, then realized Angel was gone. "Angel! Where did you go?"

She came back with two bottles of cold beer. "Would it be a better idea with beer?"

I took one. Hell, I'd already gotten into Gabe's house. How much more of a crime could drinking his beer be? I didn't think he'd care about my coming into his house or drinking his beer, since he had given me the key.

I wasn't so sure he'd be as understanding about my snooping through his office. I twisted off the beer cap and drank a long swig.

Liquid courage. Just like my fake boobs, I often had the need of fake courage. Trying to sound brave, I said, "All right, let's do it."

Gabe had a one-story, four-bedroom house. It was a pretty standard, southern California layout. From the front door, a living room and dining room opened on the right. The fourth bedroom-turned-office was on the left. Past that was an archway that led into a kitchen/family-room combo and a hallway that opened to a bathroom and the three remaining bedrooms. Berber carpet and white tile covered the floors, the walls were white, and the furniture was standard.

But every time I came into Gabe's house, I felt another root sink into the floor, anchoring me to him and his life.

Cripes, I was overwrought. I turned and went into Gabe's office, heading around the massive desk to his big leather chair, and I turned on the fancy green lamp.

Soft light filled the room. The wall across from Gabe's desk held framed portraits of him as a uniformed cop getting accolades, shaking hands with the mayor of Los Angeles and other VIPs. There were more recent photos of Gabe with a few TV stars.

Gabe did a little consulting on scripts that had private investigators, bounty hunters, or cops in them. It was a sideline of his PI work. Truthfully, Gabe did need an assistant.

I felt a germ of guilt wiggling in my gut. I smothered that sucker with a drink of beer.

If Dee hadn't been rude to me on the phone, maybe I wouldn't have been compelled to snoop.

I looked down at the surface of his desk while Angel headed first for the door to the walk-in closet on the far wall. She put her hand on the doorknob, but a single twist proved it locked. Then she moved to the filing cabinet in the far corner of the room. "Locked. I think I can open both of them."

I glanced over at her.

She started digging around in her purse.

Uh-oh. The last thing I needed was to have Angel breaking the locks on the closet and the filing cabinet. I wouldn't be able to explain that. Besides, Gabe's cases were private, just like my clients'. Well, Gabe saw all my clients' information because he ran the security check.

Enough. I was making myself more crazy than usual.

"Angel, leave the filing cabinet and closet. Come here and help me."

She put a bobby pin back in her purse and came around the mahogany desk. "Nice computer. Let me see if I can boot that up while you look for papers and stuff."

Before I could answer, Angel found the hard drive and turned the computer on. I got up out of the chair and let Angel sit there. The computer would keep her busy and out of trouble. I turned my attention to the stacked horizontal set of files on the right of Gabe's desk. I started there. The first shelf had bills and stuff. Boring.

I went to the second shelf and pulled a stack of papers down. A fax from Blaine of the permission sheet from Fireman Bob to do a background check. A few other pending items that meant nothing to me. I put those back.

The third shelf had a large envelope. A note on the outside said, "Mr. Pulizzi, please find the lease agreement inside. Thanks." What lease agreement? Stunned, I turned over the envelope and looked at the flap.

Sealed.

Damn. *What now?* I couldn't open it without Gabe's knowing. What lease agreement? This wasn't about Dee. Was Gabe looking to open an office for his PI business? He hadn't said anything to me.

At least not since I had been avoiding giving him an answer about working with him. God.

"Gabe's computer is locked up tight."

Taking my attention from the envelope in my hand, I turned to look at the computer screen and read Enter Password. "Bet Grandpa could crack it."

Angel sat up in the chair. "Want me to call him?"

"No." I shook my head. "Angel, we can't break into Gabe's computer. He's running a business that might have sensitive information. Let's just look for information on Dee." I dropped my gaze back to the envelope in my hand.

"What's that?" Angel started to shut down the computer.

"I don't know. Says it's a lease agreement. I don't know anything about it."

After shutting down the computer, Angel picked up her

beer and took a drink. In the soft light of the green lamp, her green eyes glittered. "Let's open it."

I opened my mouth to protest, when we both heard a noise. The sound of a key in the front door, then the door swinging open.

Omigod! Fear, guilt . . . Gabe was going to kill me! I started to move, to stuff the envelope back in the filing shelf. But I didn't move fast enough.

"What are you doing?" a female voice demanded.

I snapped my gaze up to the doorway. A woman. Swear to God, she looked like a bad copy of Catwoman. She had a black capelike coat on over black leggings and a black tank top.

8

I stood in Gabe's home office, holding the large envelope I'd picked up while snooping through his desk, and stared at the Catwoman clone. Why was there another woman in Gabe's house? How many women had a key to his house? She obviously had the alarm code, too.

What the hell was going on?

Finally, the woman moved, lifting her hands to her face, and said, "Samantha Shaw. Caught snooping."

A flash blinded me. "What . . ." I blinked and saw dancing black spots. That flash had to be a camera. "You took a picture? Who the hell are you?" I shoved the envelope into its file slot.

Catwoman grinned. "Oh yeah. I'm going to download it onto the laptop and show Gabe just what his girlfriend is doing. Gabe is a man of few words who respects privacy." Over Gabe's desk, she ran her gaze down my shirt and back up. "Do you always wear stained clothes? Tacky. Gabe will notice; he notices everything."

Angel started to stand up. I put my hand on her shoulder, pushing her back into the chair. The bitch had to die, but Angel wasn't going to be the one who killed her.

And I knew who the bitch was; I recognized her voice from our chat on the phone earlier at Angel's house. "So you are Dee." I sized her up. Under the capelike coat, she had white blonde hair cut in a Meg Ryan style around her face. Her black heeled boots took her to about a five eight height, same as Angel. Nervous energy kept her twitching and shifting.

She looked a tad younger than Gabe was. Which made her more than a tad younger than me. "What are you doing here, Dee? Where's Gabe?"

She checked the picture in the viewing screen of the camera, practically bouncing with joy at what she saw. "Waiting for me, of course. He needs his laptop. He's teaching me how to write up the report for the client."

"Uh-huh. So Gabe's on the stakeout and sent you home to get his laptop." I squeezed Angel's shoulder to keep her from leaping over the desk and smacking Dee into next week. Then I let go and walked around the desk. "Translation: you were getting on Gabe's nerves, so he sent you on a fool's errand." That's what I wanted to believe. That Gabe tired of her and sent her away.

Dee sucked in her full cheeks and glared at me.

I pushed harder. "Does Gabe know you were answering his cell phone, Dee? Did you give him the message that I called?"

She narrowed her eyes and protectively clutched the digital camera she held against her flat stomach. "You can't threaten me. I'm getting the laptop and I'm going to show Gabe what you really are."

I turned and sat my butt on the desk. God, I was sore. "Go ahead," I waved my hand at Dee.

Her mouth fell open. "Huh?"

"Get the laptop. Run back to Gabe. Show him your evidence."

Her smile faltered, then spread as her confidence returned. "I will." She pulled her black shoulder bag around, stuffed the camera in it, and pulled out a key. Watching Angel and me with a sharp stare, she made a point of moving close to the wall and as far away as possible from where I was sitting on the edge of Gabe's desk. She made her way to the closet door that Angel had tried to open earlier. She pulled out a key ring and unlocked the door, then left the key in the lock and reached inside for the light switch on the wall, flipping it on.

I watched this, amused as hell.

OK, pissed as hell, too.

Dee studied the interior of the walk-in closet. It was lined with shelves, and there was a gun safe in there. I would have bet my last dollar that Dee didn't have the combination to Gabe's gun safe. She found the laptop in its carrying case right away.

But she seemed to be looking for something else.

I slid off the desk. Quickly, I looked over at Angel.

Her grin practically lit up the night.

"What are you looking for, Dee?" I was two steps away from the closet.

She glanced back at me. "Batteries. Gabe was very specific. He said, 'Always have backup batteries on a stakeout.'" She turned back around to scan the shelves while muttering, "Batteries, batteries . . ."

I had ahold of the door. "You have a cell phone, right, Dee? And it's charged?"

"Yeah." She spotted the extra batteries deep in the closet. She took a big step in, reaching up to snag them. "Mission accomplished!" she announced.

I slammed the door and turned the key still sitting in the lock. Without the key, Dee couldn't unlock the closet from the inside.

Angel clapped. "Well done, Sam!"

I turned around and looked at Angel. "She sure can scream, can't she? Gabe should soundproof that closet."

Angel arched an eyebrow. "Screaming stopped. Guess she figured out to call her boss on her cell phone. Good thing you practically drew her a map."

I smiled. "Checkmate. There's no way Gabe hired that," I jerked my thumb to the closet, "to train as a PI. Damn it, I fell for it. Telling me about Dee, giving me a key, practically giving me an engraved invitation to snoop. He's just making a point."

Angel laughed. "I believe you made an excellent counterpoint. How do you suppose he knew we were coming here right now?"

Good question. I thought about it for a second. "He probably guessed it wouldn't take us long, after Dee wouldn't put my call through." Gabe knew me pretty well. But that was a risky way to time it. Gabe didn't take those kinds of risks. I looked around. "Gabe is a security specialist. House and business alarms, that kind of thing. He set something up to notify him when we got here." Hell.

She thought about that, then asked, "So how far away do you think he is?"

I shrugged. "Let's get out of here." Quickly, I set the key to the walk-in closet down on his desk, got my purse, and winced at the banging on the closet door.

Angel glanced at the door. "Hey, are you sure Gabe will get her out? I mean, what if he doesn't show?"

The phone on Gabe's desk rang.

I looked up at Angel. "He'll get her out, Angel. Gabe's hero streak runs too deep to leave a woman, even Catwoman, locked in a closet."

Angel picked up her purse and laughed. "This is fun."

"Or insane." I made sure to set the alarm before we left.

We got into our separate cars. I smiled as I pulled out of Gabe's housing tract onto Grand Avenue. Gabe was trying to manipulate me into making a decision about working with him and getting my PI license. Using that Catwoman clone. He'd think again about playing with me when he had to leave his stakeout to rescue Dee.

Of course, Gabe would get even with me.

My cell phone rang. Pulling the phone out of my purse, which was on the passenger seat, I debated answering it. It could be Gabe. A very pissed-off Gabe.

I took my eyes off the road to glance at the caller ID. I was safe—it was Angel. As I put the phone to my ear, I glanced in my rearview mirror.

She wasn't behind me.

My stomach flipped and I said into the phone, "Don't you dare go back to your house!" Zack and his gun could show up again.

"I'm not. I'm going to drive by Hugh's house, then go stay at my mom's place."

Relief settled my stomach. "Chicken." I put the phone on my shoulder and used both hands to turn my T-bird into the dirt parking lot in front of our house. "You don't want to be around, in case Gabe shows up for a little game of revenge."

She laughed.

I parked the car and then took hold of the phone. "Why are you spying on Hugh?" I knew part of it was Angel's restless energy. She should be safe enough at her mom's house for the night, so I wasn't worried about that. With her mom and my mom on the cruise, she'd have the place to herself.

"I don't trust him. Hugh's up to something. He practically burst a blood vessel screaming at me last Friday. I think Brandi left him and he's desperate."

I bit back a sigh. "Angel, Zack's out there somewhere and he's got a gun. Hugh's not your biggest problem right now." Much as I detested her sniveling weasel of an ex-husband, I didn't want Angel distracted. She needed to stay focused to stay safe. "We need to think about what we're going to do tomorrow if the police don't find Zack."

Silence. Then, "Still, a girl's got to have fun." She hung up.

Crap. I thought I had hurt her feelings. I laid my head on the steering wheel. It had been a long day. In the last two days, I'd thought Angel had been kidnapped, dealt with a crazy romance fan, stumbled onto Angel being threatened by a man with a gun for unknown reasons, and locked my boyfriend's new assistant in the closet. Now I had hurt my best friend's feelings and was probably going to be dealing with my pissed-off boyfriend very soon.

"What a day." Lifting my head from the steering wheel, I looked at the muted yellow light coming through the front window of Grandpa's small house and consoled myself with having gotten the best of Gabe. Now he had to leave his stakeout to rescue his assistant. That would teach him to hire Catwoman. I got out of the car and stomped up the steps.

I pulled my keys out and unlocked the front door. Angel might be mad at me, but she wasn't stupid. She'd be OK. Tomorrow, I'd apologize for brushing off her worries about Hugh. Opening the door, I was glad to be home.

Ali ran out from the hallway and across the living room to greet me. She sniffed my shirt with her elegant nose.

"It's Diet Coke and wine spray, Ali."

Satisfied, she licked my hand, then turned and went back to the boys' room.

Grandpa had his nearly bald head bent over his computer screen. He waved a blue-veined hand at me. I walked through to the dining room, set my purse on the glass-topped table, and sank into a chair. "Hi, Grandpa. How are the boys?"

He leaned back and turned to look at me. "They were disappointed that the skateboard pro didn't show up. Apparently, the guy fell in practice and had to get some stitches. That's the rumor they heard there, anyway. We cheered them up with a game of poker."

I smiled. "We" consisted of the same group that I had confiscated the sex-toy kit from earlier that night. What a day. Tiredness sank through my skin into my bones. "I bet you did. Whoever cheated the best, won?"

"Sammy, we're a bunch of old men—would we do that?" He laughed at himself, his face crinkling up. Then he said, "You look beat, and your shirt looks worse."

"So I've been told." I leaned back in the chair and rubbed my eyes. "What are you doing?"

"Getting some information on Zack Quinn. Where's Angel? She's not staying at her house, is she? I thought she'd come home with you."

I decided not to scold him for Internet-snooping on Zack. "Angel's going to stay at her mom's house because she's a big redheaded chicken." I quickly told him the story of going to Gabe's house, then locking Dee in the closet.

Grandpa's milky blue eyes widened. "You locked Gabe's new assistant in a closet inside his house?"

I smiled at the memory. "Yep."

"Well, then." He turned back to his computer. "Guess I'd better give you what I have before Gabe gets here."

I frowned at Grandpa's bony back. "You mean you want to escape to your room before he gets here."

"Hey, I'm a magician. I know when to make my exit." He reached into a side drawer of his rolltop desk and pulled out a yellow tablet. He handed it with a pen to me.

"You aren't going to get arrested for hacking, are you?"

"Pshaw!"

Alrighty then, I guess that was my answer. I scooted around in my chair, got the tablet positioned on the table, and said, "Let's just hope the police find and arrest Zack Quinn."

Grandpa started reading from his computer screen. "Zack Quinn lives in an apartment on Poe Street over by the police station and Swick Matich Field." He rattled off the address.

I wrote it down. Swick Matich was one of the older parks in Lake Elsinore. It was really just a field in a V of a couple of roads that somehow got dubbed a park. There wasn't any playground equipment, but these days it was carved up into three diamonds for Little League. There were some lower income apartments in that area, and the police and sheriff's station was practically across the street.

Adding to the ambience was the lake, just a few streets over from the other side of the park. On cool nights, a damp breeze blew off the lake. But on a hot day after fish kills, the sick smell of decaying fish lay like a heavy, rank fog over the field. Lately, Lake Elsinore had been spared that particular misery.

"Sam, are you paying attention?"

"Sure." Now, anyway. "What do you have besides Zack's address?" I was glad Angel wasn't there, or I'd have to tie her up to keep her from going to Zack's apartment to confront him. I just hoped the police would get Zack's address, find him at home, arrest him, and make this whole thing go away.

But I was going to be prepared in case that didn't happen. One thing I had learned from my life, and from Gabe, was to be ready to take care of myself and my family. Angel was part of my family.

Grandpa went on, "He's worked at Daystar for two months."

I looked up. "That's all?" Then I frowned. "How do you know that?"

"I kind of peeked into his files."

"Ugh. Grandpa, you are going to get into trouble!"

"Nah. I got his Social Security number and birth date. I've already made some discreet inquiries to see if he has any criminal past." He turned to look at me. "I bet he does. Using a gun to threaten Angel in her house—that's pretty bold."

The entire top of my head tightened. "There weren't any marks on the door to indicate forced entry into Angel's house. The back door was open, though, so we think he used lock picks. A real pro could do that." Or I thought he could. I'd have to ask Gabe.

Don't think about Gabe.

Going back to concentrating on Zack, I added, "But why? What did he want? What does he think Angel has?"

He shook his head. "What does Angel think, Sam?"

"She doesn't know. She's frustrated, too. Right now, she's venting her frustration by stalking Hugh." I still felt bad for brushing her off about Hugh. "Vance said this Zack could be a stalker, but that doesn't seem right."

"Why not?"

"I guess because he doesn't really seem to want Angel. He wants something else." *Where is it?* he had demanded. Where was *what*? What was Zack talking about? "And he thought Angel should know what he was looking for." I shook my head, tired.

"Angel's only contact with Zack was at the casino?"

"Yes, she hadn't met him before last Friday."

Grandpa sighed. "Zack could be a crazy, Sam. I'll have

more information in the morning." He started shutting down the computer.

"There's nothing more we can do tonight, anyway." I stood up and kissed Grandpa's dry, weathered cheek. "Thanks, Grandpa. I'm going to say good night to the boys, take a shower, and go to bed."

He looked up at me. "Aren't you forgetting something, Sammy?"

I wracked my brain. "What?"

He stood up. "Gabe." Grinning, he turned and shuffled down the hall.

Damn. "He might not show up tonight!" I said.

Laughter floated back down the hallway before Grandpa's bedroom door shut.

I stopped into the boys' bedroom. TJ was reading and Joel was listening to his CD player with earphones in. Ali was stretched out on the bedroom floor. She opened one eye when I walked in, then went back to sleep.

Joel saw me from the top bunk and pulled off his earphones.

"What happened to you, Mom?"

I looked down at my shirt. What to do? For now, I decided that I'd skip over Angel's being threatened with a gun. "Spilled Diet Coke on myself. I heard the skateboard pro didn't show up at the park."

Joel sat up. "It was even in the paper that he was going to be there. That sucks."

Skirting Ali, I went to the bunk beds. I was too tired to suggest a better word than "sucks." "Yeah, I'm sorry, Joel. I'm sure the event will be rescheduled. The city is trying hard to make that skate park work." The city of Lake Elsinore had commissioned the skate park for a price well over three hundred thousand. Then they charged folks for using the park. Guess they hadn't been paying attention to the economy and the fact that Lake Elsinore has a large pool of macaroni-and-cheese income folks. Turned out the skate park was in the red, so now the city was subsidizing the park.

Lake Elsinore was like that. Sure, our city had had some pretty harsh failures. We had built a minor league baseball stadium with multimillion-dollar cost overruns. Then there was the much-touted Camelot Shopping Center that was now just two boarded-up buildings that were once a movie theater and a KMart. But Lake Elsinore just kept jumping in with both feet, and trying to compete with the surrounding areas.

So I was pretty sure the city would get the skate pro back for Joel and TJ to see. They didn't want to add the skate park to the failure list.

"TJ had fun. He was hanging out with a girl."

"Shut up, Joel," TJ snapped from the lower bunk.

I smiled at Joel. "Why don't you turn off your CD player now? It's getting late."

" 'K. 'Night, mom."

" 'Night, honey." I sat down on TJ's lower bunk. "Hey—"

TJ cut me off. "Mom, is Angel in trouble? I heard Grandpa on the phone to you. And besides, you got stuff all over your shirt—that usually means you are on a case."

True. I did have a knack for ruining clothes. Much like I believed TJ had a knack for changing the subject when he didn't want me asking questions about girls.

What to tell him about Angel? I had told them when I thought Angel had been kidnapped because there was no way I could have hidden it, or my worry. But now I didn't really know what was going on. I skirted it a bit. "Someone broke into her house tonight. We really don't know why.

Just to be safe, she's staying at her mom's house tonight. We'll sort it out tomorrow."

TJ's face was tight and serious. "So how did you ruin your shirt?"

I grinned. "I swung a six-pack of Diet Coke at the guy who broke into Angel's house and scared him off." OK, not exactly accurate, but I didn't want to mention the gun to TJ and Joel.

Some of the tension left TJ's face. "Really? Mom, that's pretty good."

Joel leaned over from the top bunk. "Cool, wait until I tell my friends. Their parents have stupid jobs."

Uh-oh. This was what happened when I bragged to my kids. "This wasn't a job. I just happened to be there." I didn't even want to think about what kind of rumors Joel's story would morph into.

"But it's 'cause you're a PI," Joel insisted.

"I'm not a PI, Joel. I just do part-time work for Gabe." Until I locked his assistant in the closet. Wonder what my sons would think of that escapade. Maybe I should look into bookkeeping as a side source of money to keep building Heart Mates.

I leaned down and kissed TJ goodnight. "You guys get some sleep." I resisted asking TJ about the girl at the skate park. That particular subject was going to require a little finesse to get actual answers out of TJ. I leaned down and petted Ali on the way out.

Too bad Ali couldn't talk in peoplespeak. She could tell me what girl my son liked.

In my bedroom, I stripped off my clothes, dropped my white shirt into the bathroom trash can and took a long shower. As I let the hot water ease the ache in my neck and shoulders, the day's events splattered my mind like a broken puzzle, all jumbled pieces that I couldn't make fit.

What did Zack Quinn want? What did he think Angel had?

Who was the girl at the skate park with TJ? When had TJ stopped telling me everything? Maybe I wasn't spending enough time with the boys?

Did I hear a noise? Had Gabe let himself into my house?

Shutting off the shower, I listened but didn't hear any noise. Maybe the idea of Gabe's revenge had me a little spooked. I struggled to turn off my thoughts. I needed sleep. I toweled dry, slipped on my panties, and reached under the sink for my blow dryer.

My hand touched velvet. The sex-toy kit. I pulled it out, and saw that the white strip sealing the box closed hadn't been opened. Well, what do you know, one thing had gone right that day. I set the box on the counter and finished the job of drying my hair.

By morning, my hair would revert to blonde-streaked, frizzy waves, but at least it wouldn't be as bad as if I had slept on it wet. I pulled on a T-shirt, then looked at the box.

Where is it?

Could *this* be "it?" Could the sex-toy kit be what Zack was looking for? But that didn't make sense. Mitch had given it to Angel. As far as I knew, Angel hadn't seen Zack the dealer again after we met with Mitch.

But maybe I should open it. Just to be sure. Picking up the blue velvet box, I turned off the bathroom light and went into my bedroom.

My bedside light was on and the romance novel I was reading to review for *Romance Rocks Magazine* was on my nightstand. For once, I was ahead of schedule on my reviews. Usually, I was reading both a book at work and a book at home. The book I was currently reading at work was riveting, full of suspense.

The one on my bedside table had a too-stupid-to-live heroine. A whiner. I don't know why the hero didn't kill her. Honest to God, if she complained about her hips being too slim to find decent jeans again, I would scream. What woman had hips that were too thin? Add to that that this poor creature had trouble with her shirts because her boobs were too big—and not man-made boobs either—I wanted to rewrite this book so that the girl died and came back to life only to die again. Really, I'd make a medical miracle out of her and have her die every single chapter.

I got into bed and ignored the book. I had to protect myself from the violent tendencies that it induced in me.

Putting the sex-toy kit on my lap, I thought about Angel. How pissed would she be if I opened it without her? On the other hand, what if there was something inside this box that cleared up what was going on?

All this internal debating woke up the tight ache that started between my shoulder blades and rode up to knot the back of my neck. The scuffle with Zack must have twisted and strained those muscles. I was just too tired to trudge out to the kitchen for Tylenol.

I glanced over at the stupid book on my bedside table. I had to read the whole book to write a review. That was my policy, though right now, I hated my policy.

Dull kill-me-now-so-I-don't-have-to-read-about-this-heroine book, or sex-toy kit. Oh yeah, like I had to think about this decision. If I made Angel read one chapter of the book, she'd understand. Besides, with my ambition for getting one-up on Gabe escalating, it would be foolish to overlook that this sex-toy kit might have something to do with Zack threatening Angel. If I opened this box and found answers that led to solutions . . .

Not only would Angel be safe. Gabe would be impressed.

A win-win situation.

Smiling, I reached for the sex-toy kit on my lap and broke the seal.

No turning back now. I lifted the top. The box had a spring hinge that snapped open with a faint crack.

Well.

So that was what a vibrator looked like. Actually, there were two of them, secured onto a dark blue velvet bed with little elastic bands. Who knew vibrators came in colors! One was mint green and shaped pretty much like I expected. The second one glowed a lavender color and had a protrusion at the base . . . like a real man, I guess. Sheesh.

I didn't see anything that would drive Zack to breaking in to Angel's house. Unless he had problems with women having vibrators.

Men could be strange.

Taking my eyes off the vibrators, I looked at the top of the box. There were elastic pockets that held some small bottles. I pulled them out and read the labels: massage oil, edible chocolate paint, and lickable raspberry spray. These actually looked like fun. They would complement Angel's lingerie line.

The two sides of the box had pockets. Carefully, I pulled open one pocket—velvet-lined handcuffs. Check-ing the other side—a second set of handcuffs.

Now, these I might have a use for, especially if Gabe showed up tonight in an Italian temper. If I could slip these cuffs on him . . .

Grinning, I tried to picture the scenario in which I

could succeed in handcuffing Gabe. I didn't think it would be as easy as locking his assistant in the closet.

Tucking both sets of handcuffs into their pockets, I sighed. All of it looked . . . well . . . normal, I guess. For a sex-toy kit that was supposed to be a sample. Nothing here to induce Zack to tear Angel's house apart and threaten her with a gun.

Sample. Wait, wasn't there supposed to be a catalogue of all Mitch's merchandise inside? That would have Mitch's contact information, so where was it? I slid my hands around the vibrators, bottles of oils, and paints. . . . I couldn't find any more pockets.

Maybe Mitch had forgotten to put the catalogue in?

Face it, this was a wild goose chase. It was driving me crazy trying to figure out why Zack was after Angel. I had hoped for an easy answer.

The sex-toy kit was just what Mitch had said it would be. Sex toys. I'd just tell Angel that I had looked in it out of desperation to find answers. With everything else going on, she wouldn't care.

Using my right hand, I rubbed the back of my neck but couldn't reach that spot between my shoulder blades. With my head bent and my gaze on the colorful vibrators, I wondered if I should go to the hallway closet and drag out the heating pad. I hated falling asleep with it plugged in because of the fire danger.

There was something to be said for batteries. I grinned, remembering Gabe's assistant so diligently looking for batteries in the closet—right before I slammed the door and locked her in.

Hmm, batteries. Vibrators. That would work. . . .

I stopped trying to reach the spot between my shoulder blades and studied the vibrators. Not the lavender one with the . . . uh . . . appendage. But the mint green one. . . .

I reached into the box and slid it from the elastic band holding it in place. It was cool and smooth. The casing was made of a moldable silicone. Turning it around in my hands, I saw the base had a battery compartment and a little switch.

I moved the switch.

With a low hum, it started moving. Vibrating. Interesting . . . I was too tired to think sexually interesting right now. Besides, this was Angel's and—ugh—some things just weren't meant to be shared.

But as a massager? My muscles cried out for relief. I set the rest of the sex-toy kit on the floor and slid it under my bed but still in easy reach. When I was done with the "massager," I would put it back in the box, close it, and shove it back under the bed.

Next, I arranged my pillows, put the "massager" where it would hit the perfect spot on my upper back and neck area, and lay back on it.

"Oh, yeah." It was perfect, vibrating against that tight, painful knot. I groaned, then reached over to turn out my bedside lamp. In the dark, I closed my eyes. Just for ten minutes.

A ringing jarred me awake. Confused, I tried to turn off my alarm, but the noise didn't stop. Wait, that was the phone ringing. I levered up on my right elbow and reached for the phone with my left hand. "Hello?"

"Surprise."

Either there was one hell of an echo in my phone—

Or there was a man in my room.

9

Fear slammed down on my chest. How could I hear a man's voice on the phone and in my bedroom at the same time? Flinging the phone back on the hook, I looked around in the dark. How long had I been asleep? Was it morning? Who was in my room? Male voice. I tried to make out the shapes in the room. My desk, my bookcases, a large man—

Oh God. There was a man in my bedroom!

Something touched my left hand. Something cool, long, and round. I closed my hand over it. A weapon! I jumped up out of bed, switched the weapon to my right hand and raised it over my head.

The light by my bed snapped on.

Blinking, I tried to see the threat.

Gabe leaned against the wall by my bedside table, holding his cell phone. Faded jeans and a black muscle shirt made him look too damn good for the middle of the night.

He stared at my raised right hand. His hard mouth curved. "What exactly is that you are planning to attack me with?"

"Huh?" I had just had a year scared off my life. And what pissed me off more was I had known Gabe would show up eventually. I took a quick look at my alarm clock. Five a.m. Jeeze. The man did not play fair. Using his cell phone to call me while standing right next to my phone? At five a.m.—that was just evil. Lowering my arm, I looked at my hand to see what weapon Gabe meant.

The vibrator.

Heat rushed into my face, making me dizzy. "Oh, this?" How did I explain a mint green vibrator? I must have fallen asleep while using the vibrator on my sore neck. "It's, uh . . ."

Gabe's eyes darkened. He took a step toward me. "Don't you know the cardinal rule of weapons, babe? They can be turned back on you."

His voice had thickened. Omigod, he knew what it was and it turned him on! "No! I mean, I was using this as a massager. For a spot I couldn't reach!"

He arched an eyebrow. "Well, now, you should have called me. I would have reached that spot for you."

Oh God. Humiliated beyond words, I could not believe he'd caught me with a vibrator! It looked . . . desperate. Pathetic. And there Gabe stood, looking hot and dangerous, ready to pounce. All smug with his "you should have called me." Trying for a shred of dignity while I stood in my black T-shirt holding a vibrator that practically glowed green, I said, "I did call you, stud. Your *assistant* answered your cell phone. Explain that." How did I get rid of this vibrator? Drop it? Toss it casually on the bed? Damn.

Gabe's smirk spread out into a full devil grin. "So you were calling me for my stud service? Sorry I missed that, but I'm here now." He took another step.

The man was stalking me, closing the distance between us slowly. Just one step away, he was taunting me. Gabe had the supreme confidence that he could seduce me into wanting him. Which was true. But I was not going to be played. Annoyance started to edge out my embarrassment. "Don't worry about missing my call, stud." I held up the mint green vibrator. "You replaced me with Dee, and I replaced you with Mr. Green Pleasure here. It all works out."

Gabe went stone still one step away from me. The light from the lamp in my bedroom backlit him in the predawn hour. Olive skin over hard bones; a nose that might have been broken in a street fight—not disfigured, just with a slight bump; dark eyes that took in his environment almost without any effort on his part. His mouth pulled tight. His eyes darkened to a near black. He closed the last step between us. His dark eyes zeroed in on my face. "Am I that easy to replace, babe?" The question was silky.

Too silky. I'd stirred the dormant ashes of Gabe's considerable temper. He was so close, I felt his body heat mixed with anger. I fought to keep my voice steady. "Why should you be any harder to replace than me? How long did it take you to find Dee?"

"Not long," Gabe answered in that same silky voice. "But then, I was looking for an assistant, not your replacement."

"Oh?" OK, we had a match here. My own temper flared hot. "Give me a break, Pulizzi! You were baiting me with your Catwoman clone. You all but drew me a map with your intention to replace me with your newest hero-worshipping trainee. Do you think I'm stupid enough to believe that you didn't know she was answering your cell phone? You have caller ID on there!" I was doing that whisper-yell thing. On one level, I knew the boys were asleep down the hall so I whispered. But I was so damn pissed that I *yelled* the whisper. I consciously made my throat unclench and added, "Giving me your house key was a nice touch."

Gabe's shoulders relaxed a notch and he quirked up the left side of his mouth. Devil smirk, a smirk that just forced horny women to zero in on that mouth with erotic fantasies. "Yeah, I thought the house key might get your attention. The best part had to be sending Dee in to get my laptop and extra batteries. Taking the digital picture was her idea."

Picture. Crap, I'd kind of hoped that getting locked in the closet would have made Dee forget about that picture. "You saw that? Never mind, it doesn't matter."

Gabe's grin widened. "Keep that thought in mind."

Huh? Uh-oh. There was most likely only one reason Gabe had shown up here in my bedroom—revenge. I hadn't seen the picture Dee took, but I knew what I had looked like last night. My white shirt had a wine-and-soda dye job, my hair had to be wild from my fight with Zack . . . "Where's that picture?"

"Could be anywhere by now." Gabe oozed smugness.

God, it was too early for this. "What have you done?"

"Hey, I'm not the one playing with sex toys. Not that I have anything against sex toys." He grinned, then snatched the vibrator out of my hand.

Heat shot up into my face. "Give me that back!" I reached for it.

Gabe took a single step back. "Be happy to." His eyes gleamed with wickedness. Then he turned the vibrator over in his hands. He flicked the switch on, but nothing happened. Raising his gaze, he said, "Looks like you've worn out the batteries."

This was not happening. I was dreaming. If I pinched myself, I would wake up. I took a step and tried to grab the vibrator.

Gabe caught me around the waist with his free hand, tugging me to him. Looking down into my face, he grinned. "You look kind of sunburned."

"Shut up." Now I sounded like my kids. I wanted to die of embarrassment. Staring at his throat, I admitted, "I fell asleep with it on the back of my neck. I didn't—"

"Babe."

Trying to act like an adult woman, I looked up into his face. Make a joke, I told myself. Make this bearable. Pretend to be sophisticated enough that it didn't matter. "Just tell me you didn't take a picture of me with that." I glanced at the stupid thing in his left hand.

He smiled. "Only in my head, sugar. I have lots of those pictures in my head."

OK, I could breathe. Maybe survive this. "Guess I can't censor those."

Gabe lowered his face close to mine. "Stop being embarrassed."

"I can't help it. It's not even my sex-toy kit. I just—"

He blinked once. "Sex-toy kit? You have a sex-toy kit? This just keeps getting better. I think I've died and gone to heaven."

"It's not mine!" Getting flustered, I tried to wiggle out of his arm around my waist.

He tightened his arm, bringing me up to meet his mouth. The touch of his lips sent shards of electricity along all my nerve endings. They pooled wet heat in my belly. I put my arms around his neck, kissing him back.

He lifted his head to look at me.

I met his heated gaze. This was part of Gabe's sexiness. When we were together, even when I was naked for him, I wasn't embarrassed or worried about my flaws. He made me feel sexy. Sex toys stretched the limits of that feeling, though. "I really did fall asleep using it as a massager."

"Don't ruin my fantasy."

"Really?" I watched his face. "That's a fantasy?"

"It's going to be a reality, first chance we get." He shifted me until I stood. Then he took my hand. "Right now, though, you need to tell me what's going on. Why do you have a sex-toy kit that's not yours? What happened to your shirt in that picture last night? And why are you sore now?"

I had a bit of trouble shifting. My mind had a disturbing tendency to get stuck on sex and Gabe. "How do you know I'm sore? Oh, I told you I used the vibrator to massage my neck."

He tugged me toward the bed and pulled me down to sit beside him. "That, and you are stiff. I can feel it. What happened, Sam?"

He sat on my left. He set the vibrator on the other side of him. My mind was starting to get up to speed. "That's why you are here? Because of my shirt in that picture?"

He rubbed his thumb over the back of my hand. "It worried me. Ruining clothes for you is like a national broadcast that you are on a case. You aren't exactly working for me now, so how could you be on a case?"

He still had ahold of my hand. I felt the tension in his fingers. "I'm not on a case. Well, not for money for your agency. But something weird is happening with Angel." I told him the entire story of walking in on Zack threatening Angel with a gun. I kept my voice level when I told him that Zack had had the gun pointed at my face. Unlinking my hand from his, I leaned down and fished out the velvet box from under my bed. "That's why I looked through this sample sex-toy kit. I thought maybe there was something in here that Zack wanted." I refused to be embarrassed now.

Gabe dropped his gaze as I opened the box and asked, "Who gave that to Angel?"

"A man named Mitch St. Claire. We were watching Rick Mesa's group, the Silky Men, perform when he approached us. Well, he approached Angel, really."

"Does this Mitch St. Claire have any connection to Zack?"

I shook my head. "Not that we know of." I glanced up at Gabe. "I know it was a long shot. I just can't figure out what Zack wants. It was stupid. I was looking for easy answers." Truthfully, I remembered that gun in my face. The desperation of Zack behind that gun. What did he want? I shuddered at the memory of staring down the barrel of that gun.

Gabe touched my shoulder. "That's not stupid. The answers often are the most obvious ones." He turned slightly, so that his thigh pressed into mine. "Sam, is it possible Angel's not telling you something?"

"No." I said it without thinking.

"Are you sure? Think, babe. If Angel made a mistake, she might not want you to know."

Anger rushed up. "I am sure." I bit off the words. I had made misjudgments in the past. My husband was a prime example. Then there was the time Blaine hadn't wanted to tell me about his past problem with drugs because he had thought I would judge him. But Angel knew better. She knew I'd help her if she needed me. "I'm sure," I repeated.

Gabe moved his hand from my shoulder to the back of my neck. Slipping to the inside of my T-shirt, he rubbed the tense spot. "OK, so this Zack Quinn is breaking into Angel's house to look for something she has, but neither of you know what that is. Then he breaks in again and uses a gun to demand to know 'where it is.' She still has no idea what he's looking for?"

"I know it sounds crazy. He came in the back door." I

ran my fingers over the edge of the velvet box on my lap. "Can you open a lock without the cops being able to tell?"

"Yes. But not just anyone can."

Gabe's warm hand felt like bliss on my sore muscles. "That has to be how he got in. The door was sitting open and he ran out of it."

Taking his hand from my neck, Gabe pulled his phone off his belt. "I'm going to change my plans and stay here."

I wanted to grab his hand and demand more neck rubbing. "What plans?" I grinned then. "Oh, that's right, with Dee locked up in your closet, you had to leave your cheater to rescue her."

Gabe grinned while scrolling through his phone numbers in his cell phone address book. "That case is finished. I'm going to teach Dee how to write up the report tonight. Today, we have another case. A guy with severe back pain had to go out on workman's comp, but oddly enough, it's not the kind of back pain to keep him from repairing the roof on his folks' mobile home in Hemet. As luck would have it, Dee and I will be shooting a video for Dee's modeling career in that very same mobile home park. And that's just so convenient, if I happen to catch severe-back-pain-guy on tape working on his parents' roof."

Incredulous, I said, "Dee's still working for you?"

He looked up from his phone to me. "She took a little convincing after being locked in a closet, but she finally agreed. Besides, she has a brand new bikini and is excited to try it out on videotape."

Good for her. She could be buried in it. Bet she wouldn't look so good in that bikini *dead.*

Gabe found the number and started dialing. "I'll call Dee and tell her we're going to hold off on that."

Part of me wanted him to do just that. Part of me wanted him to never ever see Dee the Catwoman in a bikini. But that was the same part of me that had called Gabe last night because I was scared. The gun in my face had tripped something inside me and I had wanted to run to Gabe and have him hold me, then fix everything.

Not good.

"No." I put my hand over his dialing finger. "Go on your case. Vance will probably have found Zack. Angel's at her mom's house. Everything is under control."

Something feral rolled through Gabe's eyes and stamped down hard on his face. "Under control?" He shut off his phone, dropped it on the bed, and reached for me, taking hold of my shoulders. "A man held a gun to your face and you think it's under control? Then you were too chicken-shit to call my cell phone back after Dee answered and demand to talk to me? No, babe, this is not under control."

Startled by the depth of his feelings, I shot back with, "I am not chicken-shit. OK, I am, but not like that. I would have called you if I—" I broke off. If I what?

"If you *needed me?*"

He dragged me closer. Close enough to see that he had taken time to shave his hard jaw smooth. "Tell me you didn't need me after looking down the barrel of that gun."

I glared at him. "I did call you!" Then I got it. "Don't turn this back on me. You're mad at yourself because you didn't answer your phone. The hero inside you just can't stand that you missed a rescue-me call." I jumped up, dumping the sex-toy kit on the floor. Glaring down at Gabe, I said, "Maybe if you weren't trying to make me jealous—"

Gabe unfolded from the bed to his full six-foot-plus height. "Jealous?" His voice sank down to that silky death tone. "You have me arranging my entire life around you, and you think this is about jealousy? Maybe," he leaned forward but didn't touch me, "I'm tired of being second string in your life." He turned, went to the bedroom door, and yanked it open.

"Second string? What the hell are you talking about?" Honest to God, I didn't know!

He turned back, looking every bit the part of the oh-so-done Rhett Butler in *Gone with the Wind*. "I won't beg for your love, Sam." He was gone.

My chest hollowed with shock. I took a step to run after him, but the toe of my left foot caught on the sex-toy kit. I stumbled and fell to one knee. The skin of my left knee burned across the carpet.

I hated that sex-toy kit. Picking up the velvet box, I hurled it out of my way. It hit the wall two feet from my bedroom door and thunked to the ground. Stuff spilled out of it. I didn't care. I got to my feet; I had to catch Gabe. To stop him. To wipe that wounded look off his face.

I stepped on something pebbly hard. Yelping, I lifted my foot and looked down at a black jeweler's bag that was a bit smaller than an index card. I started to ignore it and rush out when a hard glitter caught my eye.

I knew Gabe was already gone. I was too late. Something terrible, knotty, and acid-tasting was ballooning up my throat. Through a hot film of tears, I stared at the glitter spilling out of the loosely tied end of the jeweler's bag. Sinking down to my knees, I reached out and touched the black bag. It was velvet, just like the sex-toy kit lying open on its side. Next to that was the lavender vibrator with the appendage. The end of the vibrator, what I assumed was the battery compartment, gaped open like a perfectly round mouth. The black jeweler's bag must have fallen out after the sex-toy kit hit the wall and spilled out the vibrator.

I picked up the black velvet bag, put my fingers inside the opening, and pulled the gold strings open. Then I turned the bag over and dumped out the contents.

The just rising morning sun streamed through my bedroom window and caught the icy fire in the most gorgeous diamond necklace I'd ever seen. It had three strings of beautifully cut diamonds in what I guessed was a platinum setting. It looked like it belonged around the neck of Jennifer Lopez in one of her fabulous low-cut gowns. Instead, the necklace rested cool and hard in the palm of my hand. I stared at it. An answer. Here was the answer to what Zack was looking for at Angel's house.

But all I saw was Gabe's wounded face. I knew what I felt for Gabe. But I also knew that Gabe was healing from the nightmare of the murder of his wife and unborn son. Once he healed from that, he'd want a family again. A wife and children of his own.

I was just a stepping stone in that process. I was five years older than Gabe, I already had my children, and I was a miserable failure at love. Heart Mates and reviewing romance novels were the closest I could get to love.

Closing my fingers over the sparkling diamond necklace, I couldn't stop myself from whispering. "I do need you."

I had to pull myself together. I had two sons who needed me, a best friend in serious trouble, a business to run, and a life to live. I stuffed the necklace into the pouch and placed it back in the lavender vibrator. After that, I reassembled the sex-toy kit and closed the box.

Getting up off the floor, I tried to think. *Vance. Call Vance.* I went to my purse, dug around, and came up with Gabe's house key.

Shaft of pain. *Ignore it.* Holding the key, I got out my wallet and found Vance's card. I called the police station, punched in Vance's extension, and got his voice mail. OK, here goes. "Vance, it's Sam Shaw. I found a diamond necklace inside a box that Angel and I got from Daystar. That must be what Zack Quinn was looking for. I will bring it by the police station on my way to work this morning." I hung up.

OK. So far so good. Next, I dialed Angel at her mom's house. And held on to the key to Gabe's house.

"What? Who gets up this early?"

"Angel, it's me. I opened the sex-toy kit and found a diamond necklace. I called Vance. Meet me at the police station—"

Angel woke up. "A diamond necklace where? I'll be there ASAP!" She hung up.

I set the phone down and squeezed the key in my hand. What next? Clothes. Couldn't go to the cop shop and work in a T-shirt and panties. I went to the closet and pulled it open. Dressing quickly, I put on a pair of black jeans, a pink tank top, and a jacket over that. Put on minimal makeup, fluffed my hair, and took a deep breath.

I squeezed Gabe's stupid house key in my hand. Mail it back? Drop it off? Give it to Blaine and tell him to return it? What did I tell my kids? Hey, boys, I just got dumped by your hero. Want some Fruit Loops?

Stop it. Just stop it. I stuck the sex-toy kit in my purse and forced myself to leave my bedroom. Grandpa's door was still closed.

Hell. I was up before Grandpa. That meant I had to make the coffee. I stopped halfway down the hallway and sniffed.

So why did I smell coffee? Angel couldn't have gotten here that fast. Did criminals looking for diamond necklaces break in and make coffee?

I doubled back to my bedroom and set my purse on the bed. Returning to my closet, I found my big can of pepper spray. After positioning my finger on the nozzle, I went back out in the hallway and walked as softly as I could in my boots. The doorway to the kitchen was on my right. From there, I could see the back door was closed, with the dead bolt lock turned.

But the smell of coffee was stronger. The kitchen was a long galley kitchen that opened into the dining room. There was a sliding glass door there someone could break in through. Or the front door . . .

Finally my common sense kicked in. I had an alarm system, and better yet, I had a crack guard dog. If someone had broken into my house, they'd be ground meat by now, or at the very least, I'd have heard Ali's warning barks.

The coffeemaker had a timer. Sometimes, Grandpa set the timer.

I squeezed Gabe's house key in my left hand, while dropping my right hand, which held the pepper spray, to my side. "Idiot," I muttered. Taking a breath, I tried to pull myself together and walked into the kitchen.

Gabe leaned against the counter with his back to the window over the sink. He sipped coffee. And watched me with a subzero expression.

Stunned, I stopped cold. My mouth fell open. "Uh . . ."

He arched a single eyebrow. It was a signature look for dealing with me.

"I thought you'd left."

"You would." He took another drink of coffee.

My stomach squeezed up a splash of acid. I didn't know what to do. I wanted to escape. To not face all the being-adult-about-a-breakup crap. I didn't want to be adult. I squeezed the house key.

House key. Gabe's. Adult women returned their boyfriends' house keys. Unless they were Angel, in which case they used said house keys to fill up their boyfriend's house with Vaseline and toilet paper.

I knew I'd better return the house key. My feet felt like

lead bricks in my pointy-toed boots. I took a step and held out my hand. Unclenching my fingers, I turned my hand palm up. "Here's your house key."

He glanced down at the key, then he slammed his frost-bite gaze back into me. And didn't move.

I could spray him. That would have zapped that icy look right off his face. My right hand actually twitched around the can of pepper spray. He stood there so damned sexy and mysterious, making me squirm because I didn't have the guts to tell him I loved him. God, I really wanted to spray him.

"Try it, Sam. Go ahead."

I turned around, took a step to the stove and slammed the can down beside it. It made a satisfying thunk. "What are you, Dirty Harry now, Gabe?" I smacked the key down next to the can, but it barely made a sound. I had the urge to pick up the can of pepper spray and bang it on the counter over and over. "Get your own house key." I turned to storm back to my room.

Gabe caught my left elbow, then shoved me up against the old olive green refrigerator. It hummed against my back from the vibrations of the ancient motor. Gabe's face was so tight, I saw white lines around his mouth and nose. But his voice was soft. "I don't want my house key back."

"You don't?" That was too weak and hopeful. Using the fridge to pretend I had a backbone, I said, "I played that love-your-man game once, Gabe, and came out looking like the town dupe. I'm not going to do it again. Besides, we both know that I'm just a stepping stone for you." There. I told the truth. "You can take your house key now."

I heard the chugging of the refrigerator motor behind me. In front of me was dead silence.

"I smell coffee," Grandpa's voice was cheerful as he walked into the kitchen. He stopped when he got to my right shoulder where I was pinned up against the refrigerator. He had on gray slacks, a yellow-and-green-plaid shirt, and a crinkly smile that never wavered. His milky blue gaze slid from me to Gabe, who had both his hands placed flat against the fridge just above my shoulders. Grandpa made a swift about-face. "Forgot something," he said, and went back down the hallway.

Great. I stared after him, willing him to turn around and come back.

Gabe's voice climbed up from silky death to baffled when he said, "Stepping stone? You are a stepping stone?"

Since Grandpa had bailed, I had no choice but to turn back to Gabe. He looked like the words didn't fit in his mouth.

"Stepping stone. Stopover. Rebound. The one you bang while your heart heals, then you move on. Come on, stud, this should all be old news to you." My face burned hot enough to fry an egg on.

He rolled his eyes. "This is what I get for falling in love with a woman who reads romance novels. I should be shot."

"You have been shot," I pointed out. That was what had led him to taking an early retirement from the LAPD and landed him here in Lake Elsinore to open his PI business. I didn't like thinking about Gabe's being shot, so I turned to his romance novel comment. "Don't be so smug. I've seen you read one or two of my books."

He leaned his head down. "I read them for the sex."

"Whatever. Are you done threatening me? I have a full plate this morning. You know, break up with my boyfriend, hurl the sex-toy kit at my bedroom wall, then discover a diamond necklace in the vibrator, get the boys ready for school, dash off to the police station to explain the necklace in a vibrator to Vance—"

Gabe thawed and slid his hands behind my head and back, pulling me toward him. "Slow down. Diamond necklace in a vibrator?" He shook his head. "We'll get to that in a minute." He took a breath. "Stepping stone. Christ, I don't even know how you dreamed that one up."

I decided to help him out. "You will want a wife and kids again." I was older. I knew what I was talking about. "Gabe, look at how good you are with TJ and Joel. As time goes by, you're going to realize that it wasn't your fault . . . what happened. And you'll want it all. You were meant to have kids."

He was silent. One of his hands found the sore spot on my neck and gently rubbed it. "That's the biggest load of bullshit I've heard since I've been off the streets."

I blinked. "Excuse me?"

The vicious ice mask over his face dissolved completely. "Bullshit," he clarified.

Reaching out, I shoved at his chest.

He didn't move.

"Listen here, stud. I am not bullshitting you. I'm trying to be realistic. I'm trying to be an adult. And damn it, when I push you, move!"

He grinned. "Touched a nerve, huh? And do you know why, Sam? Because you are scared of what you feel for me."

"I could be a lot madder at you if you'd stop rubbing my neck." I swear, if he made me cry, I was going to get the pepper spray and make him cry. I hated being this vulnerable. "Stop smiling like that! I fell for that happily-ever-after stuff once. I won't do it again."

"Yes, you will." He shifted his fingers from massaging my neck, tunneling them deep into my hair and pulling me to his mouth.

I sank into his kiss when the phone rang.

Gabe stepped back and I hurried to the other end of the kitchen, snatching the phone off the hook. "Hello?"

"Flat tire." Angel announced. "I'll be there as soon as Auto Club gets their sorry butts out here and changes it."

"OK, I'll call you if I leave before then and you can meet me at the police station."

"One question. How did you find the necklace?" Angel sounded both irritated and excited.

"I threw the whole sex-toy kit against the wall. When it fell, one of the vibrators broke open, spilling out the necklace."

"Cool." She hung up.

Gabe leaned against the wall where the phone was, watching me. When I hung up, he said, "It was all part of my master plan, babe. I meant to get you that pissed off so you would throw the sex-toy kit and discover the diamond necklace."

I was surrounded by insane people, and it was barely six A.M. Narrowing my gaze, I said, "You meant to get me naked and play with the sex-toy kit."

"That, too."

10

I walked Gabe to his truck. He leaned back against the door and pulled me into his arms. "You will call if there are any problems?"

I looked at his face and felt my heart catch. It was getting harder and harder to keep our lives separate. Gabe was making it harder. "All depends who will be answering your cell."

His mouth twitched. "I'll tell Dee that if you call, she's to give me the phone."

Gee, thanks. What had he told Dee yesterday? Piss off my girlfriend if she calls? I shoved it aside. "I'll be fine. Angel and I are going straight to the police station with the necklace."

He arched an eyebrow. "Leave the necklace in the sex toy kit, Sam. Give it all to them."

I sighed. "Yeah, yeah, evidence and all. I know." I just couldn't wait to explain to Vance why Angel and I had a sex-toy kit. Vance already thought I was a trailer-trash bimbo Barbie. On the other hand, Vance hated that I appealed to a part of him he wanted to deny. A part of him that wasn't so high-nosed and sophisticated and desired a woman like me, who wore tight jeans and had breast implants. Seeing Gabe's steady gaze on my face, I said, "I'll take the diamond necklace in the sex-toy kit. Give Vance a thrill."

Gabe's hand, which had been resting on my back, flexed. "I've changed my mind. I'm going with you."

I shook my head. Vance and Gabe had gotten into a slugging match not too long ago. If Vance starting shooting off sex-toy innuendoes about me in front of Gabe, there was no telling what would happen. They both had guns! "Go film your workman's comp guy. Vance may have already arrested Zack if he found him. And once Angel and I give Vance the diamond necklace, there's no reason for Zack to threaten Angel." But it bugged me. "How did Zack know there was a diamond necklace in there, when Mitch St. Claire gave that box to Angel and me? It just doesn't make sense."

He used his hand to cup my chin. "Not your problem. You have an open house to worry about tomorrow night."

I smiled. "You remembered."

"Don't insult me, sugar. I'll see you tonight." He brushed his mouth over mine, then added, "Unless you need me sooner, then you'll call, right?"

I stared back at him. "Gabe, once I give the—"

He still had ahold of my chin. "Sam."

Stubborn Italian. But he's also the Italian who remembered my open house at Heart Mates because it was important to me. I forced the words out. "I'll call you if I need you."

He laughed. "That looked like it hurt. Later, babe." He turned, opened the door, and got into his truck.

I went back inside. The boys were sitting at the table eating cereal. Ali crunched her breakfast in her spot by the sliding glass door while Grandpa drank coffee and read the paper.

"Hey, Mom," TJ said between bites of Fruit Loops, "Grandpa said the skate pro is in the paper. He had an accident in practice and had to get stitches. He's going to reschedule the demonstration in a week or two."

I smiled at TJ, while wondering about this mystery girl Joel had said TJ liked. "Great, TJ. It'll probably be in the newspaper. Do you boys have your homework? I put lunch money out for both of you." I went to the coffeemaker, got down a cup, and poured some coffee. How long would it take Angel to get there? Auto Club should have had her tire changed by now.

"I have a permission slip for a dance." Joel waved the white paper back and forth while drinking down his orange juice.

I took the permission slip and read it over. Dance on Friday night. I got a pen, signed the permission slip, and handed it back to Joel. "Do you have your homework?"

Exasperated, he answered, "I didn't have any homework, remember? You left your pepper spray on the counter."

I smiled. "Thanks, Joel."

TJ got up and took his bowl to the sink. Tilting his head toward the can of spray, he asked, "Did you think Gabe was a robber or something, mom? Grandpa said you should have expected him to show up, since you locked his assistant in the closet."

"Grandpa said that?" I glared at Grandpa. "What kind of example does that set for the boys?" I demanded of him.

He laughed, folding up the newspaper and going to his computer. "Probably lets them know that no one should mess with their mom."

I grabbed the pepper spray from the counter by the stove.

Joel shut the dishwasher. "Hey, Mom, do you know what Gabe's gonna do to get even?"

No. The only clue I had was that it probably had something to do with that picture Dee took of me. "This isn't a game, Joel. Gabe and I are adults. Now it's almost time to go to school."

Joel and TJ laughed all the way to their bedrooms. Sighing, I took the pepper spray and my coffee to the table and sat down. "Grandpa, I can't believe you told the boys that I locked Dee in Gabe's closet!"

He had signed on to his Internet service. "Don't start on me. I figured it was better to tell them that, than about the diamond necklace you found in a sex-toy kit."

"Gabe told you." He had told my grandfather! It was my morning for hot embarrassment. "At least now we know what Zack wanted from Angel." I frowned, looking at my watch. "Where is Angel?"

Swiveling his chair, Grandpa fixed his milky blue gaze on me. "He told me because he loves you, Sam. He wants someone watching your back while he's out of town working. Call Angel if you are worried about her."

I dropped my gaze to my coffee. All true. Gabe wasn't a liar and wouldn't say he cared about me if he didn't. But telling my grandfather about sex toys? Nothing much embarrassed Gabe. Or Grandpa. I played with the can of pepper spray and said, "I'll give Angel a few more minutes."

"All right," Grandpa said and turned back to his computer screen. "Here's what I have on Zack so far. He was arrested as a juvenile for theft and breaking and entering. His record was expunged."

Unease spider-skittered up my back. "Any adult arrests? How old is Zack?"

"No adult arrests, and he's twenty-two. He was sixteen and seventeen when he got into trouble."

"How did you get the information, Grandpa? If his record was expunged—"

"There's always a trail, but I found this out by connections. Found the arresting officers who remembered him. They said that Zack was following older kids, had average intelligence but didn't think things out, and that he believed he was owed by society."

"Connections" meant Grandpa's Triple M society of magicians that spread far and wide. If the National Security Agency ever found out how much information that network of magicians accessed, they'd become a secret weapon. I had learned to trust that information, but I didn't like what I was hearing. "Guess Zack grew up and is trying to think for himself now. He must have stolen that necklace from someone at Daystar, but how did he come across Mitch's sample sex-toy kit?" I bit my bottom lip, realized what I was doing, and took a sip of coffee. "Mitch carried the sample kit in a briefcase. I guess Zack could have found an opportunity to stash it in there—maybe not realizing that Mitch would give that box away. But then, how had he planned to get the necklace back? And how would he have found out that Mitch had given it to Angel? From there, he'd have to get Angel's address—"

Grandpa cut in, "Sam, the main thing is to get the necklace to the police."

Snapping my gaze up, I nodded and tried to let go of the puzzle. "And maybe they've already arrested Zack, anyway." And I could make Vance satisfy my curiosity about Zack and the necklace.

Joel rushed out. "Mom, I have to get to school early to turn in my dance slip!"

Grandpa stood up. "Come on, guys, I'll drop you off on the way to my meeting. I have important news."

Meeting, my ass. Grandpa was going to Jack in the Box to huddle with the gossipy senior citizens in town and to tell them all about the sex toys and the diamond necklace.

I hugged the boys good-bye, then watched as Ali ran out with them to Grandpa's Jeep. She raced around, barking and playing with them. At last they were all settled inside. Once Grandpa started the Jeep, Ali ran back up the steps to the porch and sat next to me. We watched them leave.

I looked down at my watch. It was about twenty minutes to eight. "Come on, Ali." We went inside. I headed down to my bedroom, where I got my purse and double-checked to make sure the sex-toy kit was inside.

The doorbell rang.

"Finally, Angel's here," I told Ali.

Ali barked and ran to the door.

I reached in and took the sex-toy kit out of my purse to show Angel the necklace. Hooking the strap over my shoulder, I hurried down the hall to the door.

Ali stood impatiently at the door, and looked back over her shoulder at me.

"I'm getting there, Ali." Shifting the sex-toy kit to my left hand, I opened the door. "What took so long? I was just about—Zoë!" What was Zoë doing here? Where was Angel?

Zoë clomped past me into the living room. This morning she wore a bright yellow sleeveless T-shirt with green cargo pants and combat boots. She had the length of her thick black hair pulled through a black baseball cap of some kind.

"Zoë, what are you doing here?" How did she know where I lived? Why was she here?

The tightly toned muscles in her upper arms rippled as she thrust two framed pictures at me. "Your sons like skateboarding, right?"

Shifting the velvet box under my right arm, I took the pictures. "My sons?" I stared at Zoë. "What do you mean, my sons?" How would Zoë know about TJ and Joel? I glanced down at the top picture in my hand. It was a signed eight-by-ten shot of the skateboarding pro who had been scheduled to do an exhibit the night before. The top one had, "To Joel," written across the picture, and a signature. The second framed picture was the same thing, only with TJ's name.

Apprehension rolled my gut over and tightened up my sore neck muscles. Zoë knew I had two boys, and she knew their names and their interests.

Ali whined low in her throat and nudged my leg.

I looked down at my dog. She cocked her head and stared at me. She didn't know what to make of my confusion. Neither did I. "Zoë, what's going on here?" I held up the pictures.

Her gaze was on the sex-toy kit under my arm. "It's business, Samantha. I do something for you, you do something for me." She looked up at me. "I met TJ and Joel at your office, remember? They told me they liked skateboarding. Since that pro couldn't be at the skate park last night, I thought your sons would like signed pictures. Now give me R. V. Logan's real name and address."

Ali made a low rumble in her chest at the boys' names. Not a growl exactly, more like a warning that she was paying attention.

I put my hand on her head and struggled to keep calm. "How do you know the boys were at the skate park last night?"

"I saw them there."

My brain screamed *stalker!* Psycho romance stalker-fan. Or was she some kind of pervert who liked teenage boys? Struggling to keep calm, I took a couple of steps to the coffee table and set down the signed and framed pictures and my purse. Then I moved the sex-toy kit from under my arm and tucked it inside my purse. Ali sniffed around the items I set on the table, while I fixed my sight on the pepper spray on the kitchen table and moved past Zoë in that direction. With my gaze on the can of spray, I asked over my shoulder, "You went looking for my sons?"

"You make it sound sinister. I saw that there was going to be a skateboarding exhibition in the paper. I am into extreme sports and went to watch. Obviously, since I like the sport, R. V. Logan likes the sport, so I took a chance that I might run into him there. Instead, I saw your sons."

OK, maybe I shouldn't turn my back on a lunatic. I pivoted around with the pepper spray in easy reach of my right hand. Ali headed toward me, her toenails clicking dully on the linoleum. Zoë stood a step closer to the coffee table. "Zoë, how did you get those signed pictures?" I didn't even want to know how she thought she'd recognize her beloved R. V. Logan since she claimed she'd never seen him.

She glared at me across the room with her deep-set brown eyes. "You're not very grateful. I overheard that the pro skate guy had an accident and went to the hospital, where he was getting stitched up. The hospital people were as ungrateful and suspicious as you are. But I managed."

I'll bet. She had probably read Stephen King's book *Misery* to get some ideas on how to manage. I had to get her out of my house and keep her away from TJ and Joel. I tried to phrase my words carefully. "Zoë, I appreciate your thoughtfulness in getting the boys these autographed pictures, but I'd rather you stayed away from them. Now, I'm on my way out to work. You need to leave."

She barely blinked. "I will leave just as soon as you give me R. V. Logan's real name and address."

I closed my hand around the pepper spray. The knotted muscles in my neck and shoulders had developed into a full-blown headache. Turning for a second, I watched Ali stretch out on her blanket by the window while I debated in my head. If it came to a choice between my sons and Vance, otherwise known as romance writer R. V. Logan, Vance would lose in a heartbeat. But I didn't think it was coming to that yet. And I needed Vance to cooperate when I took the diamond necklace to him. I looked back at Zoë in her multipocketed cargo pants and yellow sleeveless shirt. "Zoë, I don't know who R. V. Logan is. I just don't know how else to convince you." *Except with this pepper spray,* I thought as I tightened my grip on it.

Her face hardened. "You're a liar, Samantha Shaw." She turned and stormed out the open front door.

I hurried across the room, slammed the door, and leaned back against it. Ali got up and came over to me. She sniffed the can of pepper spray still clutched in my right hand, then sat down to let me pet her.

Finally I sighed. "Come on, Ali. Let's go call Angel. If she hasn't been snatched by aliens, then she can meet me at the police station once she gets her tire changed." I headed toward the phone on the wall.

Ali barked and raced to the kitchen. I picked up the phone, punched in Angel's cell phone number then leaned around the corner to see Ali with her nose in the seam of the fridge. Apparently she thought we needed a beer break. "No beer, Ali."

She kept her nose in the seam and wagged her tail.

Angel's cell phone started to ring in my ear.

Someone knocked on the front door.

"Finally," I hung up the phone. Ali followed me to the door, wagging her tail. She apparently liked this game. Probably she thought the winner got a beer.

I pulled open the door and groaned. Detective Vance blocked out the morning sun. He was dressed to arrest in his dark pants, serious white shirt, and snazzy tie. His coat covered his shoulder holster and emphasized his wide shoulders which narrowed to a trim ass. If he'd been five minutes earlier, he could have arrested his lunatic fan.

What a morning.

"Vance, I was just on my way to the police station." Or I would have been if I had talked to Angel. I opened the door to let him in.

"I'm not taking any chances, Shaw." He came into the living room and bent over to pet Ali.

"Whatever." I ignored the implication that I'd somehow lose the necklace. "Did you find Zack? It had to be the necklace that Zack was looking for last night."

He stood up from petting Ali. "We went to his apartment but he wasn't there. He didn't show up there overnight. Oddly enough, I found out that a diamond necklace was stolen from Daystar last Friday night and the suspect is Zack Quinn. He hasn't shown up for work since his shift ended on Friday."

I stood there, thinking. "So Zack's still out there."

"Looks like it. I got your message on my voice mail this morning that you just happened to find a diamond necklace. A necklace that was stolen the same night you and Angel were at the casino. Quite a coincidence."

My scalp tightened, contributing to my headache. That's why Vance had shown up at my front door—cops don't believe in coincidences. Why the hell wasn't Angel here to help me explain this? "I just found the necklace this morning. That must be what Zack was looking for at Angel's house, but we didn't know we had it!"

Vance stood in the living room between the pressed wood coffee table and the TV set against the wall. "That happens to a lot of folks, Shaw. They can never quite figure out how they came to possess stolen property." Smug arrogance laced every word he said.

The best way to end this would be to get it over with. Give him the necklace in the vibrator. . . .

Oh crap. "Uh, there's a reason we didn't know about the necklace. See, this man at Daystar came to the table Angel and I sat at. He had a proposal for Angel's lingerie line." I took a breath.

Vance unfurled a small smile that had his flat cheeks flirting with dimples. "Selling diamond jewelry that fell off the back of a truck?"

"No!" Outraged, I put my hands on my hips. "Cut it out, Vance. You know Angel and I aren't criminals." I suspected he was letting me twist in the wind to get a little revenge. Angel and I had made him the butt of his cop buddies' jokes. Plus Vance and I had a little sexual chemistry, and I kept choosing Gabe over him.

"I have no such knowledge, Shaw. Why are you stalling?"

Hell. "I'm not stalling. Anyway, Mitch—"

"Wait." Vance's face shifted into cop mode. He reached up into his shirt pocket and pulled out a notebook and a pen. Opening the notebook, he said, "What's the name?"

"Mitch St. Claire. But I don't know if he knew what he had. I mean—"

Vance cut me off. "Where in Daystar were you?"

Getting annoyed because I wanted to get this over with, I said, "The Nova Lounge."

He wrote and then looked up. "Friday night?"

"Yes."

"All right, what did Mitch give you?"

"He gave it to Angel, as a sample to see if she wanted to sell his products through her lingerie parties for Tempt-an-Angel."

Vance made a note, then fixed his eyes on me. "What products?"

I met his gaze. There was no going back now. "Sex toys."

The only sound was Vance clicking his pen on and off. His expression remained cop-blank. No dimples surfaced. After a few seconds, he blinked and said, "Sex toys." *Click. Click.*

I had finally pushed Vance off balance. "Actually, it's a box of sex toys. I found the necklace in one of the vibrators."

The clicking stopped. "This morning? How did you discover the necklace in a vibrator?" He moved in. "I'll need details."

If he touched me, I thought I'd see blue sparks. Then it dawned on me. He thought I'd found the necklace while experimenting with the vibrator. "Jeez, Vance, I hate to burst your bubble, but I found the necklace when I threw the sex-toy kit against the wall."

"Hmm."

Did I hear a sizzle? "Hmm what?" Outrage rolled up my throat. "It's the truth! I tripped over the stupid kit, got mad, and threw it against the wall. Stuff spilled out of the sex-toy kit and I saw the necklace. That's what happened."

"So you woke up this morning, got out of bed, and tripped over a sex-toy kit that just happened to be there?"

Second time this morning I'd been called a liar. Vance was less blunt than Zoë, but still. "That's what happened." I folded my arms over my chest.

"Sure. We'll write that down. It'll look better in my report."

"You have a dirty mind, Vance." I reached for my purse on the coffee table to give him the sex-toy kit and get this over with. The doorbell rang.

Angel. *Finally.* Letting go of my purse, I went to the door and yanked it open.

Angel strode in wearing a pair of black leather pants and a tan tank top. "Auto Club ran late this morning.

Fireman Bob happened by, though, and he changed my tire. Then the Auto Club guy showed up while Fireman Bob was changing my tire and they got into an argument about the right way to change a tire. I had cancelled my Auto Club call, but the guy didn't get the notice. Typical screw-up."

I shut the door. Two men fighting over changing Angel's flat tire wasn't that big of a shock. But Fireman Bob was a Heart Mates hottie. I wondered if Angel was interested in him.

Angel glanced at Vance, then back to me. "I thought you said we were going to take the necklace to the police station."

Vance said, "I thought it prudent to come here and get the necklace myself."

"Prudent. What a tight-ass word." Annoyed, I said to Angel. "Vance is suspicious of us. Like we'd call and confess we had a diamond necklace if we had stolen it."

Vance shut his notebook. "Get the necklace, Shaw."

Angel took in the tension between us, then looked at me. "I want to see it, too."

I just wanted it gone. Out of my house. Out of my life. As soon as I dumped this on Vance, he could go out and find Zack. Angel and I could get back to our lives. I moved to the coffee table, opened my purse, and peered inside.

Wallet, calendar, lipstick, breath spray, keys-with-Gabe's-house-key, receipt for new shoes, hairbrush. My heart kicked up and slammed throbs of pain into my head. Reaching in, I dug around. Pulled out my hairbrush, a diet bar, case of pressed powder.

Gone. The sex-toy kit was gone.

Vance said, "Shaw, what are you doing?"

Where was it? I had had it when I answered the door for Zoë. I glanced at the two framed, signed pictures. No sex-toy kit sitting out on the table. I'd set the framed pictures down by my purse.

I distinctly remembered putting the sex-toy kit in my purse.

Omigod. When I moved to the dining room to get the pepper spray, Zoë must have seen the blue velvet box in my purse and stolen it!

"Shaw, stop stalling. Where's this sex-toy kit and diamond necklace?"

Furious, I let go of my purse and stood up. "Gone. Your greatest fan, who believes you are her heart mate, stole it."

11

Detective Logan Vance didn't look like a too-handsome sun god. Right at the moment, he looked like an extremely pissed-off cop in a suit. Before he could explode, I said, "It has to be Zoë who took the sex-toy kit and the necklace. I had it in my hand when I opened the door for her, then I stuck it in my purse and set my purse on the coffee table." Babbling now, I picked up the two framed pictures and held them up between us. "She brought over these autographs and demanded I give her R. V. Logan's real name and address in exchange!" The woman was crazy.

Angel said, "That yoga freak was here? And she stole the sex-toy kit?" She turned to Vance. "What are you waiting for? Go find her!"

Vance had developed a throbbing twitch at the outside edge of his left eye, and his hands clenched into white knuckled fists at his sides. He ignored Angel and fixed his stare on me. "Did she see the diamond necklace?"

Setting the pictures down, I shook my head. "No. It was inside the vibrator, and that was inside the box."

Vance reached down to pull a folded piece of paper

from his suit pocket. He opened it and stuck it in my face. "Is this the necklace you found, and lost?"

I looked at the paper. It was a faxed picture of the exact necklace. Was I going to jail? "Yes. At least that's what the necklace looked like."

Angel grabbed the paper from Vance's hand. "Are those real? How many carats?"

Vance took the paper back from her. "A quarter of a million dollars' worth." To me, Vance said, "The two of you had better start explaining. So far, you've led me on a wild goose chase. Now I want answers. Start with who was in the two cars that were pulling out onto the street from your house just as I pulled in."

"I don't know what's going on!" My thoughts spun frantically. "Two cars? You probably passed Zoë, but no one else was here. Grandpa already left to take the boys to school." I felt like I was sinking in confusion. Nothing made sense. How had Zack gotten that necklace into the sex-toy kit that Mitch gave us? Why? Obviously, it was stolen, but why hide it in there? Was Mitch involved? What about Zoë? Could Zack have sent her to find the sex-toy kit and steal it back?

Vance kept his gaze locked onto me. "Two cars, Shaw. A black Lincoln Navigator SUV and a green Ford Focus. A female in the Ford and a male in the SUV."

Damn, he was good. I'd never have gotten all those details as I passed two cars. "Zoë must be in the Ford Focus. We just have to find her." My heart pounded viciously. I swallowed, unable to believe how bad this looked, and how furious Vance was. "I never saw a man. Chances are the SUV that you saw was just someone turning around in the dirt lot in front of our house."

Angel tilted back her head. "I've met Zoë, Detective. The woman is nuts."

Vance pulled air deep into his lungs, raising his swimmer's shoulders up to his ears, and then he let it go. He walked to the love seat, sat down, and said, "Start from the beginning with how you met Mitch St. Claire to how the necklace disappeared this morning."

I went to the couch adjacent to the love seat and sat down. Ali put her head in my lap, while Angel sat on the other side of me. I studied Vance as he arranged his pocket-size notebook on his knee. I didn't know a whole lot about police procedure and territory, but I suspected that Vance had called either the Temecula police or Daystar security and told them he had a lead on recovering the necklace.

And once again, I had made Vance look bad. I would be lucky if I didn't end up in handcuffs. Taking a breath, I recounted the whole mess of Mitch's giving Angel the sex-toy kit, then how I took it home and only just this morning found the necklace in it. I described every detail I could remember.

Vance looked at Angel. "Do you have contact information for Mitch?"

Angel shook her head. "His information was supposed to be in a catalogue inside the sample kit." She looked at me.

I shook my head. "There wasn't any kind of catalogue."

Angel shifted back to Vance, "Mitch has left a couple of messages on my answering machine, but he didn't leave a phone number."

"Do you have caller ID?" Vance asked.

"It was blocked."

"How did he know about your lingerie business?"

Angel shrugged. "He said he had heard about me at the casino. I was promoting my business there. The Silky Men wear my lingerie and promote it as well."

"I see. And did you give out your address?"

She shook her head. "Phone number on my business card, but it wouldn't be that hard to find my address."

Vance frowned. "Something's not adding up. Why you? According to Daystar security, they believe that Zack Quinn stole the necklace, based on the victim's story that she picked Zack up for a night of sex. She had the necklace on when they went up to her room, and it was gone when she woke up from a deep, probably drug-induced, sleep."

I frowned. "It makes sense to me. Zack is the obvious suspect, so he had to find another way to get the necklace out of the casino, in case the victim woke up too soon and he was caught. So he paid someone to pose as an entrepreneur and pass the necklace in a sex-toy kit."

With a deadpan stare, Vance asked, "Then what? Run to Angel's house and steal the necklace back? That's too risky. Too many things could go wrong. And why Angel? How did they know about her lingerie business? Could they be sure she'd accept the sex-toy kit? It'd be much easier just to pay this Mitch St. Claire to walk the necklace out of the casino and meet him somewhere later."

Crap. There was a reason Vance was a detective, while I only worked part-time for my PI boyfriend. Or at least I had worked part-time with Gabe until he had hired an assistant.

Angel said, "But the fact is that Mitch did give me a sex-toy kit with a diamond necklace in it. What's your explanation, Detective?"

Vance shifted his gaze beyond me to Angel. "That's what I'm trying to find out. Had you and Sam told me that a man gave you a sex-toy kit at Daystar the day Sam thought you were missing, we might have the answers right now."

"I forgot! It didn't even cross my mind." Lord, I felt stupid.

Vance closed his notebook and faced me. "Unless Zack paid the two of you to get the necklace out of the casino for him. And when you found Angel missing, you thought he'd kidnapped her because the two of you were double crossing him. That would be an excellent reason to not mention the sex-toy kit to me." He stood up.

I jumped to my feet. "That's stupid! Angel and I didn't even know the diamond necklace was in there. Why would I call you and tell you I had it this morning, then?"

He shook his head. "Hell if I know, Shaw. I'm just a dumb cop." He closed the distance between us. "But if you want to keep your ass out of jail, then you call me the second you hear from Zoë. Then I'll . . ." He trailed off as he realized that he was the very person Zoë was trying so hard to find.

"You'll what?" I demanded. I was not going to be threatened by Vance. "Autograph her collection of R. V. Logan books? Give her a bookmark? Dedicate a book to her?"

His jaw tightened. "I'll send a uniform to get the necklace from her." Then he added, "My writing never interferes with my job as a cop, Shaw. I do my job."

"Then find Zoë."

"Do you have her full name? Address? Phone number? Place of employment?"

I blinked, seeing the problem. "The name she gave me is Zoë Cash. She's taller than I am, with black hair and brown eyes. Big-time into yoga and romance reading." I struggled to think of something that would help. I didn't even know if Zoë lived in Lake Elsinore or had come here to find me, and, ultimately, R. V. Logan. "Wait . . . she said she had just been to a romance convention. *Romance Rocks Magazine* holds a convention every year. Zoë knew who I was from the reviews in that magazine, so I'm sure it's their convention. Maybe you can find out more about her through that." Somehow.

"That's all?" Vance drilled home his disgust with his stare.

"I wasn't interrogating her, Vance! I was trying to help you by getting rid of her."

"You just never get it right, do you, Shaw?" He turned and left.

Angel stood up next to me. "He's not going to help us."

I hadn't even left my house yet and the day was a complete disaster. "I should call Gabe. He told me to call him if there was a problem with turning the necklace over to Vance." I headed toward my kitchen phone.

Angel passed by me and went to the coffeepot. "And tell him what, Sam?"

With the phone in my hand, I watched Angel get down a coffee mug and fill it up. "That a crazy romance fan stole the necklace." Then I admitted, "That probably doesn't happen to a lot of people." I hung up the phone. With Dee in the picture, hell, with the picture Dee had taken of me the night before, when she had caught Angel and me snooping through Gabe's office, I wasn't excited to tell Gabe my latest failure.

Angel went to the refrigerator and pulled out the milk. "Let's try to find Zoë first. The two of us can outsmart that lunatic. We'll get the necklace back." She poured some milk in her coffee, then put the milk carton away.

I stood by the phone and thought out loud. "Once we take the necklace to Vance, he'll believe us. Then he'll concentrate on finding Zack so that you are safe." That made sense. "I'm sure Zoë took that box to blackmail me. I mean, she's really focused on finding R. V. Logan. If she was working with Zack, she'd have taken the sex-toy kit the first time she saw it." I knew she'd seen it at Heart Mates the day I was painting and again the day before, when Angel and I were getting ready to look at it.

Angel took a sip of her coffee. "So how do we find her?"

"She usually finds me." *Think!* What had Zoë told me? Any hints as to where she might be? "She went to the skate park last night." How could that help us? "Wait!" I hung up the phone and ran down the hallway to my bedroom. Once in there, I went to my desk, snatched up my Rolodex phone tree, and hurried back out to the dining room. "I can call around my phone tree and see if anyone in here knows anything about Zoë."

Before Angel could answer, the phone rang.

I picked it up. "Hello?"

"Boss," Blaine said, "there's a line of people waiting to sign up at Heart Mates. What are the chances of you making an appearance?"

Work. Heart Mates. Ignoring Blaine's sarcasm, I asked, "A line? Really? How did that happen?"

"Word on the street is that we have signed a sizzling hot fireman who is looking for love. Four women want to sign up before the open house tomorrow night so they can come to the preparty mixer for our clients. Strangely enough, they are expecting to see you here."

Wow. Talk about a fast gossip grapevine. Excited, I answered, "OK, I'll be there. I'm leaving right now." I hung up. Then I looked at Angel.

Nothing like being torn between my best friend, work, and that nagging feeling that I should call Gabe. "Let's take the phone tree to work. We can make calls from there."

Angel finished off her coffee and took the cup to the sink. "Maybe Zoë's there already, waiting for you."

"Ha, we should get so lucky." But just in case, I grabbed

the can of pepper spray that I'd left on the dining room table and stuck it in my purse. One way or another, Zoë was going to give me that sex-toy kit with the diamond necklace back.

Blaine was on the phone when Angel and I got to Heart Mates, saying, "Yes, ma'am, we did recently add a fireman to our client list." He looked at me and winked. "We can set you up with an interview today at ten o'clock. Will that work for you?"

I turned to the right. The old metal folding chairs in the little waiting area were empty. Where were the potential clients? Let's see, all I had to do that day was interview possible new clients. Find the crazy romance fan who stole the missing diamond necklace in a vibrator so I could prove to Vance that Angel and I had nothing to do with the burglary of the necklace. Find Zack before he found Angel again. And get Heart Mates ready for the open house the next night. How hard could it be?

I heard Blaine hang up. I turned around with a questioning look.

"The new clients are in the interview room, boss. I put in the advertising videotape we made for tomorrow night and let them preview it. I'm still putting the finishing touches on it."

Dang, Blaine was good. I'd never have thought of that. "Great." I held out my hand. "Do you have their interview sheets?"

"Right here." He reached to the side of his desk and picked up four clipboards. "Oh, and Gabe faxed over the clearance for our fireman."

When had he done that? Busy boy, my Gabe. "Good." I turned to Angel. "Why don't you go in my office and start calling anyone you know on my phone tree to see if they know anything about Zoë. I'll clear out these interviews and be right in to help you."

Angel took the Rolodex from me.

"Boss?"

I had started reading through the first potential client and said, "Hmm?" *Abby Rochester. Divorced . . .*

"Don't you want to see the clearance that Gabe sent over?"

Looking up from the interview sheet, I took in Blaine's bland expression. He looked the same as ever. The front of his brown hair was feathered with the length pulled back into a ponytail. Thick neck, average face. Wore a blue work shirt. All looked normal except that his mouth twitched. "Why?"

"Gabe has a new business stationery."

"So?" Oh crap. Maybe he had listed Dee as his new assistant or something. I held out my hand. "Let me see it."

Blaine picked up the fax sheet from his desk and handed it to me.

I looked down and saw a picture of myself centered at the top of the page. It was the picture Dee had taken the night before in Gabe's home office. My wild, shoulder length, blonde-streaked hair matched the wide-eyed shock in my eyes and tight pull to my mouth. The stained white button-down shirt made me look like I had rolled in the mud days ago. Worst of all, I was holding the large envelope I'd taken from Gabe's desk and looked guilty. "Pulizzi's Security and Investigative Services. When you need the real thing, not a TV-sitcom knockoff." The air evaporated out of my lungs.

Angel leaned in, read over my shoulder, and burst out laughing.

I looked at Blaine. "Get that smile off your face! How many places do you think Gabe sent this to?"

His smile widened. "He sent me a download of the picture in my e-mail. No telling where-all Gabe has sent the picture."

"Men." They think they are so funny. I smacked the stack of four clipboards down and went to the coffeemaker at the end of Blaine's desk. "He probably only sent it to you," I glanced up at Blaine. "Gabe wouldn't hurt my business." Or I didn't think he would.

"Dee might," Angel pointed out.

I filled my heart-stamped mug with coffee. "True, and she might be the type to hold a grudge for getting locked in the closet."

Blaine bounced his gaze between Angel and me, then settled on me. "Who is Dee and what did you do?"

Holding my cup of coffee, I snagged the clipboards. "Angel can fill you in. I'm going to see if the ladies would like to do a group interview or do one at a time. I have a business to run." Trying to look dignified, I opened the door to the interview room and went in.

I was just finishing up the interviews with my four new clients when Blaine stuck his head in. "Boss, Zoë's on the phone for you. She's says it's urgent and you will want to take the call."

I jumped up. Things were looking up. All four ladies had signed on for Heart Mates dating packages and Zoë was calling. As soon as I found out where she was hiding, I was making a phone call to Vance and saving Angel's and my butts. "Thanks, Blaine! Can you take it from here? The ladies have picked the dating packages they want and would like to do a videotape for potential dates to view." I tried to keep my voice calm, but I was desperate to get to the phone before Zoë hung up.

"Got it covered." Then he turned to the ladies, smiled, and said, "We could do a group interview video . . ."

His voice trailed off as I shut the door. I didn't want to lose any more seconds going to my office, so I grabbed the handset from the phone off Blaine's desk. "Zoë!"

In my ear, Zoë said, "Samantha, I have something of yours, even if it is kinky. Fake diamonds in a vibrator? You'd think a woman who reads romance novels would have better taste."

Angel came out of my office and sat on the end of Blaine's desk while I said into the phone, "Zoë, listen, that necklace isn't—"

Zoë cut me off. "I'm done playing nice, Samantha. If you ever want another diamond-laced orgasm again, tell me R. V. Logan's real name and address and I'll return your sex toys. I'll call back in five minutes." The phone disconnected. I pulled it away from my ear and stared at the handset.

Angel asked, "What did she say?"

I looked at her. "She said she'll trade the sex-toy kit with the necklace for R. V. Logan's real name and address. She'll call back in five minutes. The woman is crazy." I slammed the handset down. "She has no idea what she has. She thinks the diamond necklace is fake." Disgusted, I walked out from behind Blaine's desk and into my office. I got my purse out and found Vance's business card.

Angel came in just as I picked up my phone. She asked, "What are you doing?"

"Calling Vance." That way he could be ready once I had a place to meet Zoë.

Angel reached across my desk to the base of the phone and hung up. "No. You and I will meet Zoë, give her what she wants, then we will take the necklace to Vance. If Zoë sees the cops coming, she'll run."

She was crazy enough. God. "Vance can send a plain-clothes or—"

"You didn't get a phone number, Sam. So you'll have to set up a meeting anyway. Then the police would scare her off. Wackos like Zoë can smell cops. Listen, Sam," Angel said while keeping her finger on the hang-up button. "No one I called this morning knows who Zoë is. I don't think she lives in Lake Elsinore. If she rabbits, we'll never see her again. Zack's not going to believe that someone stole the necklace from us. We're in deep shit here."

She was right. If Zoë took off, we were toast. What would Gabe do? He'd probably set up some kind of sting. Why couldn't Angel and I do the same thing? The two of us should be able to outsmart one psycho stalker-fan. I pointed out the one flaw that I could see with her plan. "But we can't give her Vance's name and address. We already have enough problems without pissing off Vance more. Who do we tell her R. V. Logan is?"

Angel smiled. The first smile I'd seen that day. "I have the perfect candidate. We'll tell her that Hugh is R. V. Logan."

I choked on the very idea of Angel's ex-husband writing a romance novel. "Hugh?"

"Sure. Once we give her the name and get the sex-toy kit back, it won't matter how fast she figures out we lied."

When the phone rang again, I snatched it up. "Zoë?"

"Well? Are you ready to deal?"

I fought down a wave of sheer, butt-kicking anger. At first I hadn't been too sure of Angel's plan. But now I was ready to take on Zoë Cash. "Yes. I have what you want."

"Tell me R. V. Logan's name and address."

"No way, Zoë. I'll meet with you and exchange the information for my stuff. Do you know where Smash Coffee is?"

"You are trying my patience, Samantha." I heard clicking noises in the background, then, "Is that a coffee shop that's located on Grape Street?"

I guessed that Zoë was on a computer, surfing the Internet to find Smash Coffee. I'd seen Grandpa do that. "Yes. In the Wal-Mart shopping center. Be there in a half hour."

"Fine. But you'd better have what I want, or you'll never get your sex toys back." She hung up.

Angel looked up at me. "I'll drive."

Angel parked her Trans Am in front of Smash Coffee and we got out of the car. I glanced in the backseat. "Angel, maybe you should roll up the windows and lock the car." She had stacks of white folded towels neatly lined up on the seats.

Angel went around the front of the car. "It's locked, and I have the alarm on. Besides, who would steal plain white towels for a beauty shop? I took those out of my mom's dryer at her house last night. She must have forgotten she brought them home to wash before she left for the cruise. I'll drop them off at the shop later today in case they are running low."

I followed Angel into Smash Coffee. Inside, it had the look of an outdoor patio. The walls were painted a light pecan color and trimmed with glossy white molding. Leafy green plants trailed along the ceiling and the top of the walls to create a sort of jungle effect. The floors had a rough-finish tile that matched the pecan walls. Glass-topped, wrought-iron tables and cushioned chairs were scattered on the left side of the shop.

The right side of the shop had a long counter that rested on several clear glass containers of coffee beans. Behind the counter were rows of sparkling machines, presumably for grinding and making coffee. On the end of the counter stood a nose-high glass bakery case filled with breads and pastries.

My stomach growled.

"Samantha! Angel!" Dominic Danger called over his shoulder. He turned on a noisy machine, then took the tall silver container out and filled a Smash Coffee cup. When he turned to face us, he flashed a smile that advertised his white teeth in his tanned face.

"Hi, Dom." I looked over at the tables while Angel chatted with Dom. There was a group of four women dressed in work-out clothes, chatting together. They had the worn, sweaty look that suggested they'd done some kind of exercise. Ugh.

A man in jeans and a T-shirt read the paper. He looked familiar. He raised his head and we both recognized each other at the same time. Fireman Bob. I smiled and did a little wave, trying not to think about him looking up my skirt. At least I had my black jeans on today—he couldn't look up those.

"Samantha, what would you like?" Dom called out. "How about my new Brownie Blaze?"

I didn't see Zoë. Turning to Dom, I smiled. "I think I have enough of a brownie butt. How about black coffee?"

He grinned. "Caramel nut flavor? No calories."

I nodded and glanced at my watch. It had been a half hour. Where was Zoë?

Dom went to work behind the counter, filling our orders. "Sam, I was just telling Angel, you have got to see Anastasia. She gets more gorgeous every day. See her pictures there on the counter?"

Sure enough, there was a framed eight-by-ten photo of a gray cat wearing a collar studded with blue sapphires to match her eyes. I rolled my own eyes at Dom's back. Anastasia was a cat that had been dumped on me as a kitten. After she peed all over me.

It had taken me a while, but I finally found her a perfect

home. Dominic Danger adored the kitten. Anastasia lived like a princess with Dom, even getting regular pedicures.

I looked over to Angel to see her reaction.

She ignored the picture. "Do you think Zoë will show?" She looked around the room, then her gaze returned to the fireman. "Be right back."

With mixed feelings, I watched her go over to chat with Fireman Bob. Bob was bringing in new clients, and I had signed him only yesterday. What if Angel liked him? What if he dropped out of my dating service?

What if he made Angel happy?

"Samantha!" Zoë burst through the door. "Oh, you are still here! I was afraid you would leave. I've been shopping."

Uh-huh. She had exchanged her green cargo pants for a bright orange crepe skirt that she wore with her sleeveless yellow muscle shirt. I needed my sunglasses to look directly at her. "Zoë, I'm not leaving until I get back the property that you stole from me this morning."

"You'll get it back when I get what I want." She swept to the counter. "I'd like some green tea, please."

Dom looked her over. "That blend of colors looks marvelous on you."

"Oh." Zoë blinked, then added, "Thank you. I . . . ah . . . wore it for someone special."

Dom nodded as he began steeping the green tea for Zoë. "Excellent choice."

Hmm, maybe my opinion of Zoë's outfit was colored by the fact that she was crazy. Hard to say.

"Here you are, ladies," Dom set three cups on the counter. "Coffee for Sam, chai tea for Angel, and green tea for our lady in orange-and-yellow fire."

Zoë actually blushed, then picked up her cup and said, "Samantha will pay."

Dom met my gaze and grinned, which made him look like a little boy. "She's got character."

"Yeah, like right out of a Stephen King novel." I pulled a ten out of my wallet and paid while Angel cut away from Fireman Bob and followed Zoë to the tables closest to the door.

I picked up my coffee and Angel's tea, then went to the table and took a seat with my back to the window.

From my right, Zoë said, "Samantha, do you have the name and address?"

Angel jumped in, "Do you have the box? With everything in it?"

Zoë stared across the table at Angel. "I'm negotiating with Samantha."

Angel leaned across the table and hissed, "You're going to be negotiating with my gun if you don't hand it over."

"Angel!" I glared at her. "You didn't bring it!"

Keeping her green eyes fixed on Zoë, she nodded that she had brought it.

Great. I was sitting between two crazy women. And one of them was my best friend. I got the index card out of my purse and tried to calm everyone down. "Here's the name and address of R. V. Logan." I waved the card. "Let's make a trade."

Zoë snatched the card out of my hand and rose. "You'll get your toys just as soon as I verify this information." She started to leave.

Angel jumped up to catch her. I leaped up from my chair to stop Zoë before Angel could use her gun to stop her.

We all froze at the loud explosion.

12

After the explosion, all I heard was a buzzing in my ears. Sort of like a bunch of bees stuffed inside my head. I looked around Smash Coffee to see what had fallen or exploded.

Fireman Bob sprang to his feet and started running toward the door with his cell phone pressed to his ear and his gaze fixed on the window behind me.

Confused, I turned to look.

I saw the flames through the stenciling on the plate glass window. Angel's Trans Am was on fire. "Oh God." It didn't make sense. I looked at Angel.

She stared out the window, her green eyes big enough for me to see the reflection of the flames dancing in them. I took hold of her arm. Then I turned to Dom, who stood transfixed behind the counter with the phone to his ear. "Call 911!" I shouted. Then I realized that was what he was doing with the phone to his ear. God.

He looked over at me. "Talking to them now."

Angel yanked her arm from my hold and ran.

"Angel!" I ran after her.

She didn't even look at her car, but instead she stared toward the street. "What?" I followed her gaze.

"Zoë. She's gone."

The firemen got the fire out, saving the surrounding cars and property from damage.

Angel's red Trans Am was a blackened, smoking mess.

The sidewalk in front of Smash Coffee was crowded with people. They had wandered over from the Vons and Wal-Mart anchor stores, and the smaller health food, shoe, hair, and nail shops, and one of those all-in-one privately owned post office places.

I made my way through the curious onlookers to where Angel stood in a group of serious-looking cops and firemen.

Angel turned to me. "They found a homemade device in the backseat."

My chest seized up into a painful lump. "My God, you could have been killed!" I'd been in the car, too.

Bob turned to look at me. "Not likely, Samantha. Chances are good that the device was only put in there when the arsonist was sure no one was inside."

From behind me, a voice said, "There was a pile of towels and rags in the backseat. And the window was left down. Seems almost like perfectly planned conditions for a car fire."

I turned around to see Detective Vance. He had taken off his suit jacket and had his sleeves rolled up. His brown gaze had little sparks of gold fury and was fixed on me. "You can't think Angel did it!"

"Sure I can, Shaw. Mr. Danger tells me that the two of you were meeting with a woman named Zoë. I can only conclude that is the same Zoë who supposedly made off with the stolen diamond necklace. The same Zoë I told you to call me about if she contacted you." He clamped his jaw shut, visibly struggling to control himself. A bulging throb had developed by his right ear. "What kind of trouble are you two in? Or are you trying to help your friend get out of financial trouble?"

"What? I mean, Angel's not in financial trouble! And we were going to call you just as soon as we got the necklace. We had a plan! Zoë was supposed to give us the sex-toy kit back!" Too late, I realized I had shouted.

Silence dropped like a gunshot.

A heat separate from the smoldering of Angel's car rushed into my face.

Vance clamped his hand around my arm. "Let's go inside Smash Coffee. Both of you." He included Angel in his forceful invitation.

No one was inside the coffee shop. It was quiet and cool. We went to a table and sat down. Vance immediately demanded, "I want to know exactly what's going on, Shaw. I put my reputation on the line for you—twice!" His jaw bulged as he clamped his mouth shut and took a breath. "First, when you thought Angel was kidnapped, and again, when you left that message that you had found a diamond necklace that turned out to be the same necklace stolen from Daystar. I told both the Temecula police and Daystar security that I had a good lead on that necklace and their suspect. Now both are missing."

Good Lord, I hoped he wouldn't shatter his jawbone. "Vance, we still have a chance to find Zoë and get that necklace!"

Vance took in a breath, visibly getting control of himself. "You said Zoë was supposed to give you the sex-toy kit back. Did she?"

I was getting a little worried about Vance. He had the look of someone who could snap, pull out his gun, and shoot someone. OK—shoot *me*. "Well no, but—"

"No, but." Vance's voice went up a notch. "No, but. That's always your answer."

Angel slammed her purse down on the table. "Detective, we gave Zoë Hugh's name and address and told her he was R. V. Logan. All you have to do is go over there and wait for Zoë to show up."

He turned his gaze from me to glare at Angel. "And I'm supposed to believe you?" Vance leaned forward for emphasis. "The deal was that you were supposed to call me when you heard from Zoë, not send her on a wild goose chase sure to piss her off more. Which leads me to believe you two are trying to get that stolen necklace back for your own purposes—like trying to appease Zack Quinn after you tried to double cross him. In the meantime"—he turned back to Angel—"your car is firebombed just when you are in debt. Is it possible that you really didn't think I'd take a look at your financials?"

Cripes, what was Vance talking about? "Angel didn't set the car on fire! She was right here with me in Smash Coffee!"

He shifted his steely gaze back to me. "Could have arranged it, while she gave herself an alibi. All I need is the evidence, and believe me, whatever dumb scheme the two of you have cooked up, I will get the evidence." He stood up and stormed out of Smash Coffee.

Angel got up, walked behind the counter and rummaged around, then returned with two cans of Diet Coke. "Zoë's gone and Vance thinks I firebombed my own car." Angel handed me one of the cans of Diet Coke. "He won't listen. All because he has unresolved lust for you, and now thinks you might be walking the shady side of the law. For a stick-up-your-ass detective, that's just the kind of thing that pisses him off. Now he has to redeem himself by proving he can set aside his lust and go after you, and by extension, me."

I opened the can, making a mental note to pay Dom for the sodas. Outside the window, the firemen were reloading the fire hose into the truck. Vance and another man, who I guessed was some kind of arson investigator, were taking pictures of Angel's car. Angel had already called her insurance agent, who had said he'd be there soon and take care of having the car towed.

Wait until the insurance agent heard Vance's theory of Angel's being responsible for firebombing her own car. That was going to put a serious crimp in Angel's getting the insurance money for the car.

"Vance isn't going to do anything to help us." Angel paced around the table and took a drink of her soda. Then she stopped pacing and looked down at me. "Since Hugh doesn't get home from work until three, Zoë will keep going back to his house until she finds him. All we have to do is go to Hugh's and wait for Zoë. Then we can get that sex-toy kit from her."

I barely listened to Angel as I thought about Vance's words: *trying to get your friend out of financial trouble*. Then Gabe's words: *is it possible Angel's not telling you something?* I tried to think it out. Finally, I looked up at her and said, "Angel, come sit down for a minute."

She sank into a chair, leaned her arms on the table, and said, "Sam, we have to go now. I don't want to miss Zoë at Hugh's house."

I ignored her agitation. Besides, as she had pointed out, Hugh shouldn't be home until 3:00, so we had time. "What did Vance mean? Are you in financial trouble?"

Angel turned to look out the window at the burned-up wreck of her car. "I'm in a lot of debt. All Vance had to do was get my credit-card statements to figure that out."

I stared at her pale and strained face. "What happened?"

"Remember my mom's accident?"

It took me a second to make the transition. We'd been talking about Angel and her finances and now suddenly we were talking about her mom's car accident over two decades ago. It had been bad; her mom had been severely injured and she'd lost a nearly full-term baby. "Yes, but that was years ago."

"She's having problems with her back and hips. Her insurance doesn't cover chiropractic care and one of her medicines. I'm paying for it."

It hit me then. The guilt. It had been more than twenty years ago when Angel was ten years old. She had fallen off the swing set at school and broken her arm. When the school called her mom, Trixie, she had insisted on talking to Angel. Angel was in pain and was crying.

Racing to the school, Trixie was hit T-bone fashion on the driver's side. The nearly full-term baby boy she'd been pregnant with had died, and Trixie had been severely injured.

A couple of months later, Angel's dad told her that her being a crybaby had killed his son and left him saddled with a crippled wife. He'd walked out the door for his long-haul trucking route and never returned.

Since that day, Angel had never again been a crybaby or relied on anyone else if she could help it.

Bringing myself out of the past, I thought of the cruise Angel's mom and my mom were on right then. "And the cruise?"

"I charged it on my MasterCard. Mom can't afford it. But the cruise is good for her. She needs to stay off her feet for a week to let her hip rest and get the swelling around the nerves down. If she were home, she'd work. Standing while cutting hair is the worst for her."

"You should have told me." I had known that Trixie was having chronic pain, but she'd told me it was under control. I certainly hadn't known that Angel had spent her savings to take care of her mom.

Angel didn't appear to see anything outside the window, but rather, her expression looked turned inward. "I'm making Tempt-an-Angel work, and I still have some stocks that I haven't sold yet. I have everything under control."

I had said the exact same thing to Gabe this morning and he'd blown a gasket. Now I understood it. Angel and I had been friends for too long for her to carry this burden by herself.

I'd think about how I wasn't letting Gabe help me later.

Right at that moment, I had to help Angel. I had somehow missed that my best friend was worried and going into debt to help her mom. I reached out and took hold of Angel's hand. "No, you don't have it under control. But you and I are going to deal with this. Together. Let's see if Dom can give us a ride to Heart Mates. We can get my car, then go to Hugh's house to wait for Zoë and get that necklace."

We piled into Dom's bright yellow Mustang. Since I had the shortest legs, I sat in the backseat. I let Angel and Dom talk while I pulled out my cell phone.

Maybe I could convince myself that Zoë's stealing the sex-toy kit wasn't a call-Gabe problem. But Angel's car getting firebombed definitely was a problem. I dialed Gabe's cell-phone number and hit send. "I'm calling Gabe." I announced.

"Bet Dee answers," Angel glanced back at me, then turned to tell Dom the whole Dee story.

I ignored them both, though I was glad to see that Angel had regained some of her spark.

"Pulizzi Investigations. How can I help you?"

Dee! I gritted my teeth and tried one of those deep yoga breaths. "Dee, this is Sam Shaw. Put Gabe on."

"I don't think so."

"Listen here—" I stopped when I realized she had hung up.

Angel turned to look at me.

"What we have here is a failure to communicate." I redialed Gabe's cell phone.

No answer.

"Caller ID." I closed my eyes and leaned my head against the headrest. "Killing her is too good."

Dom stopped at a red light and looked back at me. "Sounds like the girl has a crush on the hero."

I opened my eyes and stared at Dom. "I know. So does Gabe. Don't think he doesn't know it. He knows it. He's having a grand time being admired and fought over. Having Dee and me get into a battle over him? Men love it. The only thing he'd love more is if we agreed to have a threesome." God, I was pissed. No little girl was going to outmaneuver me with my boyfriend. Even more, I wasn't going to let him put me in this position. Gabe knew she had his cell phone.

I dialed the phone, this time calling Gabe's pager unit, and pressed a button to go to voice mail. "Quit playing games, Pulizzi. I'm tired of getting hung up on by your assistant. I have bigger problems right now. A woman named Zoë stole the sex-toy kit with the diamond necklace in it and someone just firebombed Angel's car. Vance is out for blood, specifically Angel's and my blood. If you get a little time from chasing around Dee in her bikini, you think you could give me a call?"

Dom grinned in his rearview mirror. "Sex-toy kit? If you have handcuffs in that sex-toy kit, you should handcuff your bad boy and spank him."

I rolled my eyes. I needed some Tylenol and a margarita in a five-gallon bucket.

* * *

It was two o'clock by the time Dom dropped us off at Heart Mates. I stormed in, pissed that Gabe hadn't called me back. I had left that message five minutes ago! What the hell was going on?

"Sam, I faxed Gabe the security releases for the new clients. Do you know when he can process those? We need those cleared for the ladies to come to the client mixer before the open house tomorrow night."

I stopped in front of Blaine's desk and said, "You are absolutely correct. Gabe's on a case, but why don't you call his cell phone and ask to talk to him." I reached over and picked up the handset of Blaine's phone. "I'll dial for you." I punched in the numbers and handed Blaine the phone.

"Something wrong, boss?" Blaine asked as he took the phone.

Angel said, "Gabe hired a new assistant who answers Gabe's cell phone and won't let Sam talk to him."

Blaine raised both eyebrows up to his hairline. "No shit?" He studied me for a minute, then said, "Went to voice mail. Guess the assistant recognized Heart Mates' number on the caller ID." He hung up the phone and grinned.

I reached up to rub my forehead. Murderous thoughts were giving me a headache. "Forget Gabe. Right now, Angel and I have to leave." I dropped my hand and looked at Blaine. "Can you handle things here?"

Blaine's grin vanished. "What's wrong?"

Angel answered, "Some asshole firebombed my car."

"Your Trans Am?" Blaine's expression tightened into one of horror. "When? Where?"

"At Smash Coffee." She took a breath to launch into the whole story when her cell phone rang.

While Angel answered her cell phone, I filled in the details for Blaine, until we both heard Angel say, "Hugh, that bastard!"

Blaine and I both turned to look at her. She shoved her cell phone into her purse and said, "Come on, Sam. We have to go to my house."

I didn't move. "What's going on, Angel? Who was that on the phone?"

She shifted back and forth, her energy practically a living thing. "That was Mitch. He was supposed to call me yesterday to set up a dinner to talk about the sex-toy kit. He got busy and never called."

I'd forgotten all about that. Understandable, with Zack-the-gun-wielding-jewel-thief after us. Then Zoë stealing the necklace. Then the car. "Wait—did you get any information from Mitch? Caller ID? Where is he?" My heart pounded and I was determined not to screw it up this time. I didn't see how Mitch could be involved, but he had given Angel that sex-toy kit.

"Caller ID was blocked. And Mitch hung up after he told me that he went by my house to leave some flowers as an apology for not calling me back for dinner. But before he got out of his car, he said he saw a man run out of my gate and jump into an old Mercedes and race off. The man he described sounded just like Hugh. Mitch said that we'd talk about the sex-toy kit later this week, but that he didn't want to get between me and a boyfriend and hung up."

It didn't make sense. "But what would Hugh be doing at your house? Isn't he at work?"

Angel brushed her long red hair off her face. "Hugh drives around doing security checks in his security guard job, so he could slip in a drive by my house. He saw me last night watching his house. Knowing Hugh, he's probably getting even in his warped mind. For all I know, he turned on the gas and ran out." She took a breath. "I just want to check."

I studied Angel. I knew something had been the matter with her at Daystar the Friday before. Now I knew she was worried about her mom, but it was also something to do with Hugh. "Angel, that fight you had with Hugh on Friday, what happened?"

Her leather pants squeaked as she shifted. "It was like I told you, he was screaming at me for causing him to be denied the private patrol license. That everything was my fault. Last night, Brandi's car wasn't at his house. I think she's left him and he blames me."

I frowned. I wanted Angel to let go of Hugh, but I had to admit that he had started it this time with blaming her for his being denied his license. And if he had been at her house, we'd better stop by and find out why. "OK, your house is on our way to Hugh's anyway." I turned to Blaine.

He waved his hand. "Go. Just be careful."

"Thanks, Blaine. You're the best." Angel and I hurried to my T-bird.

Once I had maneuvered the car out to the street, I took a breath. God, I was so mad. And scared. Angel and I were on our own. Gabe was . . . hell, I didn't know. And Vance wouldn't help us. I tried to sort things out as I drove. "Do you think Zack threw the firebomb into your car?"

Angel settled her purse on the floor and answered, "He's the one who wants the necklace and thinks we have it. He used a gun last night, so I guess he'd throw a firebomb into my car."

We were making good time. I turned left from Main Street onto Graham, which would turn into Lake Street a little further down the road. "None of this is making sense." I slowed a bit to pass the Elsinore Middle School. I thought out loud. "Here's what we know: Someone stole a diamond necklace from a woman at Daystar Casino. We found the necklace in the sex-toy kit. Zack Quinn is the suspect in the theft, and he has broken into your house twice to get that necklace."

"But Mitch is the one who gave me the sex-toy kit."

I turned right off Lake Street, then right again onto Angel's street. "But he doesn't seem to know about the necklace."

"Right," Angel agreed.

I pulled into Angel's driveway, then turned to look at her. "That's another reason you wanted to come to your house on the way to Hugh's. If Mitch came by here, maybe he was really looking for the sex-toy kit and the necklace."

Angel nodded. "At first, I was just mad about Hugh's being at my house. But then I wondered why Mitch came by my house. I mean, it's easy enough to find my address in the phone book. So he could have meant to leave flowers but got spooked seeing Hugh . . ." She shrugged.

I filled in the rest. "Or he could have been here to break in himself and gotten spooked by Hugh." Dumbass Hugh. That'd be just like him to try to get into Angel's house to cause damage, and end up actually saving Angel from something worse.

I turned off the car engine. "OK, let's go see if Hugh did anything to the house, or if we can spot anything else odd." Maybe, just maybe, we could catch a break and clean up this mess. I touched Angel's arm. "But we have to be careful. We don't know where Zack is." I reached past Angel into my purse and pulled out my defense spray.

Angel reached down to her purse and pulled out her gun.

I met her gaze. "Show-off."

We got out of the car and went to the atrium gate. Everything looked normal in the atrium and the front door appeared tightly closed. Angel opened the gate and went toward the front door.

Just to hear myself talk, I said, "It's possible that Vance already went over to Hugh's and caught Zoë. Maybe he has the necklace and knows we were telling the truth."

"I'm not relying on Vance." She held her gun in one hand and used the other hand to test the door. "Locked." She used her key to open it. "I'm not going to let Hugh, Zack, or anyone else destroy my life."

"Yeah, there's a lot of that going around." I thought of Gabe's assistant and her phone games. I was mad, but part of me was beginning to think Dee was pulling a fast one on him. I couldn't figure out how, though. And Dee made me mad, too. But I was *furious* that someone was doing this to Angel.

She turned the dead bolt and pulled her key out of the lock, then she looked at me. "Ready?"

My mouth went dry at the prospect of going back into the house where I had looked down the barrel of a gun. "As I'll ever be." I hoped that sounded brave. I suspected it sounded fake.

The living room looked the same as we had left it. The wood floor was discolored where the Diet Coke had spilled. The house had an abandoned feel to it. It smelled stuffy and slightly sweet, probably from the Diet Coke on the floor. But there was no gas odor, so Hugh hadn't gotten in and turned on the gas. Something was going right at least. "No sign of Hugh," I commented. "Let's hurry. We don't want to miss Zoë at Hugh's house."

I followed Angel in the door, my boots clicking on the wood floor. The urge to turn and run squeezed my chest, but I ignored it. We walked through the living room to the swinging doors of the kitchen.

Anxiety tightened my neck. It would be a long time be-

fore I forgot the feeling of looking down the barrel of
Zack's gun. My natural cowardice surfaced.

Angel didn't seem bothered by the memory of Zack.
Holding her gun, she moved through the swinging doors.
Then she called back, "Everything looks OK. Stove is off.
Door is locked."

Angel came back out, passed me, and headed across the
living room toward the hallway.

Shaking off my fear, I caught up to her, following so
close I could smell the herbal scent of her shampoo. We
went into the hallway and headed left toward her bedroom.

The phone rang. Terror squeaked in my throat like a
mouse. Angel looked back at me, her mouth quirking in a
grin. "It's just my phone. The answering machine will get it."

All right, I was done being a chicken. A ringing phone
making me squeak was damned embarrassing. "I'm fine,
just clearing my throat." I lifted my chin, and tightened
my finger on the nozzle of the pepper spray. There was no
one in Angel's house. I forced a weak smile. "Lead on."

"Relax, Sam, no one's here. Hugh's long gone." She
turned and started toward her bedroom.

Right. Relax. As I followed close behind her, I tried some
of that breathing stuff Angel's Yoga teacher droned on
and on about. In, nice and slow . . .

Slam.

I smacked into Angel's back, jamming my pepper spray
into my stomach.

I heard a hissing noise. Uh-oh.

Just as I blinked, searing pain hit my eyes. "Shit!" I'd
sprayed myself in the eyes. I dropped the pepper spray.
"Ouch!" I squeezed my eyes shut. Tears welled up, my
nose filled, and the burn . . . I slid to my knees. "Why did
you stop?"

"Sam." Angel wrapped her hands around my arms, dragging me up.

"I can't!" God, it hurt. Burned. It was hideous.

"Stop it!" Angel yelled at me. "Hurry." She dragged me off my knees. Automatically, I got my feet under me and followed her. "Here." I heard water. "Wash your eyes out."

I cupped my hands and scooped water onto my eyelids, forcing my eyes to open. God, it hurt. Burned. Hurt like putting in contacts doused in cayenne pepper. Even my throat and mouth burned. Man, to think I had accidentally sprayed Gabe once. Finally, the burn calmed down.

The phone rang.

And rang.

I felt around until I touched something that I thought might be a towel and held it to my eyes. My wits were returning. I knew Angel had led me through her bedroom and into the bathroom. Here I'd been afraid of running into Zack, when I should have been afraid of myself. Slowly, I took the towel away and forced my eyes to open.

The phone had stopped ringing.

The bathroom was blurry, but I could see. Sort of. The big wood-framed mirror revealed swollen red-and-black eyes. Red from the pepper spray, black from mascara and eyeliner.

Not my best look. Hot tears kept up a slow but steady stream down my face.

Looking down, I could make out the brass curving faucet, the porcelain sink, Angel's perfumes and lotions, and her hairbrush. My vision cleared little by little though everything had a blurry halo. My eyes continued to sting. "Cripes, Angel." I looked around the bathroom but didn't see her. "Angel? Why did you stop like that?"

Finally, I spotted her just outside the bathroom door in the bedroom. She appeared to be staring at her bed but she blocked my view. "Angel?" I nearly laughed when I said her name—though I could see only her back, she did have a fuzzy halo around her body. Almost like a real angel.

"Do you want the good news or the bad news?" Her voice was flat and strained.

I used the hand towel to wipe away more tears and said, "What are you talking about?"

"The good news is that I found Zack."

"Huh?" Having just proved that I was more of a danger to myself than the Zack I feared so much, I wasn't in the mood for stupid jokes. I took a step, using one hand to push Angel so I could stand beside her.

Angel went on in the same flat voice, "Bad news is that he's dead."

I forced my stinging eyes to focus on the bed.

Omigod! There was a dead man on Angel's bed! *Dead man.* He had to be dead, since there was a hideous black hole in his forehead.

The phone on the nightstand rang.

13

The ringing phone sounded sinister.

Probably because of the dead man on Angel's bed. Zack had been shot through the head, but there was no blood. He must have been killed somewhere else. Terror seized my lungs and I had a hard time getting a breath.

The phone rang again. Both Angel and I turned to look at it. The caller ID screen said, "Blocked."

I was pretty sure it wasn't a sales call. Angel stood closest to the phone on the nightstand. On the third ring, I couldn't stand it anymore. "Answer it."

She reached over and snatched up the receiver. She held it between us so that I could lean in and listen. "Hello?"

"I see you've found Zack," a male voice said.

He could *see* us? How? New terror burned in my chest. "Who is this?" I demanded into the receiver. Chills ran down my back.

"Samantha Shaw. You two surprise me. Most women are easily romanced into submission."

His voice throbbed with anger. A voice I had heard before. I struggled to place it, but Angel had the answer.

She demanded into the phone, "Mitch, what the hell are you doing?"

Mitch? Mitch St. Claire from the casino? That's where I had heard the voice. But what was going on? The phone call from Mitch to Angel about Hugh—it had been a ruse to get Angel to come back to her house. An acidlike taste of fear mixed in with the aftertaste of pepper spray.

Mitch said, "I'm cleaning up, Angel. Zack screwed up. I never tolerate screwups. He put that necklace in the wrong sample sex-toy kit. I gave him a chance to fix it and he failed." He sighed. "Zack didn't grasp the importance of the details. It's not just about fucking the mark. Any man with a functioning dick can do that. It's the finesse!"

Stunned horror spun around in my brain. Mark? Who was Mark? What did Mitch mean? My brain just wouldn't process anything.

Angel's entire body shook. "So you killed him? You murdered Zack and put him on my bed!"

We heard Mitch suck in a breath. "If you don't want to end up like Zack, get that necklace. I have a client waiting. And this isn't the kind of client that waits patiently."

Angel ripped the phone from between us and yelled into it, "We don't have the—" She slammed the phone down onto the nightstand. "He hung up."

I couldn't breathe. I stared at Zack. There was a big bandage on his right arm and a partly healed cut on his left index finger. Those had to be from his two break-ins to Angel's house. But it was the hole in his forehead that made me nauseated and panicked. Burnt bloody edges of skin caved in around that black hole. "Oh God." Sweat pinpricked under my arms and down my back. The room started tilting at a sickening angle. "We have to get out of here. He murdered Zack and he's watching us!" I didn't want a hole in my head.

"Mitch. That bastard. It was him all along."

I turned my head, still seeing a bit of fuzz around the edges of my vision. Was that from the pepper spray or from shock? "He lied about Hugh to get us here. To see Zack dead." My thoughts spun in a kaleidoscopic blur. I had thought it was Zack who was after the necklace, but obviously Mitch was behind the whole mess. I looked around the room. "Is he here?" Was he hiding in the closet? Fear boiled the sick feeling in my stomach. How did he know Angel and I were in her house?

Angel grabbed my hand. "Let's get out of here, Sam."

No need to tell me twice. My fight-or-flight reaction told me to run like hell. We ran out of the bedroom, through the hall, and into the living room, where my boot heels slid on the wood floor. Angel let go of me. I got my balance and the two of us raced out the front door.

We didn't bother to close it.

At the car, Angel said, "Give me your keys."

I reached into my purse and tossed my keys over the hood. I dropped into the red vinyl seat on the passenger side of my T-bird, then grabbed Angel's purse from her so she could drive. She started the car, put it in reverse, and screeched the tires backing out of the driveway.

Hanging on to the dashboard, I thought, *Boy, Blaine would be pissed if he saw this.* When Angel straightened the car out, I struggled to get my seat belt on. My hands shook so much, I couldn't get the metal part into the lock. "What do we do? There's a dead man in your house! We're going to get blamed for this."

Angel hit the gas again. "How did Mitch know we were there? Or did he start calling my house every few minutes after calling me with that story about Hugh?" She expertly wove the car out onto Lake Street. The day was cool and the lake shimmered like smooth gray glass, reflecting the Ortega Mountains that rose over it from the other side.

I didn't have an answer. All I could think about was dead Zack with a really ugly hole in his forehead. But wait . . . what if he wasn't dead? I looked at Angel. "What if he wasn't dead? We have to go back!" My mind hopped, skipped, and jumped.

"He was dead. No pulse."

"You *touched* him?"

She stared at the road. "Yes, I touched him. If he wasn't dead, I would have killed him."

Cripes. My head throbbed while my stomach did a queasy roll every few seconds. "I'm calling Gabe. I'll use your cell phone so Dee won't know it's me." I opened Angel's purse, pulled out her cell phone and dialed the number.

Dee answered, "Pulizzi Investigations."

I was ready for a fight. "If you hang up, I will drive out to Hemet and kick your ass. Put Gabe on."

"We are busy."

She was so dead. "Dee, listen to me very carefully. If I drive out there, after I kick your ass, I am going to tell Gabe that you are not letting me talk to him when I have an emergency. I know he told you to put my calls through."

"Fine." Then nothing. Just silence for an endless minute.

Gabe came on the line. "Babe? Why are you calling on Dee's cell phone?"

"What?" I had no idea what he was talking about. I had dialed *his* cell phone number. "Never mind. Angel and I found Zack Quinn dead on Angel's bed. He had a bullet hole through his forehead." Hot tears stung my eyes. Blinking, I fought to control myself.

"Where are you?"

"In my car. We can't drive Angel's car because it was

firebombed." I felt the edge of hysteria bubbling in my brain. I took a breath and tried to order my thoughts.

"Give me the short version, Sam. We're getting in my truck now to come home."

His voice was flat and controlled. I had to be in control, too, if I wanted to keep Angel and myself alive. In the background, I heard doors slamming, then the truck engine turning over. "OK, this morning, Zoë Cash stopped by the house. She's trying to get R. V. Logan's real name and address out of me. I refused. Apparently, she stole the sex-toy kit and left. Vance showed up right after her, and he was furious when the necklace was gone."

"Christ," he hissed into the phone.

I tried to believe that he was commenting on traffic, not my losing the necklace. "Angel and I made arrangements to meet with Zoë to trade R. V. Logan's real identity for the sex-toy kit with the diamond necklace. Only Angel's car burst into flames and Zoë got away before we could get the sex-toy kit back."

"This just gets better and better."

I was pretty sure that sarcasm was directed at me, not the traffic. Going into defensive mode, I said, "I tried to call you! Catwoman wouldn't put you on the phone! After that, she wouldn't answer calls from my cell phone or the Heart Mates landline. And I left a message on your beeper service. Anyway, Angel and I came up with a plan." Before he could give me his opinion on that, I went on, "But we stopped by Angel's house first and found Zack on her bed with a hole in his forehead. Then the phone rang and it was Mitch St. Claire. The man who gave Angel the sex-toy kit at Daystar." I shivered. Had Mitch been in the house? Was he following us right now?

Gabe broke in, "Tell me what he said."

"He knew Angel and I had found Zack, like he was

watching us or something!" I had to control myself. I focused on Lake Street, noticing that we were going through the green light at Riverside Drive. We passed Burger Basket and Del Taco. "He said he killed Zack because Zack screwed up. Something about putting the necklace in the wrong sex-toy kit. And that if we didn't want to end up dead like Zack, we'd better get the necklace." I tried to remember the last part, "He has a client waiting—and it's not the kind of client that waits patiently." Whatever that meant.

"Listen to me, Sam. You are in the car with Angel, right? Drive to my house. Use your key, get inside, lock the door, set the alarm and stay there. I'm on my way."

My brain kept going, working on it, trying to make sense of the mess. "Wait, Zack stole the necklace for Mitch. Mitch said Zack put it in the wrong sex-toy kit. Angel and I were never supposed to have that necklace." It wasn't our fault.

"Sam, get to my house. Now. Do not waste any time."

Shit. I felt the urgency in his voice. We were in serious danger. New fear sprang to life in my heart. "The boys! Grandpa!"

"Don't say anything else. Nothing. You and Angel haul ass to my house and lock yourselves in. I will call Blaine and send someone out immediately to look after them. Sam, trust me."

Trust him. What choice did I have? And what was Gabe trying to tell me? Don't talk. Don't say anything more? "All right."

"I'll take care of TJ and Joel, Sam." Gabe hung up.

I stuck Angel's phone back in her purse, put it on the floor, and picked up my purse. I had to find Gabe's house key.

Angel looked over at me. "What?"

Still searching for the house key, I said, "Gabe wants us

to go to his house. We are not supposed to say anything else." I found the key on my key ring and put my purse down to look at Angel.

She turned her head, meeting my eyes.

We had been friends for a very long time. I saw in her green eyes the same conclusion I had reached—that there might be a listening device in my car. Almost certainly, there was a tracking device. That was most likely how Mitch had known we had taken his phone-call bait and were at Angel's house when he called.

Just like there must have been a tracking device on Angel's car. The burned-out wreck of Angel's car and the bullet hole in Zack's head were clear evidence that Mitch St. Claire was not playing nice.

We pulled up in front of Gabe's house. Worry for Grandpa and the boys gnawed at me. I had my seat belt off and the car door open before Angel turned off the engine. I ran up to the door and jammed the key into the lock. I shoved the front door open, went to the wall, and deactivated the alarm.

Angel came in holding both our purses. She closed the door and locked it.

I reset the alarm. Then I went into Gabe's office behind the front door and picked up his phone.

I doubted there was any kind of bug on Gabe's phone. I punched in the phone number and held my breath. One ring. Two—please let them be all right.

"Hello?" TJ answered.

Thank God. I tried to force a normal voice past my dry throat. "Hi, TJ," I hoped my voice sounded normal. "How was school?"

"Fine. What's going on, Mom? Gabe called and Grandpa locked up the house and set the alarm."

Relief sagged through me. They were safe. Except for

the worry in TJ's voice. "I'm not exactly sure, TJ. But re-member there's been some people breaking in over at Angel's house?"

"Is Angel all right?"

"Yes, TJ. She's right here with me at Gabe's house. We are fine, I promise." What was I supposed to tell him—that we had found a murdered body on Angel's bed? No. At least not until he had to know. Start with something he could handle. "While Angel's car was parked in front of Smash Coffee, someone tossed in a device that started the car on fire." Tons of people had seen that, so TJ and Joel were going to hear about it soon enough. Better to hear it from me first.

"Mom?" Joel's voice came on.

I guessed he had picked up the second line in my room. "Hi, Joel."

"Who set Angel's car on fire?"

"We're working on that. Gabe will be here in a little bit to help us. Are you guys OK, Joel?"

"Yeah. Was it a big fire? Did the car explode, like on TV?"

I smiled. "Not like TV. Just flames, no explosions. Let me talk to Grandpa now, OK?"

"Mom," TJ's voice sounded like a man's. "You and Angel be careful."

"We will. I'll try to be home by dinner." I waited while the boys went to get Grandpa.

"Hi, Sam. Gabe called. Everything is locked up and Ali's inside with us. Plus, you know, I'm armed."

"Armed with what?" I knew that came out as a screech. After seeing that bullet hole in Zack's forehead, I never wanted to see another gun.

"Switchblade and a pen that shoots pepper spray."

I closed my eyes and sat down on the edge of Gabe's

desk. All I wanted was for my grandpa and sons to be safe. "Grandpa, you guys stay there, OK? Gabe sent a guy over to keep an eye on the house. Don't leave the house," I added.

"Sammy, stop fussing. We're fine. Gabe filled me in a bit. I'm doing some research on the Internet, trying to find out who this Mitch St. Claire might be. You and Angel stay where you are until Gabe gets there."

They were fine. Alive. Fine. "OK, Grandpa. I'll talk to you later. Bye."

I hung up and went looking for Angel. I found her in Gabe's kitchen. It was actually a combination kitchen and family room. She had turned on the big screen TV to a news station and was currently looking through Gabe's refrigerator.

Even under tremendous stress, with her life crumbling around her, Angel was beautiful. Her black leather pants hugged her long legs, her tan tank top showed off slender, toned arms and nice perky breasts. But I could see the restless tension in her tight shoulders and the anger in her stiff back.

I also saw a rare fragility in her. It tugged on my heart. I walked around the bar and across the kitchen to her. "Let's sit at the table." There was a kitchen table by a door that led to the backyard.

Once I got her to sit down, I went back to the fridge and pulled out two bottles of water. Then I went to the table, sat down across from Angel, and slid one of the waters across to her.

Angel took it and unscrewed the lid. After taking a sip, she said, "So this is all one big mistake? Zack put the diamond necklace he stole into the wrong sex-toy kit. I was never supposed to get that necklace." She turned her gaze to look out the window that was set in the top half of the door.

"That's what I got from what Mitch said. I guess that Zack and Mitch realized it. Then Mitch sent Zack to break into your house Friday or Saturday night to find the sex-toy kit and get the necklace back. Zack had to be panicked when he couldn't find it."

Angel turned her eyes to me. "So he tried again last night, broke in and waited for me to get home. Then used a gun to scare me into telling him where the necklace was, but then you showed up and we chased him off."

I took a drink of my water, hoping it would stay down. "Remember this morning when Vance insisted there were two cars at my house? We know one was Zoë, right? What if the second one was Mitch, and he put a tracking device, and maybe a listening device, on my car? You were no longer at your house, so he'd have no way to find you but through me. He had the flyer to my open house at Heart Mates. Finding me would be easy."

She rolled the cold bottle of water between her hands. "How did he know where my car was? Assuming he threw the firebomb in there. Unless Zoë did it before she came into Smash Coffee."

"I don't think Zoë's involved. It doesn't make any sense. If she was involved, why would she contact us? She has the necklace. I think Zoë is exactly what she seems to be, a crazy fan." I twisted the cap on and off my water bottle as I tried to make sense of this. "So how did Mitch know where your car was? What would be the point of blowing it up?"

She stopped rolling the bottle. "Anger."

I thought about that. "We pissed him off."

Angel nodded. "And everyone in town knows Hugh and I don't get along. It'd be easy for Mitch to find that out and then use it to manipulate me into racing over to my house to see his ultimate threat—Zack dead on my bed. It looked like an execution. I'll bet there's no evidence on that body to link him to the killing, but it's a definite threat to me. To us."

"God Angel, I'm so sorry about the necklace! I can't believe I lost it. I would give it to him just to make him go away."

"He won't go away until both of us are dead."

My stomach cramped, but I forced myself to nod. It was true. "So we think he had a tracking device on your car? When did he put it on there? How? Did he double back to my house this morning after Vance left?"

Angel dropped her gaze and started peeling the label off her water bottle. "That's possible. I don't think he knows where my mom lives. Or he could have found the car at Heart Mates this morning."

That was logical. But what was she not telling me? "Angel?"

She looked up and opened her mouth when we both heard the mechanical whirring of the garage door opener raising the large door.

Either Gabe was home or we were in more trouble.

Angel jumped up and ran to her purse. By the time I got to her, she had her gun.

Hell. More guns. But I didn't want to get shot by Mitch, so I kept my mouth shut. I had dropped my big canister of pepper spray after I unloaded half the can into my own eyes. I dug around in my purse and came out with my key ring. It had a small canister of pepper spray.

A hallway ran along the kitchen and family room, then down to the bathroom and bedrooms. Right across from the family room was a door to the laundry room. On the other side of the laundry room was a door to the garage.

I went to the laundry room door and eased it open.

I looked past the washer and dryer to the door at the other end of the room. The handle turned. It had to be Gabe. Who else would have a garage-door opener? I held my breath. Angel stood next to me and gripped her gun in two hands.

I didn't doubt for a second that she'd shoot if it was Mitch.

Gabe opened the door and stepped in. His gaze took in both of us, then he moved to the side and Dee came in. She was carrying a large video cam bag over her shoulder. She had on a black bikini top over her size-A boobs and black gauzy pants with flip-flops. She swept past me, turning to go around the corner into Gabe's office.

This probably wasn't the time to wonder just what was on that video. I turned around and went to the couch to drop my keys with the pepper spray canister back into my purse.

I felt Gabe behind me. "Sam, what happened to your face?" He put his hands on my shoulders to turn me around.

I really didn't want to tell him about the pepper spray. "Why weren't you answering your own cell phone?"

His face tensed. "Apparently, Dee set my cell phone to forward my calls to her cell phone. And she turned my pager off, so I didn't know you left me a message."

Crap, I kind of had to admire that bit of ingenuity. "And you didn't know?"

He shrugged. "Never looked. Had other things on my mind today."

"Yeah, like bikinis."

His mouth twitched. "I like women in bikinis. But that's not what was on my mind."

"Work?"

"Sex toys. And you."

"Oh." Guess Dee's bikini didn't compete with Gabe catching me with a vibrator. Oh boy.

"Now, what happened to your eyes? They are all red,

and you've got black stuff running down your face and on your clothes. You're a mess."

I glanced down to see blotches of mascara on my pink tank top. Looking back up, I said, "Crying?" Which was only slightly less humiliating than spraying myself with pepper spray.

"Nice try. Looks more like pepper spray. Then I could believe you were crying." He zeroed in with his dark eyes; his hands on my shoulders went rigid. "Did someone get you with pepper spray?"

I gave up. "Yes. Me. I sprayed myself."

His grip on my shoulders eased. "You're OK?"

I forced myself to nod. I didn't have a hole in my forehead, so all things considered, I'd say I was OK.

"I'm going to call Vance and tell him about the body. Then we will meet him at Angel's house. You and Angel will tell Vance that you were scared and came to my house to call the police."

I nodded, then looked past Gabe to where Angel was sitting on the barstool. "Vance will believe us now, Angel. Once he sees Zack—" I shuddered at the memory. "Anyway, he'll know we've been telling the truth." That was the only good news in this whole mess. Now we had proof—Zack. I could show Vance the cut on Zack's finger, which I guessed he had done with the knife the first time he broke into Angel's house. Surely they could do a DNA test on the blood on the kitchen towel. Then there was the bandage on Zack's arm where I'd hit him with the wine bottle.

Angel nodded and slid off the barstool and walked over to sit on the back of the couch. "We think there's a tracking device or something on Sam's car. Maybe there was one on mine, too. Vance will see those, too."

Right. At least we had proof this time. I looked up at Gabe. "Why did you tell us to come here?"

"Because I thought the same thing. It's what I would do if I were desperate to get a diamond necklace back." Gabe arched an eyebrow. "What I'd like to know is how Mitch got you to Angel's house."

He never missed anything. "Mitch called Angel and said he had stopped by her house and saw a man fitting Hugh's description running out of her atrium, and getting into a car just like the one Hugh drives." And we had fallen right into that trap.

"That didn't strike you as strange?"

I sighed. "Not as strange as seeing Angel's car suddenly burst into flames."

Gabe moved his hands on my shoulder to the tight place behind my neck and rubbed gently. "At least you and Angel are safe. For now, anyway. I'm going to call Vance." He dropped his hand, turned, and went to the phone.

I sat next to Angel on the back of the couch. Neither one of us wanted to go back to her house, to where we'd found Zack.

Gabe hung up just as Dee walked back into the family room. "Everything's put away," she said.

Gabe looked at her. "Get your stuff. We'll drop you at home on our way."

Her face flushed with color. "But I'm your assistant!"

He met her gaze. "Not anymore."

Detective Vance met us in front of Angel's house and zeroed in on me. "Where's the dead body, Shaw?"

Gabe and Angel stood on either side of me. Gabe said, "Have you been inside yet?"

Vance shook his head. "I was waiting for the uniforms. Unlike you, I have procedures to follow."

I felt Angel move, probably ready to tell Vance off. To cut her off, I said, "The body is in Angel's bedroom. It's the room on the left side once you get to the hallway. It looked like he'd been shot through the head."

Vance reached into his shirt pocket and took out his notebook. "Who found him? What time?"

Angel said, "Sam and I found him."

Vance wrote something down, then looked up. "And why did you leave?"

Angel's voice lifted to a brittle sound. "Because we got a phone call threatening us. We were afraid the killer was watching us. So we left."

"Why didn't you drive to the police station if you felt threatened?"

I'd had enough. "Maybe because you haven't been exactly helpful, Vance. Maybe because you keep trying to blame everything on us instead of doing your job. Maybe, Detective Vance, the police haven't been able to find Zack, even though we told you he attacked Angel with a gun, then we find him dead on Angel's bed. Did it ever occur to you busy police officers to watch Angel's house? Zack had broken in there twice in just a few days!" God, I was furious. Red-hot, tired of everyone blaming me, furious.

A marked police car pulled up. Two uniformed police officers got out, a female with short blonde hair who looked like she was in her late twenties, and a newbie-looking man with a buzz cut and a tendency to bounce.

Vance waved the cops over, then glared at me. "Don't any of you move." He turned with the uniforms to go into the house.

We stood on the sidewalk leading up to the atrium. "Gabe," I looked over at him, "are Angel and I in trouble? What should we have done? We were just so scared that we wanted to get to someplace safe. If there's a bug on my car, we didn't want Mitch to find us or to lead him to Grandpa and the boys."

He looked down at me. "Babe, you have to start thinking. You are reacting, not taking control of the situation. But you and Angel are probably all right." He pinned me with a look. "We called the police as soon as you got to my house."

His lecture stung a bit. But he was right. Angel and I had kept reacting to everything that happened. And we should have called the police on our cell phones as soon as we got outside the house or in the car. I nodded to Gabe, understanding that Angel and I needed to have our stories straight. "Right, when we got to your house, we told you to call the police while we tried to calm down. We were very scared."

Gabe opened his mouth, then closed it when Vance and the uniforms came back out. The uniforms ignored us and headed for their car.

A bad feeling slid into my stomach. Kind of like the feeling I got when TJ or Joel come into the house from school with that droopy teenage shuffle. That was usually bad news.

But Vance had a fast, rolling stride. His suit moved with him, pulling nicely against his strong swimmer shoulders. His brown gaze pinned the three of us, while his jaw clenched and unclenched. The flight urge joined my bad feeling.

Vance stopped to tower over me before I could run. Somehow I had ended up standing in front of Gabe and Angel. "What?" I said, desperately trying to imagine what had him so pissed. Was there a note pinned to Zack's chest that said I had killed him? Had another body turned up? *What?*

"You have one minute to explain your game to me. Calling in false reports is a crime. Pulizzi," Vance lifted his gaze to Gabe over my left shoulder. "I'll see that your license is pulled for this."

"For what?" I demanded.

Angel didn't bother with demands or questions. She simply turned left and ran into the house.

I liked her idea. Going into a house where there was a dead body seemed better than facing Vance. Without looking at Gabe, I turned and walked up the sidewalk to the front door. I heard Gabe and Vance follow us. No one said a word.

We stepped into the living room. My heels clicked over the wood floor, while Gabe and Vance had a much more solid *thunk-squeak*. I assumed Angel had gone into the bedroom. I headed toward the hallway.

Why wasn't Vance stopping us? Cops were touchy about crime scenes. He'd been pissed that I'd gone into Angel's house and walked around when we thought Angel had been kidnapped.

When we reached the hallway, my chest got that sudden empty feeling. My adrenaline kicked up another notch and confused fear roared in my head. But I kept going. I had to know. I turned left down the hallway and stopped when I got to Angel's bedroom door.

Angel stood about three feet from her bed, looking down. Her face was pale, with angry red splotches around her nose and mouth. She glared at the bed, then looked up at Gabe, Vance and me as we stood in the doorway.

Angel said, "Zack's gone. Who stole his dead body?"

14

I stared at the empty bed in Angel's bedroom.

Dead bodies do not get up and walk away.

Any sign that Zack had ever been on the bed was gone. The covers had been smoothed out into a perfectly made bed. What the hell was going on? Angel and I had seen him! The pepper spray had clouded my vision, but I knew I had seen Zack on that bed with a blackened hole in his forehead. I could still see it in my mind.

And where was the can of pepper spray? I'd dropped it after spraying myself, but I didn't see it anywhere.

I turned to Gabe, feeling desperate. "He was here. On the bed. I saw him."

Gabe watched me with dark, troubled eyes, but the rest of his face was blank. "I believe you."

"I don't." Vance stepped past me to stand at the corner of the bed, between Angel and me. He turned slightly to stare at me. "First, Angel is kidnapped, then she's not. Then you find the stolen diamond necklace from Daystar, then it's stolen from you. Angel's car is firebombed while the two of you are meeting with Zoë, who supposedly is the one who stole the necklace from you. A very convenient way for Zoë to disappear and Angel to collect insurance money." Vance took a breath and turned to glare at Angel. "Then the two of you find Zack Quinn dead on this very bed," he waved at the bed. "But somehow, in the one-hour-plus time delay it takes you to call the police and report a murdered body in your house, Zack gets up and leaves." He turned to leave.

"Vance!" God, where was he going? I knew he was furious, but he wasn't just going to leave, was he?

His shoulders tightened, but he turned. "What, Shaw?"

"You can't just leave. Can't you see? Angel's in danger!"

He looked at Angel, then me. Then he shifted to Gabe. "If I were you, Pulizzi, I'd cut my losses. These two are trouble." Looking back at me, he said, "I have real cases with real dead bodies to solve. Have a nice life." He left.

"You're wrong, Vance!" I shouted after him. "Angel and I had nothing to do with this! It was a mistake that necklace got stuck in the sex-toy kit that Mitch gave Angel!"

Gabe put his hand on my shoulder. "Stop, Sam."

I turned on him. "Stop? Vance thinks Angel and I are in some kind of cahoots with Zack! He thinks—"

Gabe sighed. "What's he supposed to think, Sam? Look at it from his point of view. You've been set up, babe. Both of you. Whoever this guy calling himself Mitch is, he's used events to his advantage."

"But Vance should know better! He knows me!"

Gabe arched an eyebrow.

Cripes. Gabe was right. Vance and I purposely avoided getting to know each other very well. I understood his cop side. Methodical, follow the clues, by the book, cop. And he hated that the town treated him as an outsider. Not that long ago, I had misjudged Vance. He'd paid me back by kissing me in front of Gabe. It had ended predictably with the two of them fighting. So yeah, maybe Vance had a sexual response to me, but he didn't know me.

Our proof was gone, and Mitch was killing people to get that blasted necklace.

I had to pull myself together. "Fine. Let's just get out of here before another dead body appears. I have to get home and check on the boys."

When we got home, we found Grandpa surfing the Internet while Joel and Ali played hide and seek with a tennis ball. Joel told Ali to stay in the kitchen while he hid the ball somewhere in the house. Then he told her to find it. The game involved lots of running, barking, yelling, and laughing. Ali always found the ball. Once Joel had hidden the ball in the covers of his top bunk bed.

Ali had climbed up the ladder and found it.

Damnedest thing I ever saw. Well, next to a dead body that disappeared. Grandpa made live people disappear in his magic shows, but they always came back.

Ugh, was Zack's body going to come back? I had to get a grip.

Ali came racing out of the back rooms with a wet green tennis ball in her mouth. She met us as we walked into the dining room, dropped the tennis ball in front of Gabe, and then stood up on her hind legs. She put her front paws on Gabe's chest and barked.

He rubbed her ears. "You found the ball, huh, Ali?"

She barked again, jumped down, and came over to say hello to Angel and me. Ali never jumped on us, only on Gabe. Joel came in behind Ali. Seeing my son helped me to feel grounded. "Hey, Joel, where's TJ?"

He rolled his eyes. "In your room with the door closed talking to his girlfriend. Me and Ali couldn't play in there."

I smiled at Joel. For a second, all the rest of the horror

slid away as I looked at my younger son. "Ali would have found the ball no matter where you hid it."

He laughed. "I think she cheats, Mom. What's for dinner?"

Gabe answered, "Pizza." He pulled out his cell phone and handed it to Joel. "Order a couple of large ones and have them delivered."

Joel took the phone from Gabe, then asked, "Are you on the case, Gabe? About Angel's car getting blown up?"

I reached out and put my hand on his shoulder. "It wasn't blown up, Joel. Set on fire."

"Whatever." He looked at Gabe.

Gabe said, "Yes, I'm on the case. But since I fired my assistant, I don't have anyone to order pizza for me."

Joel grinned. "Do I get paid?"

"In pizza."

"Cool." Joel went into the kitchen to look for the phone number to call in the pizza.

We had to get to work and figure out what to do next. I took off my jacket, then said, "I'm going to put this in my room. Then we'll get started."

Grandpa stood up from his computer and looked at Gabe. "There's no Mitch St. Claire in any files I could find at Daystar. I'll put on some coffee."

Crap. Why, just once, couldn't some bad guy leave a clear trail of breadcrumbs that led us right to him? I headed down the hall. At my bedroom door, I knocked once, then walked in.

TJ sat on my bed, leaning against the wall. He was twirling the phone cord around his finger, then untwirling it. "I don't know if I can go anywhere tonight. My mom's . . . uh, hang on." TJ covered the mouthpiece. "I'm on the phone, Mom."

I set my purse and my jacket on my bed. "So I see. Who are you talking to?"

His face closed up tight. "A friend. Can I go to Max's house tonight?"

I could tell from the look on TJ's face where this was going. "I'm sorry, TJ, but no. It's a school night and I want you to stay home tonight." *Besides, there's a dead body floating around somewhere in Lake Elsinore, and a seriously pissed-off jewel thief/murderer.* I opened my closet door to hang up the jacket.

"Mom! It's just Max's house. I go there all the time."

Turning around, I looked at TJ. He had stood up and angry red colored his face. With my calmest voice, I asked, "Do you want to have this discussion right now while your friend is on the phone?"

He put the phone to his ear. "I'll call you back as soon as I can." He hung up. "Mom, why can't I go to Max's house after dinner?"

I remembered being TJ's age. First year in high school, desperate to fit in, and now he liked a girl. He wasn't ready to share that part of his life with me. Lord, that stung my mother's pride. But it didn't hurt as much as the thought of something happening to TJ or one of his friends because of this mess with Mitch St. Claire and the diamond necklace. I said, "It's too dangerous, TJ."

"Mom! I'm not a baby."

I closed the distance between us. Though his whole body was rigid with anger, I put my hand on his tense shoulder. He was taller than I was, which forced me to tilt my head to look him in the eye. Time to let the boys know what was going on. "I know that, and so I'm going to tell you the truth. Someone is trying to hurt Angel and possibly me because they accidentally gave us a stolen diamond necklace. We didn't know it until I found the necklace this morning. Today, Angel and I found a dead man on the bed in her room. By the time we got back there with the police, the dead body was gone. These are very serious people, TJ. It's not just you I'm worried about either. What about your friends, what if they get hurt?"

I watched TJ assimilate this information. His face pinched tighter as he struggled with hard facts that interfered with his romantic feelings. God, I felt for him. Finally, he looked up at me. "I really wanted to go."

I hugged him. "I'm really sorry, TJ." Pulling back, I looked at him. "You like this girl, huh?"

His ears turned red. "She's a friend."

"What's her name?" I wanted to sound casual but I suspected I sounded like a mom.

"Kelly, but I wanted to go to Max's house."

I stared at him. "To see Kelly."

He shuffled. "Maybe."

I sighed. "TJ, wanting to see Kelly over at Max's house is fine. As long as there's an adult there and you aren't lying to me. Kelly can come over here once we get this problem solved." I didn't dare tell TJ that I was dying to meet this girl. To move past this, I said, "Why don't you call Kelly and Max back, then come have some pizza with us, OK?"

He sank down on the side of my bed and picked up the phone.

I hesitated a second longer. Had I done the right thing? Here we were, TJ and I, on the threshold of something important, and I didn't know if I had said the right thing. Done the right thing. I desperately wanted TJ and Joel to move seamlessly and painlessly through adolescence.

But that wasn't going to happen. I took another look at TJ.

He waited for me to leave before calling Kelly.

Yep, my son was growing up. Yet I was damn proud of him for managing his huge adolescent disappointment at not being able to see Kelly that night. I left the room, pulling the door closed behind me.

I went back down the hallway to the smell of fresh coffee. Grandpa, Angel, and Gabe sat around the glass-topped dining-room table, drinking coffee. I went to the coffeepot and poured myself a cup. "Where's Joel?"

Grandpa looked up from the table. "He's brushing Ali on the back patio. We don't want him to answer the door for the pizza."

I took my coffee to the table and sat down next to Gabe. Glancing to my right, past where Angel sat, I saw Ali sitting still while Joel brushed her. He had a brown paper bag to dump all the fur into. Both my sons were safe.

Time to get busy. Up till then, I had thought that Zack was the bad guy, the one we had to worry about. But Zack was dead, and Mitch was the one behind this whole mess. I looked to my left at Gabe. "Where could Mitch put a dead body? It can't be that easy to keep moving a dead body around. Obviously, Zack wasn't killed at Angel's house, since there was no blood. He had to be put there after he was killed." Who did that? God, who shot someone through the head, then carted the body around to scare the life out of people?

Gabe looked at Angel, then me. "We have to assume that Mitch is here in Elsinore. Zack's house would be my first guess, but I'm sure the police have looked there. What we need to do is to put what we know together. The information from a friend of mine at Daystar, Barney's information from the Internet and his Triple M group, and information from the two of you."

"But if we find Zack's body, Vance will believe us! Grandpa has Zack's address." We needed Vance to believe us. Then he could bring down the full weight of the law to find Mitch St. Claire.

Before Mitch killed Angel.

The need to *do something* ate at my insides.

Gabe said, "Sam, Vance is not dumb. He's been looking for Zack. He's checked out Zack's house probably more than once. I said it was my first guess. Face it, a town like this has a number of places to dump a body. Zack could be at the bottom of the lake, in the outflow channel, in an abandoned building, in an open field . . ."

I put my hand up. "I get it." I hadn't touched my coffee. "So where do we start?"

"With Mitch St. Claire. Barney couldn't find anyone named Mitch St. Claire registered at the hotel at Daystar, or that worked there, used a credit card there, or had done anything else traceable."

Frustration had me squeezing the cup of coffee. "Dead end."

Grandpa spoke up. "Not entirely. I've been doing a little research, looking for jewel thieves that hit casinos. I've found one that looks like it could be our guy. He seduces the woman, then steals her jewelry. He's known as the Casino Jewel Thief."

I asked, "Any chance you have a name and address?"

Grandpa shook his head. "The cops believe he's purposely picking casinos because there's so many people moving around. Plus there's the shame factor—older women being seduced by a younger man, then getting their jewelry stolen, are usually a bit slow to report the theft. They are humiliated."

I could imagine. We women did like to build our little fairy tales.

Grandpa added, "But I think he's slipped up this time by using an accomplice."

I snapped my gaze up. "He was furious at Zack when he called us at Angel's house. So why did he use an accomplice? Has he ever done that before?"

After taking a drink of coffee, Grandpa answered,

"There's no mention of a previous accomplice. The women all have similar descriptions of the man they slept with who then made off with their jewels."

Gabe added, "Which means he's changed his MO by having another man seduce the woman and steal the jewels." He looked at Angel and me. "What exactly did Mitch say on the phone?"

Angel said, "He killed Zack because Zack screwed up. I was never supposed to get the necklace. Zack put it in the wrong sex-toy kit. I guess Zack was supposed to get it back and failed."

"So Mitch killed Zack." I didn't get it. "Grandpa, was there any violence in the newspaper articles and stuff you read on the Internet?"

"No." Grandpa looked through some notes he had made. "Unless you consider plying a lonely woman with alcohol, which resulted in being hungover, violence. The Casino Jewel Thief is known for being seductive, charming, and nonviolent."

Even more confused, I tried to think it out. "But he sounded violent on the phone. Angry. On the edge. What changed?"

Gabe watched me. "Go on, Sam."

I shook my head, unable to put it together. "He said something like 'most women are romanced into submission.' " What did that mean? "Would 'submission' mean he uses charm or seduction to control women? I guess he's not a big believer in female intelligence."

Angel put both her hands flat on the glass-topped table. "He was smooth. At the time, I thought he respected a woman in business. He said all the right things, complimenting my business, showing he'd researched me. He appeared successful, so I guess I thought he was branching out from whatever business he was in. Single, no ring on his left hand. But it was all a sales pitch, a method to seduce me into selling his sex toys."

I stared at Angel, stunned by how much she had picked up. Mitch *had* said all the right things to her, getting her attention and interest. How had he known what to say? How had he picked Angel? I reached out and put my hand over Angel's.

Gabe zeroed in on something Angel had said. "Business. Exactly what was Mitch, the successful jewel thief, doing trying to hawk sex toys?"

Good question. "And back to Zack. Why have an accomplice?"

Gabe leaned back in his chair. "Putting those two questions together, the answer might be that Mitch was trying to go legit and start a business selling sex toys. Maybe training his replacement—Zack. He probably expected a cut of the profits from Zack for a while."

I was amazed that Gabe could put that together. But it made sense—criminals probably got tired of hiding from the law. But why did he need to train someone to take over for him? "Replacement? But Mitch works for himself, doesn't he?" I really didn't grasp the criminal way of business.

Gabe said, "Remember you told me that when Mitch called the two of you in Angel's bedroom, he said that Zack screwed up and that his clients don't wait patiently?"

I nodded and looked at Angel. She nodded, remembering it, too.

Gabe added, "I think we are dealing with a smart, ruthless jewel thief who is connected."

I whipped my head around to Gabe. "Connected to what?"

Gabe's mouth twitched.

Breathless, I said, "The mob? In Lake Elsinore?"

Gabe blasted me with a full-on grin. "No, not in Lake Elsinore. Mitch might be from anywhere, Sam. If he's the Casino Jewel Thief, the theory is that he goes shopping for a certain kind of jewelry. Once he spots something close to what he's looking for, he probably takes a picture of it and shows it to his client. Once the client gives him the go-ahead, he steals the piece, and gets a very nice fee from the client."

"Oh." This was not good. "Oh! That means Mitch has promised someone this necklace."

Angel added, "And that someone might be nasty if the necklace isn't delivered on time. The kind of nasty that motivates Mitch to be nasty to anyone who stands in the way of getting that necklace."

Now it was starting to make sense. "Like us." Shooting Zack in the head definitely rated as nasty. Another thought slammed into me. "That's why he had to kill Zack—he would have known about Mitch's connections if Mitch was training him as a replacement." Which made Mitch even more dangerous. I took a sip of my lukewarm coffee. "So what do we do now?"

Gabe said, "I have the victim's name and information. I'm going to talk to her, try to get as much information from her as possible. I'm sure that Mitch made the first contact with her, maybe even getting a picture of the necklace with a hidden camera, or maybe a cell phone camera, to show his contacts. Then I'll go to the casino and see what I can get there. Barney's going to follow the sex-toy trail. See if he can find Mitch that way. Maybe a sex-toy Web site—anything he can think of. I'll ask around Daystar to see if anyone else talked to a man who was selling sex toys."

"What about Angel and me?" This could take too long.

"Stay here in the house and try to contact Zoë. If we get that necklace back, then we have something to give Vance."

"Wait! That's why Vance came here when he got my voice mail that I found the necklace. He knew that necklace was connected to the Casino Jewel Thief. That's why he was so furious when things kept going wrong. He wanted to solve the Casino Jewel Thief case."

Gabe nodded.

"But why didn't he believe me about Zack being dead?"

Gabe's face hardened. "Because both of you look guilty. And Angel looks desperate." He stared at her. "You have thousands of dollars on your charge cards, your business is not making a profit, and you've sold off more than half your stocks."

"Been busy, haven't you?" Angel answered, her voice cool and uninterested.

"You weren't honest with Sam about your financial problems. That made her, both of you, look guilty." Gabe said flatly. "And stuff like taking off to Vegas when she's expecting to meet with you . . ." He stopped for a second, his eyes blazing in anger. "Pointlessly worrying her." Each word came out an accusation.

They stared at each other in icy anger. My boyfriend and my best friend.

The phone rang.

I jumped up to answer it just as the doorbell rang. As I said, "Hello," I saw Gabe get up, take out his gun, and go to the front door.

"Samantha."

My back snapped rigid. Zoë! The necklace! The need to fix this whole mess solidified in my words. "Zoë? Thank God, where are you?"

"Never mind that. You have one more chance to tell me the truth or I'm throwing this paste necklace into the lake."

I barely noticed Gabe walking back into the dining

room carrying two boxes of pizza. "No! Zoë, you don't understand! That necklace . . ."

"All you've done is lie to me!" Her voice rose to a screech. "I trusted you with my heart! I told you R. V. Logan is my heart mate, but you lied to me! I don't care what this necklace is. Tell me R. V. Logan's real name and address or I'll . . . I'll . . . that . . . creature . . . was not R. V. Logan!"

"Zoë! Calm down. I'm sorry that I gave you a fake name and address for R. V. Logan, but you have to listen to me." I fought to get my voice into a soothing tone. My heart slammed against my chest and panicked sweat trickled down my back. I had to get that necklace. In hindsight, I saw that pretending Hugh was R. V. Logan had been a mistake. "Zoë, tell me where you are."

Silence.

"Zoë?" *Calm voice, calm voice,* I reminded myself. She sounded crazier than usual. "Listen, Zoë, you might be in danger. I want to keep you safe. Tell me where you are." Angel slipped up close to me to listen. I glanced at Gabe where he stood next to the table.

His face was set as cold as Italian marble.

"I want R. V. Logan's real name and address, Samantha. No tricks."

How was I going to get her to listen to me? "That necklace is stolen, Zoë. It could get you killed."

"Tell me who R. V. Logan is."

Talk about a one-track mind. I blinked and looked over the handset into Angel's face. What was I supposed to do? Vance already didn't believe us, and telling Zoë that Vance was R. V. Logan would make things worse. Vance would kill me. But Angel could die! On the other hand, all I had to negotiate with Zoë for the necklace was R. V. Logan's identity. "Zoë, just tell me where you are. I'll come to you and tell you R. V. Logan's real identity."

"I don't trust you." Click.

She hung up. "Damn it!" I wrenched the phone from between Angel and myself, and slammed it down on the base.

"Mom?" Joel said. He came in from the backyard with Ali.

I fought to keep from screaming. I looked at Joel. "It's OK, Joel. I'm just mad at myself. Can you go tell TJ to get off the phone and come eat pizza?"

Grandpa got up and came around the table. "Come on, Joel, let's go round up your brother and take our time doing it."

Joel opened his mouth, then shut it and went with Grandpa through the long kitchen. They disappeared down the hallway.

Gabe closed the distance between us. "Still protecting your detective, Sam?"

"Huh? What are you talking about?" Hey, I was ready for a fight. Someone to yell at. Someone to blame this whole mess on.

Gabe softened his voice. "Why didn't you just tell Zoë who R. V. Logan is?"

Was he that dense? "Because it's all I have to negotiate with to get that necklace back!"

A black cloud of danger rolled over Gabe's face, darkening his eyes and thinning his mouth. "We are out of time to negotiate. Are you sure you aren't protecting Vance?"

Cold fear dropped into my stomach. Was Gabe right? Had I just endangered my best friend's life to protect Vance? Omigod. Automatically, I defended myself. "Don't be stupid!" I shouted.

Raw fury wiped out all remnants of the flat cop look on Gabe's face. His Italian heritage bloomed into hard cheekbones, flashing dark eyes, and a cold voice. "Want to talk stupid, sugar? Stupid is giving Zoë a fake name in Smash Coffee to protect Vance. Whose name did you give her?"

I glared at Gabe. "What were we supposed to do? Just give her the name? As it turns out, she didn't bring the necklace with her anyway! She said we'd get the stuff back after she verified the information." I was surprised I remembered that, since Angel's car had exploded into flames right about then.

He leaned in closer. "Whose name?"

What difference did it make? "Hugh's."

"Christ." Gabe hissed it at me. "Did you really think you could pull that off?"

"We had a plan! We were going to Hugh's house to catch Zoë when she showed up, and then we'd get the necklace back from her!"

"How'd that little plan work? About like all the rest of your plans?"

He was really ticking me off. "What'd you want me to do, Pulizzi? Make an appointment with your assistant and hire you?"

"Sugar, that would have been the first smart thing you did. But you didn't, so here I am, trying to keep you and Angel alive. And what do you do?"

I was pretty sure he didn't want me to answer that question.

"You play with the first solid lead we get, protecting Vance. Why is that, Sam? Why are you so afraid to piss off Vance?"

"I was trying to find a way to meet with Zoë! I would have told her!" I wanted to believe I would. Vance hadn't done anything to help Angel. He had called me a liar. And yet, I understood the stigma that romance writers endured. For Vance, as a cop, it would be a hundred times worse.

"But she doesn't trust you, because you've already lied to her, right? That leaves you with a missing necklace, a missing body, and a determined killer. So here's the new plan, Sam. You and Angel stay in this house. No one leaves this house." He turned and stalked off toward the door.

I followed him. "Where are you going? I thought you said no one leaves this house! Who do you think you are, telling me I can't leave my own house?"

He stopped when he had his hand on the doorknob. Every muscle in his body was pulled tight enough to snap. He turned his frigid fury on me. "I'm the private investigator that's going to save your ass. That's who I am." He yanked open the door and slammed it closed behind him.

15

The slamming of the front door was still ringing in my ears when I heard Gabe's truck roar to life out in front.

Angel came up beside me. "Your boyfriend is pissed."

"Jealous. Vance is a sore spot for him. The fact that Dee had forwarded his calls from his cell phone to her cell phone isn't helping. Gabe's got that whole hero-complex thing."

"And he loves you."

I stared at the closed door, still unable to believe he'd broken the rules this morning. We were supposed to dance around that issue. On the other hand, it made his anger at me easier to deal with. He might be mad, but at least he cared enough to be mad. And he was coming back. "Doesn't give him the right to be high-handed and so damn male." Telling me to stay home and let him fix everything. Yeah, right.

"No man saves my ass."

I turned to Angel. "I'm not against a man saving my ass occasionally, but I won't be told to stay home while he does it."

She pursed her mouth thoughtfully. "And it has to be

reciprocal. If he's gonna save my ass, I have to save his once in a while, too."

"Good point." I nodded while my mind ran over everything. "Though right now, his ass doesn't look to be in as much trouble as our asses are."

"True. Which means we'd better start thinking of ways to save our own asses. I know just where to start."

I shifted around to face her. "Hugh?" I could see why Gabe thought Angel had lied to me, but he was wrong. The truth was that I hadn't heard Angel. She'd been trying to tell me something about Hugh, and I hadn't wanted to hear it.

With a level gaze, she said, "Hugh."

The boys and Grandpa came down the hallway. Joel was first and asked, "Mom, where's Gabe?"

I decided I would continue the conversation with Angel in the car. To Joel, I answered, "He went to do some work. You guys get started on dinner. Pizza's on the table. Angel and I also have some work to do. Grandpa, can I take your Jeep?" My car was still at Gabe's house, plus it was probably crawling with electronic bugs.

"Where are you going, Sam?" Grandpa held a handful of paper plates and napkins.

I started to answer when I heard a knock at the front door. Angel hurried into the dining room and grabbed her purse, which held her gun. Grandpa set down the paper plates and napkins and pulled out his switchblade.

Why were all the people I knew so weapon-happy? "It's all right. It's probably the babysitter Gabe sent over." Gabe might be mad, but he wouldn't leave us unprotected. Chances were good he had called whoever was at the door before our little fight. I looked through the peephole, then opened the door and said, "Blaine."

My assistant walked in. "I smell pizza."

Shutting the door and locking it, I said, "How long ago did Gabe call you?" He had his blue button-down work shirt hanging loose around his jeans, but I'd have bet my car he had a gun tucked into his pants.

"At least he called me." Blaine picked up a plate and selected a couple of pieces of pizza. "More than I can say for you, boss. I closed the office."

"I'm sorry, Blaine. I should have called you."

He waved away my apology and looked at the boys, who were piling their plates with pizza. "I got some new bearings for your skateboards. We'll put them on after dinner." He bit into a fully loaded slice.

"Cool," Joel said.

"Mine needs new grip tape," TJ set down his cheese pizza and looked at Blaine. "Do you know how to put that on? I have some."

"Easy to do. I'll show you and you can put it on," Blaine said.

"Did you bring your board?" Joel asked.

Blaine got up and went into the kitchen. I heard him open the fridge, probably looking for a drink. When he came back carrying a beer, he said to Joel, "Of course I brought it. This time I'll jump over the two of you long ways."

What? "No!" I shouted. "Blaine, do not—"

All three of them were laughing. I'd been had. Cripes. Joel used the back of his hand to wipe sauce off his face and leaned across the table. "Mom can't even stand up on a skateboard! Gabe can, Grandpa can, but Mom falls off."

This brought another round of laughter.

I marched into the kitchen. "Yeah, well, maybe Mom can't pay for those boards, either." I picked up my purse and kissed both boys just to annoy them. Then I stopped next to Blaine and put my hand on his thick shoulder.

"Thank you." I meant for more than just protecting my sons.

He drank his beer. "No problem, boss. Everything is set for the open house tomorrow night. It's going to be a solid turnout." He picked up his beer and took a sip, then added, "You know that suite next to us that was available?"

The one I had been lusting for, with visions of expanding Heart Mates? After slinging my big black purse over my shoulder, I went into the kitchen to pour two glasses of milk for the boys. Even if this open house brought me enough clients to lease that suite, I wouldn't have enough money left to furnish it right. I really didn't need that much space. Setting the glasses on the table next to TJ and Joel, I glanced over at Blaine. "Of course I know the suite. Did the owner drop the price?"

He shook his head. "Nope, but a new tenant signed papers on it today. A year lease."

Damn. There went my dream of opening up the wall between the two suites. I'd even thought of asking Angel to come in with me so we could work together. It would be big enough for two businesses. And with two budgets, we could have made it look more upscale. "It wasn't the right time for us to expand, anyway."

"Sam, you never answered my question." Grandpa carried a glass of iced tea and set it down at his place. "Where are you going?"

"To Hugh's house. We want to find out a few things from him, including if he got any information from Zoë. We told Zoë that Hugh was really R. V. Logan," I explained.

Grandpa grinned at that, then said, "You told me that you think Zoë went to that conference *Romance Rocks Magazine* holds, right?"

I nodded yes.

"Then I'm going to see if I can crack into the conference attendance logs and find what I can on Zoë. Maybe there's a cell phone number or something. I'm going to stay on the Mitch-the-Casino-Jewel-Thief trail, too." He came back to stand between Angel and me. "You two be careful. Take Ali and check in by phone every twenty minutes."

Careful. Right. I'd dropped my can of defense spray after dousing my own eyes, and that can had disappeared from Angel's house. Mitch was good at tidying up. I repressed a shiver that revealed my terror of Mitch St. Claire. "I'll be right back." I ran into my bedroom and opened my closet door. I reached inside and pulled out the box of stuff that Grandpa and the boys had ordered for me through the Internet. I found my stun gun in the box and dropped it into my purse. There were advantages to suitcaselike purses sometimes—like room for storing weapons and sex-toy kits.

I went back out to Grandpa at his desk and kissed his cheek. "I'm taking my stun gun. We'll be careful. Tell Gabe where we are when he calls."

Grandpa studied me with his fading blue eyes. "Not *if* he calls?"

That struck me. Somewhere along the way, I'd begun to believe in Gabe and me. "He'll call. And he won't be happy to hear Angel and I left the house."

He smiled. "He won't be surprised. Just be smart. The stun gun is a good idea."

I looked over at Ali, who had stationed herself at Blaine's right leg to stare at his beer. "Ali, Blaine is not going to give you any beer. You're coming with us."

Blaine laughed. "She's waiting for me to look away so she can steal it."

"Ali," I warned her.

She sighed a huge gust of doggy disappointment, then

got up and trotted to the front door. She liked going for rides almost as much as she liked beer.

Once we got settled in the Jeep and were on the road, I looked over at Angel. "Tell me about Hugh."

She kept her gaze on the road ahead of us. "I don't believe it was a coincidence that Hugh was at Daystar last Friday night. He was so pissed at me, believing that I was destroying his work and marriage, that I think he was up to something."

"Like what?" I made a left turn onto Grand, then a right onto Lincoln. We were heading down toward the lake. Near the bottom of Lincoln, before Riverside Drive, we would take another left into Hugh's tract. Angel had a few brief minutes to fill me in. "What would Hugh do?"

Ali stuck her head over Angel's shoulder and Angel petted her. "I don't know. My guess would be that his intention was to undo any promotion I did for Tempt-an-Angel Lingerie."

"Did he know you were going to Daystar to promote your lingerie?" Did Hugh even know that Angel had a deal with the Silky Men?

"He knew. I told him that I didn't have time for his accusations because I had to leave to go to Daystar. Unlike him, I take care of my business and my family."

Damn. I knew where this was going. Angel was a smart and independent woman, but like all people, she had needs. She had been married to Hugh for years before finally leaving him. That old need to have him care had surged and . . . "You told him about your mom."

Ali licked Angel's neck, then put her head back on her shoulder. Angel reached across with her right hand to stroke Ali's head. "I told him. He screamed at me that I was a ballbuster. Said I drove my dad away, and that I drove him into the arms of Brandi and he wasn't going to let me destroy that, too."

"Oh, Angel." Now I understood her reaction when Linda Simpkins had commented that she'd seen Angel's ex-husband at Daystar the Friday night before. Hugh, the sniveling rodent, had driven a sharp blade into Angel's raw wound. God, the thing was, I could see Hugh doing exactly what Angel said—going to Daystar to try to destroy her efforts to get more clients. The man had no finesse, so to him that would seem like a good plan.

But was that really what had he had ended up doing? "So we need to find out exactly how Mitch knew so much about us—enough to know that telling you he saw a man matching Hugh's description running from your house would be pushing your run-right-home button." We would find out soon enough. I turned left onto Hugh's street, but stopped the Jeep a few houses away from Hugh and Brandi's place. I looked over at Angel. My beautiful, smart, sexy, and practically fearless best friend was struggling to stay composed. Her face was drawn tight, and her right hand stroked Ali's head gently. "Now I wish I'd brought Gabe. He'd kick the shit out of Hugh," I said.

Her mouth twitched. "That'd be fun. We should save that for a better time. Maybe get some popcorn and a camcorder."

I laughed, then got serious. "Tell me everything that happened last night when you came over here."

Angel shifted around in her seat to face me. "I parked right across the street from Hugh's house. It took him about fifteen minutes before he spotted me. He came out of the house and strolled across the street. I got out of my car and demanded to know what he was doing at the casino Friday night."

I tapped my finger on the steering wheel. "He told Gabe and me that he was just there drinking 'cause Brandi was gone."

Angel nodded. "He tried to tell me that, but I told him that everyone in town knew Brandi had left him because he's a loser."

I stopped tapping my finger and grabbed her arm. "What did he do?"

"Predictably, he said I was the loser and that he was gonna show me and Brandi. He was gonna be successful. He had friends that I didn't know about. Brandi was gonna be surprised when she came back."

"Friends?" I asked. Who could Hugh have been talking about? Was he mixed up in this whole mess as some kind of revenge on Angel?

"That's what I asked him. I demanded to know if he knew Zack Quinn. He swore he didn't know who I was talking about. I didn't ask him about Mitch last night, because we didn't realize he was involved. You hadn't found the necklace yet, and as far as we knew, Zack was still alive."

I nodded. It was true. We had just thought Zack was a crazy stalker or after something we didn't know about.

Angel went on, "I told him that if I found out he was behind Zack's breaking into my house and threatening me, I'd destroy him." She turned away from me.

"What did he say?"

She didn't move. "He said I was good at that. Look at what I'd done to my family and our marriage."

Hugh had to die. I reached past Angel for my purse on the floor of the passenger side.

"What are you doing?" Angel asked.

After I got ahold of my purse, I put it on the console between the seats and started digging around for my cell phone. Ali stuck her nose in there to check for beer. "Going to call Gabe. I need his gun to shoot Hugh."

She put her hand on my arm. "Sam."

I looked up. "You think I'm going to sit back and let him say something like that to you?"

She smiled. "No. That's why I hadn't told you until now."

I held her gaze. "Let go of my arm."

"Are you going to call Gabe?"

"No." I closed my fingers around my stun gun. As much as I wanted to see Hugh suffer, I wanted Gabe to find Mitch St. Claire more. Angel wasn't safe until Mitch was in jail. Or dead. Whatever worked. I pulled my stun gun out and held it up. "I'll take care of Hugh myself." I turned on the stunner. The sizzle popped and crackled.

"That'll work," Angel decided.

Shutting it off, I said, "Angel, I wish you had told me all this stuff. I didn't realize you were going into debt to help your mom."

"Sam, remember Adam Miller? Remember that I invested in his computer game?"

I nodded. Adam Miller was the husband of a friend of mine who had been murdered. He was also a computer geek, and Angel had invested in a computer game he had developed. But I didn't care about Adam right now. I cared about Angel. "What does Adam have to do with any of this?"

"His game is going to bring in lots of money for me by the end of the year. I'll be fine."

I set the stun gun down on top of my purse and thought for a minute. I knew what it cost Angel to tell me about her fights with Hugh. We didn't know how deeply he was involved, if he was involved at all. But Angel had been right from the start—it was too coincidental that Hugh had been at the casino when this whole mess started. I reached for her hand. "You're not fine, but you are not alone either. We're going to fix this, Angel. And we're going to start with dumbass Hugh. He may have just gone to the casino with some lame plan to tell everyone bad stuff about your lingerie." I remembered Gabe's telling me that Hugh might be more afraid of someone, or something, else than of Gabe. But who? "How far into stupid trouble do you think Hugh would go just to make himself look better? To get even with you?"

Angel looked through the front windshield toward Hugh's house. "As far as he could without having to break heads."

Damn, that's what I had thought. "OK, let's go find out the depth of Hugh's stupidity. Come on, Ali," I said as I let go of Angel's hand and opened my door.

Hugh answered the door of his town house wearing sagging gray sweatpants and a T-shirt with yellow stains under the arms. Ugh. His face was sweaty red and he was breathing like a wheezy hippo. His face deepened to purple when he saw us on his doorstep. He zeroed in on Angel. "You just don't know when to quit, do you? That crackpot broad you sent over here ruined everything! I got out of my car with flowers for Brandi and that nut launched herself at me screaming about heart mates. Brandi saw the whole thing!"

Before Angel could tell Hugh her opinion, I asked, "About Zoë, did she tell you where she's staying? Give you a phone number? Tell you anything that might help us find her?"

Hugh turned his gaze to me. "Fuck off."

Charming. I whipped my stun gun out of my purse and held it up. "Shall we try it again?" I asked nicely.

Sweat ran down his high forehead and dripped off his nose. "What's that thing?"

"Stun gun." I wondered if zapping him with all that sweat might create an electric shock that would kill him.

"Don't make this harder than it has to be. We have to find Zoë."

Hugh sneered. "She's a lunatic. She threw herself at me, yammering about how she'd convinced Samantha Shaw that we were heart mates. By the time I got her off me, Brandi marched up and demanded to know what was going on. Zoë told her that I was some pansy romance writer. Brandi laughed. Laughed!"

Damn, I thought. Zoë hadn't told Hugh anything. This was a dead end. I realized that Hugh's face was getting redder by the second.

He turned on Angel. "Brandi told me in front of that wacko that I should get some better pick-up lines and went back to her mother's." He pointed his finger in Angel's face. "You are destroying my life and I told the police that when they showed up!"

A glimmer of hope sprang to life inside me. "The police? Did they talk to Zoë here? Uniforms or a detective?" Maybe Vance had come through after all.

Hugh didn't bother looking at me. He kept wagging his finger in Angel's face. "No, a couple uniforms got here just as Zoë left. I didn't know the answer to any of their questions. But I told them that you" —he leaned closer into Angel's face—"are harassing me by sending psychos in that cheesy green Ford Focus."

Dead end. Again. Vance had sent out some uniforms just in case Angel and I had told the truth. What had he made of the information that Zoë had been at Hugh's? Frustration blanked my mind and I wasn't sure what to focus on next, but Angel was.

She knocked his hand away from her face. "I don't give a rat's ass about your whining to the cops. Tell me what you were doing at the casino Friday night or I'll zap your ass." She grabbed the stun gun from my hand and turned it on.

"You bitch." Hugh backed up and started to swing the door closed in our face. "I'm going to call the—"

A low growl cut off Hugh's words.

Ali pushed past Angel and threw her body into the door, ripping it from Hugh's hand. The door swung into the wall.

I caught the door before it could bounce off the wall and hit Ali.

Hugh backed up into the house, crossing his arms in front of his face.

Ali froze in the doorway, leaning forward so that she was within biting distance of Hugh's fat belly. She bared her wicked teeth in a vicious growl.

He shrank against the wall covered in squares of smoky mirrors. "Get it off me!"

God, he screamed like a girl. Ali hadn't even touched him. "Ali, sit."

She dropped her butt down where she was and let loose with a final growl. She looked back at me, then turned to fix her pissed-off-dog stare on Hugh. She had a good eighty pounds of quivering German shepherd muscle to back up that stare.

I stepped into the foyer and put my hand on her head. "Good girl." Then I looked up at Hugh, determined to find out just how involved he was in this mess. "Tell us what you were doing at the casino."

He lowered the arms he had crossed in front of his face. "I told you! I just went to have a drink."

Angel was having none of that. "Who did you talk to about me?" She held up the stun gun.

The high color had drained from Hugh's face, leaving behind a pale clammy sheen. "No one! Only bar talk. Jeez, turn that thing off!"

My ears hurt from his screeching. Fury poured over me. "Angel and I found Zack Quinn today. He was shot through the head, murdered. You are in big trouble and you'd better start talking."

More sweat broke out on Hugh's forehead. "I didn't do anything! It was just talk."

Omigod.

Angel moved the sizzling stunner close to Hugh's left temple. "Who did you talk to about me? You got one second!"

He turned his beady eyes on Angel. "You wouldn't dare!"

Angel shoved the stun gun to his forehead and zapped him.

Hugh slammed back against the mirrored wall, his eyes bulging with shock, and then he slid to the floor. He sat there with his legs sprawled, his head bent to the right and his mouth hanging open. Angel stepped back and looked at me. "How long do you think he'll be out?"

"Uh . . ." Hell if I knew. I watched Ali pad over and sniff around him. "Five minutes?" I'd stunned Gabe once by accident and he'd been out about two minutes.

But that was Gabe. A finely built and tuned human body.

I looked back at Hugh. Ugh. No telling how long it'd take him to recover. "Now what?"

Angel turned around and looked into the town house. The TV was freeze-framed. "An exercise video?"

I turned and followed Angel. The living room was a mess and smelled of greasy fast food and sweat. A white bag with grease stains was balled up on the coffee table next to two beers. I glanced up at the TV. Yep, looked like an exercise video. Hugh thought he could work off the fast food and beer, I guess.

Ali padded up to the coffee table and sniffed. She knocked over one can of beer and watched it roll away, obviously empty. Then she knocked over the second can. About a half cup of beer pooled out. She licked it up.

"Ali, that's disgusting," I told her. Who would drink after Hugh?

She ignored me and licked up the beer.

"Ohhh."

We all turned to see Hugh roll over onto his arms and legs, then start coughing, gagging, and, finally, heaving up his guts. Half crying, half heaving, Hugh said, "Call 911! I'm dying!"

I rolled my eyes and then wondered how we were going to get out of the house. We had to pass that . . . mess. My own stomach heaved.

Especially when I thought of my tendency toward falling into—*stop thinking about it!*

Angel picked up a gray-looking towel from the back of the sofa with two fingernails and threw it to Hugh. "Pull yourself together."

He sat back on his butt and rubbed his face with the towel. "You assaulted me! I'm calling the cops."

Angel walked over and looked down at Hugh. "Who did you talk to about me at the casino?"

Hugh glared up at her with his small eyes bugging out of his pasty face. "Get out of my way. I'm calling the police." He groaned and started to get to his feet.

Angel turned on the stun gun.

Hugh froze when he heard the sizzle. "Don't!" He screamed, falling back to his butt and putting both hands up across his face.

Ali lifted her head from the beer, whirled around, and dropped into a crouch. She growled. The fur along her back rose up in a straight line of anger.

"Ali, not yet," I put my hand on the back of her neck. I could feel her muscles were clenched and ready. She really didn't like Hugh screaming at Angel. Given the things Angel told me that Hugh had said to her recently, I was tempted to let Ali take a bite out of him.

Except that we were in Hugh's house, and therefore, it would probably be really hard to justify Ali's biting him.

Angel turned off the stun gun. "Start talking."

Hugh uncovered his face and slowly got to his feet. "I met a guy in the bar. We were talking and he offered me a job." He glared at Angel. "He recognized my potential. I have a law degree."

I let go of Ali and moved up near Angel. "Your law degree won't get you out of trouble if you are charged with being an accessory to murder." Dang, I was impressed that I had remembered that. I was learning a thing or two.

"Accessory to murder? I didn't kill anyone!"

"Zack Quinn is dead, you dumbass," Angel said. "Murdered. If you assisted the man who murdered him by providing him information, you could be charged as an accessory."

I had a feeling Angel and I weren't getting this exactly right. Hugh should have known that, with his law degree. But Hugh had barely gotten through law school. Angel had helped him with most of his homework. His father, a defense lawyer with a practice in Temecula, may have used his influence to secure passing grades for his lazy dumbass son.

Hugh's color went from pasty pale to gray. "I'm calling my lawyer!"

Angel turned on the stun gun.

"OK!" He leaned over, putting his hands on his thick thighs and panting.

I tried not to think about how much trouble Angel and I could get into for stun-gunning Hugh in his own house. We had to get all the information we could to save Angel. I got out my mom voice and demanded, "Keep talking."

"A man in the bar offered me a job to help him find clients to sell his products."

I forgot all about getting into trouble for assaulting Hugh. I looked at Angel.

She met my gaze for a second, then turned to Hugh. "What products and what was his name?"

Hugh stood up and said, "Sex toys. His name was Mitch St. Claire, and I told him all about your lingerie business." Pride filled out his barrel chest. "I get four percent of your sales of his sex toys. I'm making money off your business."

"You stupid prick," Angel said in an even voice. "You don't know what you've gotten involved with." She closed her eyes for a second as the weight of her worries bowed her shoulders in.

Color flooded into Hugh's face. "I know exactly what I'm doing! I'm a businessman. I have a law degree. I am successful."

"You're an idiot." Angel opened her eyes and straightened her shoulders. "And you may end up a dead idiot. Does Mitch know where you live?"

Hugh leaned back against the mirrored wall. "What do you mean?"

My instincts buzzed. Careful to avoid the pile of vomit, I closed the distance between Hugh and me. "He was here, wasn't he?"

"I don't know what you are talking about." He didn't meet my gaze.

I didn't believe him for a second. I took a breath, then damn near gagged. God, it reeked in there. Breathing through my mouth, I said, "What did you do?"

"Nothing!" Hugh's voice was a whisper now. "I just have to get Brandi back. She thinks I'm a loser."

"You are a loser," Angel said.

It all began to make a sick kind of sense to me. "Mitch came here looking for Angel, didn't he?"

Hugh rocked his head back and forth between Angel and me. I wished Gabe were there. He'd have known what to ask. What to do.

Still breathing through my mouth, I said carefully, "Hugh, you are in over your head. Mitch is a thief and a killer. You'd better start talking or I'm calling the police."

He sniffled loudly. "I didn't do anything. He just asked me some questions about Angel."

Yeah, right. I thought of the back door to Angel's house. It hadn't shown any forced entry. And Angel's car—how had Mitch known what kind of car Angel drove? How had he found it? How had he gotten the tracking device on it? I grabbed the stun gun from Angel. "And?"

He shrank back. "I told him about Angel and about you. Where you live, work, what cars you drove. It's business! Mitch said I was going to make lots of money, that you both are going to sell sex toys through your businesses. He does background investigations on all his clients!"

Bile rose up in my throat. Hugh had believed Mitch because he had wanted to. I'd done the same thing with my husband. God. But right now, I saw the danger we were in. I glanced over at Angel, silently warning her to let me do this. Then I turned back to Hugh. "When was that?"

"Saturday."

"Do you have a key to Angel's house?"

Hugh shuffled his feet. "I don't feel good. I need an ambulance."

I ignored his whining. "Do you have a key? Did you give Mitch a key to Angel's house?"

He looked down at the floor. "He said he needed to get into her house to replace a defective part in the sample kit he gave her."

Angel roared, "You gave him a key to my house!"

Hugh turned his face toward her. "What did you expect, after all you've done to me?"

I reached over and put my hand on Angel's shoulder; it

was a tight ball of anger. Her face had blanched in betrayal. I didn't think Hugh realized the danger he had put Angel in, but Angel had still been betrayed by the man who once claimed to love her. I shoved down hard on my sympathy for Angel. We had to focus to keep her alive. "Angel, let's get the information we need."

I looked at Hugh. "Has Mitch been back here since Saturday?"

"Last night."

Dizziness swamped over me. Hugh was an idiot, but Mitch St. Claire had played him. I hated Hugh for what he'd done to Angel, but I hated Mitch more for finding people's weaknesses and exploiting them. Swallowing, I felt Angel's hand close over mine as it rested on her shoulder. I got control and asked Hugh, "How did the tracking device get on Angel's car?"

Hugh's eyes flooded with tears. "He said he'd kill Brandi if I didn't do it."

The foyer of Hugh's house smelled like beer and puke. I didn't know why that thought had crossed my mind, except that I couldn't believe what I had just heard from Hugh.

That he had put the tracking device on Angel's car for Mitch. She could have been killed!

Angel apparently didn't have any problem grasping what Hugh had done. She let go of my hand to grab the stun gun from me and turn it threateningly on him. "You did it? You put a tracking device on my car so that Mitch could firebomb it?"

Fat tears brimmed in his small eyes and ran down his face. He sniffled, wiped his arm under his nose, and said, "He said he'd kill Brandi! I didn't think he'd hurt you. Besides, I stuck a big screw in your tire to keep you safe."

Silence fell hard. Ali walked over, her toenails clicking on the tiled entryway. She pushed herself between Angel and me.

Angel's long, lean frame practically twanged with fury and betrayal. "How the hell would a screw in my tire keep me safe? I was a sitting duck for Mitch to get me when I tried to change the tire!" She waved the stun gun threateningly.

Hugh backed up. "But the tire should have been flat before you left your mom's house. If you'd stayed at your mom's house, you'd be safe! I had to protect Brandi!"

I reached over Ali and grabbed Angel's arm before she could zap Hugh again. We needed information and we couldn't get that if Hugh was unconscious or throwing up his guts. While holding on to Angel, I said to Hugh, "Where is Brandi?"

"Her mom's house."

"You're sure Mitch doesn't have her?"

He shook his head. "I just talked to her half an hour ago. I have to convince her I didn't pick up that lunatic you two sent over here."

OK, Brandi was safe. That was one less thing to worry about. "What about Mitch? Do you have any idea where he lives? What he drives? Anything?"

"I don't remember! Do you think he'll come back? Am I in danger? Should I call the police?" His body shook with fear.

Angel snorted in disgust. She handed the stun gun to me, then turned back to Hugh. "Grow some balls for once in your miserable life. Call the cops and get your wife somewhere safe. Your dad will protect you." She gracefully made her way around the pile of puke and left.

16

I watched her go. God, Angel had guts and style. I put the stun gun in my purse and said to Hugh, "You weren't always such a miserable little rat. How do you live with yourself?"

"It's all her fault! She—"

That did it. I grabbed hold of his sweaty shirt. "Angel was the best thing that ever happened to you, and you hurt her. I'm warning you right now, if Mitch harms her in any way, I will hunt you down and stomp your balls into hamburger. Then I'll let Gabe have you."

Ali backed that up with a warning bark at Hugh.

I looked down at my dog. "Let's go, Ali." I had to grab her collar and pull her around the vomit mess. We walked out into the night.

OK, what did all this mean? Mitch had gotten his information about Angel and me from Hugh. He was trying to force us to give him the necklace.

But Zoë had the necklace.

We had to find that necklace. Hugh would call the police, and then Vance would believe us and get on Mitch. By this time, Vance must have known that some uniforms had talked to Hugh, and he had backed up what Angel and I told him about sending Zoë to Hugh's house. When we got home, I'd call Vance and—

Ali growled, then barked, yanking hard against my hold on her collar.

I heard the sound of an engine idling. But Angel didn't have the keys to the Jeep. I let go of Ali.

She raced across the dead grass and toward the Jeep, which was parked a few houses down. Oh God, was someone putting something on the Jeep? A firebomb? Was Angel in there? I grabbed my stun gun and lunged into a run.

The sound of the engine revved up, then I heard a soft thump followed by an animal yelp.

"Ali!" My heart jackhammered. *Where's Angel? What happened?* I jumped off the curb into the street and ran hard. I got to the Jeep in time to see Ali get up off the road and break into a run to chase a car that was squealing around the corner.

"Ali! No! Come here!"

She slowed down, turned and trotted back toward me. Had a car hit her? Then she had gotten up to chase the car? Did the car have Angel in it? I took another step toward my dog and tripped. I managed to get my arms up before I landed hard on the street. My forearms and elbows took most of the impact. I started to push up to my knees when Ali stuck her nose in my face and licked me.

Hugh came huffing out of the house and shouted, "Sam? What happened?"

"Ali," I said, gently moving her nose from my face. I put an arm around her neck and looked up to see Hugh standing there. He must have heard me screaming. He had his cell phone in his hand. "I don't know!" Looking around, I saw what I had tripped over.

Angel's purse.

"Oh God. He has her! Mitch has Angel!" As I got to my feet, fury washed over me. "I'm so stupid! He knew Angel would come here. You told him she had already been here. And he used you to get us to her house to see Zack's body!" Shafts of guilt slammed into me. The skin around my forehead tightened brutally. My neck muscles clenched up and my shoulders squeezed. I looked at the Jeep. Had Angel gotten in and he had dragged her out?

No, that wasn't right. Her purse lay in the path by the driver's side headlight. She had been crossing the street, intending to pass in front of the Jeep to get to the passenger side.

Angel had been mad. Maybe a little sick over Hugh's betrayal. Overwhelmed. Her life was coming apart, and the man she had once loved and slept beside had put a tracking device on her car to help out a killer. She may not have paid attention if someone slithered up behind her and . . .

What?

Clubbed her over the head?

Hugh interrupted my thoughts. "What does Mitch want?"

As soon as I heard Hugh's voice, I realized how Mitch had gotten Angel. The same way we had intimidated Hugh—with a stun gun. She would have passed out from the shock of the stun gun, and then Mitch could have gotten her under enough control to shove her in his car.

A violent shiver rocketed through me.

I looked up from Angel's purse into Hugh's face. He was still breathing hard. He smelled of beer, vomit, and sweat. To answer his question about what Mitch wanted, I said, "A stolen diamond necklace."

Then I got my cell phone out of my purse and dialed Angel's cell phone number. It rang once.

Mitch answered the phone. "Samantha Shaw. You are so predictable. I knew you'd call to save your friend."

Oh God. Painful shivers prickled my spine. He would know it was me from the caller ID on Angel's phone. It didn't matter. All that mattered was Angel. "Don't hurt Angel!"

"It's very simple. If you want her back alive, get that necklace."

Bile burned up my throat. "I don't have it! I know who does, but—"

"One hour. Call me back when you have it. Then I'll tell you where to bring the necklace. No cops, no heroics. The two of you never had a chance of outsmarting me. I know women. I made a career out of women just like you." He hung up.

Mitch was crazy. And he had Angel. I had no time; I had to track down Zoë and get that necklace. Quickly, I dialed Grandpa. When I heard his voice, I had to fight back hysteria. Grandpa had been my rock throughout my life. But right now, I had to be strong. I had to find a way to save Angel. "Grandpa." I swallowed, trying to think how to tell him quickly about Angel and get what I needed. He loved Angel, too. "I'm at Hugh's house. Angel left the house first and Mitch kidnapped her. I found her purse on the ground by the Jeep. I called Angel's cell phone and Mitch answered. He said if I want her back alive, I have to get the necklace."

"Sam, my God! Did you call the police? What can I do?"

His voice was breathless with both love and fear. "I'll have Hugh call the police." I glanced at Hugh's pale, sweaty face. He stood there like a useless toad. To Grandpa, I said, "I need to know if you've found anything on Zoë?"

I heard him flipping pages in the background. "I got her cell-phone number. She lives up in Washington. She's

part owner in a health club. She has to be staying somewhere here in town, but I haven't found it yet."

At least it was something. "OK, give me the cell-phone
number and see if you can track down where Zoë is staying." I opened the Jeep door and watched Ali struggle to
get in. It looked like her right shoulder was hurt. I hoped
she was OK.

Grandpa's voice firmed up. "Sam, what are you going to
do?"

I didn't lie. "I'm going to find her, Grandpa, and get
that necklace. Mitch gave me only an hour."

"Sam, it's too dangerous."

Softly, I said, "He'll kill Angel. Give me Zoë's number
and I'll call you back after I talk to her, OK?"

He told me the phone number and we hung up.

Still holding the door to the Jeep, I focused on Hugh.
"You have to call Detective Logan Vance at the police station right now. Find him, and tell him Mitch St. Claire has
kidnapped Angel. Then tell him everything you told
Mitch about Angel, and everything you did. He'll get you
and Brandi to someplace safe."

Hugh blinked his beady eyes rapidly. "But—"

I let go of the Jeep door and got in his face, ignoring
the smell of sweat and vomit. "For once in your wretched
life, do the right thing! You got Angel into this, you asshole!" I jammed my right index finger into his soft barrel
chest, so enraged that I could barely see. "If she dies, I
swear to God, I will come back here and rip you apart. But
if you call right now, you just might save her life." I jerked
away from him, got in the Jeep, and yanked the door closed.

I had already wasted five minutes. Ramming the key in
the ignition, I started the Jeep and put it in gear. Then I
punched in Zoë's cell-phone number, which Grandpa had
given me. I let the Jeep idle while waiting for Zoë to an-

swer. Hugh had already slunk back inside his house. He'd better call Vance.

"Hello?"

Thank God she answered. "Zoë, it's Sam. Where are you? I will tell you who R. V. Logan is. I'll give you anything. Just tell me where you are." The fear thinned my voice to begging.

"Do you have R. V. Logan with you? You've lied to me, Samantha. How can I trust you?"

Think! I had to get that necklace. Angel's life depended on my getting that necklace. Mitch had killed Zack, then made him disappear. He would kill Angel to get that necklace. "Zoë, I'm on my way to pick R. V. Logan up right now. In real life, R. V. Logan is a cop."

"A cop! Well, of course he is."

"Zoë, where are you staying?"

"What kind of cop?"

"Homicide."

"What color are his eyes?"

"Brown. He has sandy blonde hair cut short and dimples. He's sexy and smart. Zoë, please! I need that sex-toy kit and necklace back. Tell me where you are staying." I'd tell her anything.

"I don't trust you. Call me back when you have R. V. Logan in the car and I can talk to him." She hung up.

She was so dead.

I didn't know what to do. I had to find Zoë and that necklace. Where did people stay when they visited?

Motels.

I took my foot off the brake and swerved into a U-turn. I made a right on Lincoln, then another right on Machado, and headed toward Lake Street. I would start with the motels on Main Street and work my way to the ones off Railroad Canyon Road.

I needed to call Gabe. I punched in his cell-phone number and got an out of range message. Where the hell was he? I left a message on his voice mail. "Gabe, Angel's been kidnapped by Mitch. I'm trying to track down Zoë to get the necklace." I pulled the phone away to hang it up, then changed my mind and put it back to my ear. My throat thickened. "I know you're mad at me, Gabe, but I need you." Then I hung up.

My phone rang before I could put it down. Was it Mitch? Or Gabe? I didn't look at the caller ID, I just put it to my ear. "Hello?"

It was Grandpa. "Sam, I got it. Zoë's staying at the Night Haven Motel. I don't know which room."

I made a right on Lake Street and broke as many traffic laws as I could. I ran the end of a yellow light at Riverside Drive. "How did you find her?" Did they have some sort of Internet file for motels? Had Grandpa's Triple M group come through with more incredible connections?

"I started calling motels and asked for Zoë Cash."

I nearly banged my head on the steering wheel. Such a simple solution, and I had never thought of it. "Grandpa, I love you."

"Sammy, let me send Blaine to—"

"No!" I got control of myself. "Grandpa, no. I can handle Zoë. I just need to know that both you and Blaine are protecting the boys."

"I don't like it. I could take Blaine's car and meet you—"

"No." I took a breath. Grandpa loved me and was looking out for me. If I were in his shoes, I would do the same thing. "Grandpa, I need you to find out more about Mitch. I know that's not his real name, but there has to be some trail. Something. Anything that I can use to get Angel away from him." *If she's still alive.*

Grandpa used his sternest voice. "You are not meeting

with Mitch on your own. I mean it, Sammy. I'll call the police and have them arrest you right now."

I believed him, so I thought fast as I made a left on Main Street and swerved around an elderly couple crossing the street from Guadalajara Restaurant to get to their car. I left them gaping after me, but alive. I floored it through a stop sign. I hung a hard right on Franklin.

I knew what would reassure Grandpa that I'd be all right. "I've already left a message with Gabe. He'll help me. He won't let me meet Mitch alone, either." I drove past some boarded-up apartments or motels. My mind tumbled through what I knew about Mitch, picking out fragments. Selling sex toys. Using Zack to steal the necklace. Killing Zack. His anger when I spoke to him on the phone in Angel's bedroom.

In my ear, Grandpa said, "That's good that you called Gabe. Anything specific you want me to look for on Mitch?"

Something stirred in my memory, then leaped up. Mitch had said, *Zack didn't grasp the importance of the details. It's not about fucking the mark. Any man with a functioning dick can do that. It's the finesse!*

But what did it mean? How could that help? Details—OK, I got that Zack had put the necklace in the wrong sex-toy kit. And I understood now that "mark" meant the victim whom he meant to steal the jewelry from. But what about the "functioning dick" and "finesse"? What—

Wait! "Grandpa, can you find out how long it usually was between the Casino Thief's jobs, and then when was his last job before stealing the necklace from the lady at Daystar? I have an idea, but I don't have time right now." I was thinking we were wrong about why Mitch had needed an accomplice.

"I'll find it, Sam."

"I'll call you soon." I hung up. I pushed speculation on

Mitch and his reasons for having an accomplice out of my mind for now. Desperation to find Zoë, get the necklace, and save Angel pressed down on my lungs until I could barely breathe. I passed by a sprinkling of small houses. Then there was only dirt broken up by the ribbon of Franklin Street.

Lots of places to dump dead bodies. Like Zack's.

Or Angel's.

No, she was not dead. That wasn't going to happen to Angel. I wouldn't let it. Her biggest fear was of being abandoned, of dying alone. I would outsmart Mitch. But first, I had to get the necklace.

I took a left on a street that had a name, but I didn't give a shit what the name was. I wove through the back way until I came to the Night Haven Motel.

I had two options. Vance had told me that Zoë drove a green Ford Focus. I could see if I could spot the car, hoping she had parked it in front of the motel, or I could go into the office and make them tell me which room Zoë was in.

Worst case—I'd pound on every door. Or call her and hope I could hear her cell phone ring through the door. That might work, too. I pulled into the parking lot and drove past the office. The motel was a two-story terra cotta building with bright teal doors.

I had found the dead body of my friend in one of those rooms.

I shoved that thought away. No more dead bodies. All I had to do was find Zoë. There were three white cars, two blue, a burgundy, and—

There it was—the green Ford Focus. Parked toward the end of the lot where the motel butted up against the freeway. It was the third unit from the end. The blackout curtains had a two-inch gap that showed a strip of light.

I had an idea. I looked over at Ali. "OK, girl, we're

gonna lie our way in. I want you to stay with me." I was afraid to leave Ali in the car. What if Mitch showed up and killed her? That wasn't so far-fetched, since Mitch seemed to be one step ahead of us at every turn. Vance had seen two cars, a green Ford Focus and a black Lincoln Navigator, at my house this morning. I was sure now that Mitch drove the Lincoln Navigator and that he had been at my house to put the tracking device on my car. He could have spotted Zoë and followed her to the motel, or he could have put a device on her car just for some kind of insurance. I was confident he hadn't seen Zoë with the kit or he would have gotten it from her already.

But he could come to the motel to tie up loose ends. Especially if Zoë had seen him. Maybe he had even figured out that she had taken the necklace by then.

Fear yanked a noose around my guts.

No time to dick around. I reached past Ali and got my purse off the seat. "Come on," I told my dog.

She followed me out. I could see she was favoring her right front shoulder. I needed to get her to a veterinarian to have her checked out.

No time.

I quietly shut the Jeep door but didn't lock it. Ali followed me without complaint to the door of the room directly in front of the green Ford Focus. I pulled out my stun gun, then I dialed my phone and put it to my ear. "Sit, Ali." She sat by me.

"Hello?"

"Zoë, it's me, Sam."

"Do you have R. V. Logan with you?"

Lying was easy, to save Angel. "Yes."

"Put him on the phone. I want proof. I'm going to ask him a question about his book that only he would know, so this better not be a trick."

Lunatic. Probably anyone who read his books could answer whatever question she came up with. "OK, but first can you do something for us? See, R. V. Logan doesn't want anyone to see us. Can you open the door and look outside? Is anyone outside by you?" My heart banged in my chest.

The silence was suspicious. Finally Zoë said, "But he's not here yet. Why don't I look when you are closer?"

Now she was being logical. "We'll need you to look again when we get to whereever you are." I kept turning away from the door to talk, hoping Zoë wouldn't hear us from inside her room. "But can you just check now? I'll put him on the phone while you do that."

She sighed and said, "OK."

Please let me have the right room! I dropped the phone into my purse to keep my hands free, turned on the stun gun, and watched the door.

While listening in case another door opened.

The door in front of me started opening. I flattened myself against the wall. The door pulled open five inches. Then seven inches. Then it swung open.

I stepped up.

Zoë's dark eyes widened in surprise. "Wh—"

I put the stun gun to her temple and zapped her.

She slid to the ground.

I looked around and didn't see anyone. Ali started sniffing Zoë, so I pushed her away and stepped over Zoë into the room. Bending over, I hooked my forearms under her shoulders and noticed that the undersides of my arms were bloody. From tripping over Angel's purse into the street.

Not my biggest problem right now. I took a breath and dragged Zoë's unconscious body into the room. Ali followed me in and sat down to watch.

I rushed around her and closed the door. Then I looked around the room.

There were at least two dozen candles burning. The flickering light gave me a headache.

Find the necklace!

I took a breath and ended up inhaling a lungful of rose-scented candle wax. I went to the table by the window and blew out three candles. Then I faced the room. A double bed with two nightstands, each with four candles. I blew those out. The dresser across from the foot of the bed had—hell, I didn't even count the candles. I just started blowing them out and opening drawers to look for the sex-toy kit.

I got dizzy from blowing out air and inhaling rose-scented smoke.

I stood up and took a slow, steady breath. No sex-toy kit or diamond necklace in the dresser, and all the candles on top were out. I ran back to the nightstands and looked in those. No sex-toy kit.

I turned to the dressing area and bathroom.

More candles. Zoë had a serious obsession with candles. I headed for the dressing area. First, I blew out the candles ringing the sink, and then I started looking around for the sex-toy kit. No sign of it.

"It has to be here!" I rushed into the small bathroom. It was basically a shower and a toilet. The tub was filled with water and . . .

More candles. It was a wonder the smoke alarm didn't go off. I leaned across the bathtub to blow out the candles. Then I stood up. Where the hell had she hidden the sex-toy kit?

I left the bathroom and went to the closet. It had mirrored sliding glass doors. I caught a glimpse of myself. My pink tank top was ripped from my falling in the street and streaked with dirt and blood. My hair was tangled, my face . . .

Forget it. I opened the closet. Ironing board and iron, a few clothes hanging up, and a suitcase. Maybe she had put the sex-toy kit in her suitcase. I grabbed the bright yellow midsize suitcase with wheels and yanked it out.

It was heavy.

Putting it on the floor, I dropped my purse off my shoulder and unzipped the suitcase. No sex-toy kit, but there had to be twenty or thirty romance novels in there. Why had Zoë been carrying those?

The romance conference. They gave away free books. Zoë hadn't gone home, but had come right here to Lake Elsinore to hunt me down and find R. V. Logan.

Lunatic.

I closed up the suitcase and shoved it back into the closet. Where was the sex-toy kit? Tears of terror and frustration burned my eyes. What had she done with it? I had to find that necklace!

Where else could you hide something in a motel room? I looked around. The bed. Remembering my purse before I could trip over it, I picked it up off the floor, slung it over my shoulder, and ran to the bed. I grabbed hold of the gold bedspread and ripped it off.

There were two pillows, white sheets, and a brown blanket. I grabbed the first pillow.

It was just a pillow.

I threw it aside and grabbed the second one. It was heavier. It had a rectangular lump on the bottom. I couldn't get my breath. Frantic, I reached inside the pillowcase and felt a velvet box. I had found the sex-toy kit! I pulled it out.

The blue-velvet box. The sample sex-toy kit. I opened it up. Everything was just as I had put it back that morning. I grabbed the big lavender vibrator and wrenched off the end for the battery compartment.

Nothing.

It was empty. A huge sob worked up my throat.

Ali barked, then growled. *Omigod, now what?* Dropping the vibrator, I looked over at Ali. She sat at Zoë's shoulder, growling at her.

I dropped my gaze to Zoë. She was awake. She wore the same long, gauzy skirt that I had seen her wearing in Smash Coffee. But she had a hand deep into her skirt pocket.

Did she have a weapon in that pocket? A cell phone? Her hair was loose and soft around her pale face. I reached into my purse to get my stun gun, then yelled, "Freeze, Zoë!"

Her whole body went stiff.

With the stun gun in my hand, I walked around to stand at her hip and face her. She had changed her top from the sleeveless yellow muscle shirt to a white peasant blouse.

All the better to show off the diamond necklace glittering on her neck. She was wearing the stolen diamond necklace.

It had been right in front of my face when I had stunned her, and I had missed it. "Get your hand out of that pocket and take off that necklace."

She pulled her hand out and fingered the necklace. "It's mine. Where's R. V. Logan? He likes diamonds, I know he does. In one of his books, the hero made love to the heroine when she was wearing only diamonds."

This woman had serious issues. But I supposed all dedicated stalkers did. I glanced over at Ali. She was waiting for me to tell her what to do.

As if I knew what I was doing. Desperation for Angel pushed me on. "Zoë, take off that necklace. It's stolen. If you don't, I'll just zap you and do it myself."

"No." She levered herself up on her elbows. "It sparkles in the candlelight. Hey!" She looked around. "What happened to all my candles?"

I stared back at her. "They were a fire hazard. Take off the necklace."

She leaned back on her elbows to stare up at me. "Know what I think, Samantha? I think you have a crush on R. V. Logan and you want him for yourself."

"I do not!" I yelled at her. Of all the stupid comments—

She moved so fast, it caught me completely by surprise. Dropping on her elbows, she rolled on her back and popped up to her feet. Then she spun around and caught me with a kick to my gut.

I dropped the stun gun and flew back onto the bed. Ali's fierce growls pierced my shocked pain-fog. Sitting up, I saw that Ali had Zoë's right wrist in her mouth. Her right hand was wrapped around the stun gun.

Zoë had locked gazes with Ali. I stood up and yanked the stun gun out of Zoë's fingers. I turned on the stun gun. "Release her, Ali."

Ali let Zoë's wrist go.

Zoë stood up and charged me.

I caught her in the temple with the stun gun.

She froze in place, then slid to the floor.

God, this woman was a royal pain in the ass. Quickly, I dropped to my knees and rolled Zoë over to her stomach. She must have weighed more than me! And all of the weight was muscle. If I lived through the night, I'd be lucky to stand up again after that kick I took in my stomach. I hoped all my organs were still attached. I got the diamond necklace unhooked from around Zoë's neck. I stood back up and shoved it in the front pocket of my black jeans.

"Come on, Ali." I went to the door, but then looked back at Zoë.

Was she safe here? What if Mitch showed up? What if she woke up, called the police, and they arrested me before I could save Angel? I hurried back to Zoë. Hell. I looked around the room, then got an idea. I went back to the suitcase with all the books. Sure enough, there was a roll of strapping tape. Every savvy conference attendee knows that she can snag an empty box at a conference, and all she needs to do is bring a roll of strapping tape. Then she can box up her free books and send them home for the cheap book rate instead of trying to stuff them all in her suitcase.

In fact, I'd have bet the two dozen books in Zoë's suitcase were the ones she couldn't get into the box she had shipped home.

I ran back to Zoë. She still wasn't moving. I gathered her wrists behind her back and wrapped the tape around them.

I was sweating and my stomach hurt. Hell, everything hurt. Breathing hard, I dragged Zoë to the door.

How was I going to get her to the Jeep and then inside the Jeep? She was taller than me and weighed at least as much as me. Shit.

This was a nightmare.

Maybe I had to take my chances and leave her there. I had to call Mitch and tell him I had the necklace.

Then he'd kill both Angel and me.

I was in over my head.

My phone rang. Where the was my purse? I looked around, shoving my frizzy hair off my face. It might be Mitch. I had to answer! Ali went to the bed and barked. She picked up my purse by the strap and dragged it off the bed and over to me. The purse must have fallen off my shoulder when Zoë kicked me and I flew onto the bed.

I took my purse and got my cell phone out. I loved my dog. "Hello?"

"Babe? Where the hell are you?"

17

"Gabe!" I said into my cell phone as I looked down at Zoë, who was out cold at my feet. The entire motel room swayed. "Mitch has kidnapped Angel! I have the necklace, but—"

"Sam, I've already talked to Barney. He filled me in a bit and told me the motel you're at. Tell me which room you are in. I'm getting off the freeway right now. I'll be there in one minute."

I sucked in a breath. Gabe was there. He'd help me figure this out and save Angel. "I'm in the room right in front of Grandpa's Jeep on the ground floor." I didn't know the room number. I had never looked. "I knocked Zoë out with my stun gun. Twice. I have to take her with me. I can't leave her here. Mitch might figure out that she had the necklace and kill her."

Silence.

Gabe was probably debating turning his big black truck around, getting back on the freeway and the hell away from me.

Finally he said, "I knew you wouldn't stay home."

Anger surged up inside me. "Yeah, that's me, always getting into trouble. Can't learn to stay home and let the man fix everything. Especially when the man is being an ass." It dawned on me that this might not be the best time to piss off Gabe. I needed his help.

I needed him.

"Open the door, Sam."

Ali stuck her nose in the door, whined, and wagged her long tail.

I glanced down at Zoë to see that she was still out cold and opened the door.

Gabe filled up the threshold. He turned off his phone and slid it onto his belt. Then he swept his dark gaze over Ali, Zoë unconscious and bound with tape on the floor, and, finally, me.

The impact of his stare made me instantly defensive. "OK! I screwed up and got Angel kidnapped! And now I'm kidnapping the romance fan from hell, except that I can't figure out how to get her to the Jeep! I know I'm a screwup. But I have the necklace. I can fix this." My eyes filled with tears. If I didn't fix this, Angel was going to die.

Gabe reached for me, dragged me into his arms and up against his chest. "I shouldn't have left you, babe. I was wrong." He let go of me to look down into my face. "And you are wrong. You are not going to fix this. *We* are. Got it?"

I nodded stupidly. My best friend was in mortal danger, and I was suddenly worried about how I looked. My shirt was stained and torn from the street, my face tear-streaked, and . . . "I look awful." I took a step back, determined to pull myself together.

He dropped his gaze in a slow search down my pink tank top and black jeans and back up. "This looks normal for you when you're working on a case."

I shook my head. "We don't have a case."

He flashed a small, smug smile. "Actually, we do. The woman who Mitch and Zack stole the necklace from hired me to get it back for her and bring the thieves to justice. Her name is Winnie Lange."

I blinked. How the hell had Gabe managed that in an hour? "Really? I have the necklace!" I reached into the front pocket of my jeans and pulled the necklace out. It shimmered in cold beauty. "But I have to use it to save Angel."

"We will." Gabe rubbed my shoulders. "We'll save her, Sam, but it won't be easy. Whoever Mitch is, he's been very slick as a jewel thief for a while. According to Barney's research, Mitch has pulled off at least a couple dozen of these jewel heists. Barney also had some information that he said you asked for. That is that the average time between the jewel heists attributed to the Casino Jewel Thief was about three to six months. Then they suddenly stopped for almost an entire year. The police speculated that the Casino Jewel Thief had been arrested on another charge and that's why the thefts stopped." Gabe stopped talking for a second and raised an eyebrow. "Why did you ask Barney that? Do you think Mitch has been in jail, or do you have another theory?"

His faith in me, his belief that I could put together clues into a possible explanation, gave me confidence. Both in my ideas and that we would get Angel away from Mitch, safe and alive. I started explaining, "Mitch's anger got me thinking. When I called Angel's cell phone and he answered, he said Angel and I would never outsmart him, that he knew women and had made a career out of women like us."

Gabe lifted an eyebrow and glanced down at Zoë.

OK, he believed in me but he also knew my tendency to get in over my head. "Gabe, Zoë's crazy. Don't untie her. I can't reason with her. She kicked me in the stomach after I'd stun-gunned her to get the necklace back. She didn't care that it was stolen; she's convinced that the necklace would be a turn-on for R. V. Logan." I had to keep him from untying her. We didn't have time to deal with Zoë's antics, and I had no idea how far she would go.

He nodded, and returned to the subject of Mitch and his certainty that he could handle women. "But you're not like other women. You or Angel."

Did he mean that in a good way or bad? "Right. I think under normal circumstances we would annoy him, but now we're driving him to a rage."

"Go on." He watched me with his dark eyes.

I wanted to frame this right, to make Gabe see what would be at stake for Mitch if I was right. "Well, what if Mitch took on an accomplice because he suddenly developed a disability that prevented him from getting close enough to the women to steal their jewels—but he didn't want his connected friends who buy the jewels from him to know about his disability?"

Gabe's face stayed blank. He reached down to pet Ali, who was sitting beside him. "You think that's why he took on an accomplice?"

I nodded. "Yes! He felt he had to so that he could keep up his reputation as a jewel thief. And the sideline of sex toys also fits his disability in a way."

Gabe reached out and touched my shoulder. "You've thought this through. What do you think this disability is? And why do you think he has it?"

A rush of nerves skittered through my chest. But I had to know what Gabe thought. If I was right, maybe it would help us save Angel. "Well, at Angel's house, Mitch was furious on the phone. He basically said that any man with a functioning dick could fuck the mark."

I spit it out fast. "We know that Mitch's method was to charm and seduce older women, probably get them drunk and wear them out with sex. Then when they were in a sated and alcohol-induced sleep, he walked out with their jewels. It was clean and simple, and I think it fed some superiority complex he has about women." I met his gaze. "But what if one day he couldn't get it up anymore?"

Gabe winced. "Ouch, babe." He let go of my shoulder and paced to the bathroom area and back. "You could be right. Impotence in someone like you describe might send him over the edge. And that would explain the year of no activity of the Casino Jewel Thief."

But how could we know for sure? "Gabe, the woman you just talked to, do you have her number?"

He nodded.

"Call her, let me talk to her. We know she slept with Zack the night her necklace was stolen. But maybe Mitch tried before Zack."

Gabe's dark eyes narrowed. "And he failed." He pulled his cell phone out and rolled through his address book. Then he put the phone to his ear. "Winnie? This is Gabe Pulizzi. I have a solid lead on your necklace, but I have to ask you a question."

I waved at him. "Give me the phone."

"Better yet," Gabe said into the phone. "I'll let my associate ask you. Her name is Samantha."

I took the phone. "Winnie? I'm Samantha Shaw. I need to ask you if you dated a man who looked a little like Richard Gere that you met at the Daystar Casino anytime in the last few months or so." I went on to describe Mitch as best as I could remember him.

Winnie said, "Well yes, a couple of months ago. It didn't end well."

She sounded like a nice lady. "I'm sorry to ask you this, but was he impotent?"

"Yes. How did you know?"

"We're still putting it together. Was he angry?"

"I had to insist he leave. I had a room at Daystar and threatened to call security."

"Thank you, Winnie. You've been a huge help. We'll tell you more as soon as we have solid information." I said good-bye and gave the phone back to Gabe. "It was him! He couldn't get it up and Winnie had to threaten to call security. She was staying at Daystar. So now we know he's impotent. And that he tried and failed with at least one woman. He reacted angrily."

Gabe slid his phone back onto his belt and prowled the motel room, keeping an eye on the unconscious Zoë. "So he comes up with a solution by taking on an accomplice. He hires a younger, more virile man to compensate, but Zack screws up. Now he has another problem, because he's told Zack enough for him to be dangerous to his connected friends. And, hell," Gabe stopped in front of me, "he might have hated Zack for being able to do what he no longer could. It would explain the rage and his compulsion to finish the job, to get the necklace." He fixed his gaze on me. "To beat the women screwing up his carefully laid plans."

I nodded. "Because he wasn't going to let Angel and me, mere women like those he is used to seducing and manipulating, get the better of him by getting away with the necklace."

"What about the sex toys? Are they supposed to replace his limp dick?"

I cringed at his word choice, but I had been thinking that. "Maybe. Or maybe it's his backup plan. He trains Zack to take over as the Casino Jewel Thief, and to the connected people he steals for, it looks like he just wants to retire. Then he will need another job—selling sex toys. And who does he try to sell the sex toys through? Another woman that he thinks he can manipulate—Angel."

Gabe's dark gaze locked onto me. I felt the tension of those long seconds, a connection between us, a bond. Then he shifted slightly and said, "It fits. In fact, I wouldn't be surprised if he was setting himself up to eventually demonstrate sex toys to more wealthy women and make off with their jewels."

A someone-walked-over-my-grave shiver pulsed up my spine. Two things, then, were driving Mitch: deep anger over his impotence and a deep drive to go back to what he loved: stealing jewelry from women. He was a man desperate to keep his identity. The kind of desperate that fueled rage and violence, and Angel was at his mercy. "We're out of time. I have to call him."

Gabe put both hands on my shoulders. "Which brings us back to Mitch's plan. He means to get that necklace back, then he has to kill both you and Angel. He's a very pissed-off man."

I could see the threat of danger to me stripping away the veneer of civility in Gabe. He was struggling with the animalistic urge to drag me to his house and handcuff me there where he could keep me safe. I tried to use a little of Grandpa's magician's diversion technique. "Maybe I can use his problem to talk to him. Be understanding, blame all the women for his problem, something to buy time." I took a breath and addressed his needs. "Time for you to get in there and save us. You know, like a hero."

He grinned. "Clever way to stroke my ego, so I won't notice you putting yourself in danger."

I shrugged. "Did it work?" I was going to save Angel. I just hadn't worked out the details so that Angel and I would get out alive.

His grin flattened. "No. But we'll figure out a way to get Angel. First, we have to find out where she is. I have a call into Vance. I'm assuming you didn't call him?"

I looked up at Gabe. "I called you. I told Hugh to call the police, specifically Vance, to tell him all that he knows. Including that Angel was kidnapped. I figured Vance was more likely to believe Hugh." I looked down at my watch. "We're running out of time." It had been fifty-five minutes.

He nodded. "Call Mitch from your cell. Tell him you have the necklace and ask where he wants to meet you to exchange the necklace for Angel. Be very compliant and anxious to please, except that you insist that Angel better be alive and well when you get there. Tell him that if it looks like Angel's been harmed, you will bolt right to the police with the necklace."

Fear churned up my stomach. I didn't want to screw this up, but I had to do it. I went back to the bed, sat down, and picked up my cell phone. Gabe sat on my right to listen in. I dialed Angel's cell phone, then both Gabe and I listened.

Mitch answered, "Do you have the necklace?"

"Yes." *Please let me get this right.*

"Ten minutes. You have ten minutes to get to the abandoned movie theater on Mission Trail or I start hacking off parts of Angel." His voice was low, slightly angry but confident.

He was sure he had me under control. "Wait!" I frantically tried to remember what Gabe had told me. "How do I know Angel's alive?"

"Hold on."

I heard a ripping noise, then, "Ouch, you stupid prick!"

My insides turned a sick liquid.

Gabe covered the mouthpiece of the phone and mouthed, "Tape."

Oh. Tape pulled off Angel's mouth. My stomach calmed down.

Then Angel came on the phone. "He's got a knife, a gun, and a problem with women."

"Angel! Hold on, I'll—"

Mitch came back on the line, "You'd better bring the necklace. Alone in ten minutes, or I'll start with that bitch's tongue. Come to the boarded-up door on the side of the theater."

He clicked off.

I jumped up and ran for the door.

Gabe caught me by my shoulders and came around to face me. "You are not going in there alone."

"He'll kill her!" I meant to scream the words but they came out a tortured whisper.

His face went cop hard and he bore his gaze into me. "You will do what I tell you, or I will handcuff you inside my truck and leave you behind."

Gabe didn't bluff. The dangerous man beneath the almost-civil exterior was in full view now. I knew he meant it. I fought to be as tough and calm as he was. "OK. But, please, we have to hurry!"

He let go of me and glanced down at Zoë. "We can't leave her." He went to Zoë and picked up her wrist. "She should be awake by now. Her pulse and breathing are fine. I don't have time to see if she's playing possum." He scooped her up in his arms. "Check outside, then open the back of the Jeep."

I yanked open the door, feeling a draft of cool night air. No one was outside, so I ran to the Jeep and opened the back. Gabe followed with Zoë and put her inside. Then he looked at me. "I need some stuff from my truck. Get in the driver's seat. Ali and I are going to hide in the backseat."

I started the Jeep while Gabe shut Zoë's motel door and

got some stuff out of his truck. He and Ali got in the back-seat. "Go, Sam."

I backed out, passed the motel office, then made a left from the motel parking lot to the street. I was shaking so hard, it was an effort to steer the Jeep. "What do I do? I have to go in the theater." I made a right turn onto Railroad Canyon Road.

"Drive past the theater and turn around, dropping me before you come back to the theater. Then I want you to drive in and spend a few minutes searching around the Jeep for the necklace. Put it on your neck for safekeeping. Spend at least four minutes. Get out with Ali, then call Mitch on your cell phone. Tell him you are there at the theater, but that you need him to tell you how to get in. If he says anything about Ali, we know he can see you. If he gives you a hard time about her, tell Ali to wait outside."

He wanted me to stall and keep Mitch distracted. "What if he kills Angel? I don't want Ali to get hurt, either. What are you going to do?" I got into the left-hand turn lane, which would put me on Mission Trail. There was a McDonald's on my right and across the street on the left was a Burger King. Neither one of those could satisfy my desperate urge to get to the theater and find Angel. We had to get there in time. We had to save her.

Gabe's voice floated up from where he was crouched on the backseat as I made the left turn. "Kids break into that theater once in a while. I tracked a runaway who tried to hide in there. I know a way in that I am banking Mitch doesn't know about."

It was dark, after eight now, so few cars were on the street. I braked for a red light. On the right was the Thrifty's shopping center and the stoplight let people leaving that center make a left-hand turn.

If I got into the left-hand turn lane, that would take me

between the boarded-up buildings that were once the town's Kmart and movie theater. I struggled to keep my thoughts focused and organized. "So once I get in, what do I do? Give him the necklace?"

"Stall as long as it's safe with the necklace. Fumble with the clasp around your neck, that kind of thing. I'll be there, babe. I'm going to try to get in long enough before you to locate where Angel is. But I won't let Mitch hurt you."

I shuddered, and felt Gabe's hand settle on my shoulder from the backseat. The light turned green. The movie theater slid past, a silent, boarded-up ghost of Lake Elsinore's past. Of one of the big dreams of a bright future that Elsinore had a nasty habit of chewing up and spitting out.

God, I loved this town. It took real guts—fortitude—to live here.

I drove past the next traffic signal, then made a left turn onto a dark street. My hand shook when I put the Jeep in park.

Gabe opened the door, got out, and came around to my side and opened the door. "It's been only five minutes. Lock up and wait here another few minutes. Then take as much time as you dare when you pull into the theater parking lot." He leaned down and kissed me. Not a fast brush, but a seconds-long kiss boiling over with emotion.

Then he was gone, melting away into the dark shadows. I pulled the door closed and locked it. Ali made her way through the seats to climb into the passenger seat next to me. I reached out to my dog. "He'll be OK, right, Ali?"

She licked my hand.

I looked over at her. "How's the shoulder?" My dog never complained. Mitch was going to answer for hitting my dog with his car.

Ali sighed and found a comfortable spot on the seat to lie down on.

I looked at my watch. Two more minutes. I counted to one hundred and tried not to think about Zoë Cash bound up with tape in the back of the Jeep.

I would go to jail for kidnapping. My head throbbed in time to the fearful pounding of my heart. Swear to God, I never meant to get into this much trouble. It just happened. All we did, Angel and I, was take what we thought was a sample sex-toy kit from a seemingly legitimate businessman.

OK, in hindsight, it was possible we should have been a little more careful. I started the Jeep. Maybe Angel and I had been a little reckless in accepting a sample sex-toy kit from a stranger in a casino. But Angel didn't deserve to die. Alone, scared, and thinking her life had meant nothing.

I made a three-point turn and then a right on Mission Trail. At the signal, I turned right into the parking lot of the boarded-up buildings.

I didn't see anything. No cars, no lights. Behind the abandoned movie theater was the Lake Elsinore Resort and Casino rooms. But I doubted they could hear much. The theater had been soundproofed to play the movies and not bother the people in those rooms.

I turned right toward the theater and stopped. Where was Mitch's car? It could have been behind the theater, but Gabe had told me to stall. I knew the boarded-up door that Mitch wanted me to use to get inside the theater. It was the side door that faced the other boarded-up building that once had been a Kmart. In case Mitch was watching somehow, I put the Jeep in gear and crept to the front of the theater, then around the far side. Once there, I looked around, working to get a confused expression on my face.

Then I turned the Jeep around and went back to the front. I idled there, and made a show of bending down and getting my purse. I fumbled through it, then put it back. I looked around the Jeep.

Was Zoë awake in the back? I hadn't heard anything.

Finally, I leaned back against the seat and lifted my hips to get my hand into the front pocket of my jeans. I pulled out the necklace.

There wasn't much light, but the cool necklace glittered. I carefully unhooked the latch, then slid it around my neck. Bending my head down, I secured the latch.

A quarter-million dollars around my neck, yet it felt like a hard, dead weight over my collarbones.

I reached across Ali again to the floor of the passenger seat and pulled my phone out of my purse.

Ali lifted her head and watched me.

I looked at her amber eyes in the dark car. "I have to do this right." I dialed the number to Angel's cell phone.

Mitch answered, "You better be here."

My heart kicked up to a furious throbbing. Fear and adrenaline roared in my ears. "I'm here. In the front. I have the necklace. But all the doors look sealed with boards." I glanced at the front of the movie theater. The marquee had only a few letters remaining from when it had read: *This Theater is Closed.*

His voice was calm now, cooler and suave like it had been in the casino. "Very good, Samantha. Pull around the left side of the theater, the side that faces the other boarded-up building. Do it now."

Here we go. I glanced over at Ali. She watched me with her bright eyes. I inched the Jeep toward the edge of the theater, then turned right. I stopped at the door. It looked solidly boarded-up. There were a couple of big splotches of white paint to cover up graffiti; tagging was a fair-sized problem in this town. I took a breath. "OK, now what?" I wanted to scream at him that Angel better be OK. But I knew Gabe was in there, and I wanted to keep Mitch focused on me.

"Get out and walk to the door."

"Uh, I have my dog with me."

"The dog that chased my car?"

I had to fight down the sudden hot urge to scream at him that he'd hit my dog and I'd get him for that. "Yes. You . . . uh . . ." *Keep him distracted, don't get him mad,* I reminded myself. "She was hit by your car. She's not a threat."

"Leave the dog in the car."

I reached over to stroke Ali's head and said, "Stay here." She didn't like that and sat up to watch me. I hoped she'd obey me.

I got out of the Jeep and pushed the door to make it look closed, but I didn't latch it. Then I turned and looked at the boarded-up door to the theater. To Mitch on the phone, I said, "Now what?"

"The outside board will swing to the side. Push it and step inside."

That sounded like the kind of idea that ended in murder. From the cocky confidence in Mitch's voice, I knew he thought that he'd already won. "Uh . . . why don't you just meet me at the door. I'll give you the necklace and you release Angel."

"Or I could start cutting Angel up."

"No!" I fought down panic and remembered that I needed to keep Mitch distracted so that Gabe could find Angel. Maybe he'd get her out to safety, then help me deal with Mitch. "I'm coming in." My natural cowardice felt like a huge hand tugging at my back, trying to get me to turn around and run like hell. I fought down the urge and forced myself to walk to the door.

It looked like the board was bolted in several places. I reached out to the right edge and shoved.

It moved. The bolts were either fakes, or they had been cut through. My hand shook, but I pushed the board far enough to see inside.

It was one of the theater rooms. There was a glow of light to my left. I squinted and tried to see it.

"Come inside and let the board fall back." Mitch's voice came from behind that light.

I stepped in and let the board go. It slammed back into place. I blinked, trying to get my eyes to adjust. A new beam of light hit my eyes. Instinctively, I put my hand up to shield my eyes and backed up a step.

"Hold your arms out to the side."

I had left my purse in the Jeep. With only my jeans, a pink tank top, and the diamond necklace, it was pretty easy for Mitch to see that I was unarmed. I held my arms about a foot away from my sides and squinted to see into the light. "Where's Angel?" Directly in front of me, I could see shadows that I figured had to be the rows of theater seats that faced the screen.

"Walk forward."

Was Gabe there? Where was Angel? I tried to remember what the theaters had looked like. They had been simple. Screen up front with an exit door to one side of the screen. That's where I had come in. Then rows of seats—hadn't they been a red or burgundy? I couldn't remember. Projection room in the back.

I took a step forward. I tried reasoning with him. "Mitch, let's not make this any worse than it is. It was an accident that the necklace ended up in the sex-toy kit you gave us. We didn't even know we had it. Then someone took it from me, not realizing there was a diamond necklace hidden in it."

The voice behind the light said, "It was incompetence. But Zack paid for that."

I stopped walking. I had to buy time for Gabe. Had he gotten in? Was he trying to find the theater we were in? There were four movie screening rooms, I thought. God. Dust coated my tongue and tickled my nose. The air smelled putrid, like decay. Maybe a small animal had died in there. Revulsion rolled through my stomach.

"You're wearing the necklace."

Startled, I looked directly into the light, then winced. "Yes. It seemed the safest way to get it here. I didn't want to take any chances. I just want this whole thing to be over."

"It's a lovely piece, that necklace. The mark wearing it was a dried-up old biddy. I should never have sent that kid to do a man's job." He sighed.

I thought I heard a noise from my far left.

Mitch swung the light away from me, sweeping the beam across the seats in a leftward motion until it landed on Angel. Silver duct tape secured her wrists to the arms of the seat in the front row and there was a wide strip of tape across her mouth. Now that the light was out of my eyes, I could see Mitch's back as he searched for the noise.

He was between Angel and me. Angel appeared to be watching us. Was Gabe with her? I couldn't tell. If he was, she didn't give anything away.

I had to distract Mitch. He had that powerful flashlight in his left hand and a big gun in his right hand.

I didn't have any weapon, so I used words instead. "But you had to send another man, didn't you, Mitch? Your wanger is on the blink. It doesn't rise to the challenge." I held my breath, counting on him not wanting to damage the necklace by shooting me before he got it off me.

18

Mitch's long elegant back went rigid beneath his dark-colored shirt. He turned slowly, the aura of the flashlight catching the silver streaks in his dark hair. He kept the flashlight pointed down. "My *wanger*?" His Richard Gere face sneered. "Wanger. What else could I expect from this hick town? You people are a bunch of hillbillies. Wanger." He sighed.

I took exception to his comments. Lake Elsinore was the poor cousin to the surrounding areas like Temecula, Murrieta, and Corona. Lake Elsinore had all the raw materials to be a fast-growing resort town, but the character of the town resisted mightily. Those of us in Elsinore were a little sensitive to criticism. "Since you're so sophisticated, let me be more specific. You either can't get, or can't hold, an erection that is required to seduce a woman with all the romantic trappings, including enough wine or champagne to get her drunk so she sleeps through your stealing her jewelry and your escape." I took a righteous breath of anger and added, "I have a college degree." OK, it was just a two-year AA degree from Riverside Community College, but it was a degree. I had to keep Mitch's attention on me.

Where was Gabe? What was he doing?

Mitch dropped his gaze down to my breasts, then lower, then crawled his stare slowly back up. "Impressive—looks and deductive reasoning . . . and yet I'm the one who will walk away with the necklace. Now, let's get down to business. Take off that necklace. I want you to set it on the armrest of the first seat on your right."

Gabe had told me to stall, so I kept trying. "But what—"

Mitch raised the gun to point at my face. "Now. I'm done playing with you. Get that necklace off."

"All right." I tried to sound reasonable. I reached up behind my neck and fumbled with the clasp. My hands shook. I strained to listen, but all I heard was the roar of my own fear pounding in my ears.

And it smelled in there. The stench of rotting meat . . . or something like that. Ugh. I breathed through my mouth, trying to get my shaky fingers to work the clasp behind my neck. To show Mitch that I was cooperating, I took a step toward the row of seats.

My right foot hit something.

"Oh!" I let go of the necklace clasp and struggled to catch my balance. The toe of my right foot was wedged beneath something heavy and the momentum pitched me forward. My knees landed in a mass that gave a little beneath the impact and my hands hit the threadbare dirty carpet. Because my knees were higher than my hands, my butt was up in the air.

The smell was worse down there.

I had a bad feeling. A sick, greasy, horrible, fall-into-an-occupied-grave feeling. I turned my head to the left to see what my knees had fallen onto.

Zack. I'd found Zack. I was kneeling on a dead man.

A painful scream rocketed up my throat.

Another scream came from behind me. "I want my necklace! It's mine! Give it back now!"

The scream in my throat froze as I recognized the voice. "Zoë! No! Get out of here!" How had she gotten free? I scrambled off Zack's stomach, yelping when a something pointy bit deep into my right hand. It was a nail sticking out of a board that was on the ground next to Zack.

"Sam, watch out!" Angel yelled.

I looked up in time to see Mitch sighting his gun on me. It slammed into my mind that if Angel had yelled, then the tape was off her mouth. Which meant Gabe had to be there to have gotten the tape off her mouth.

Mitch must have had similar thoughts, because he turned his gun from me to Angel.

I looked over in time to see Gabe throw his body across Angel just as Mitch fired the gun. The loud bang and flash stunned everyone for a breath of time.

"Christ," I heard Gabe groan out the word, then he was gone from view. Just melted down to the floor. He must have had ahold of Angel's arm because she slid off the chair and was gone, too.

I didn't know if Gabe had meant to escape to the floor, or if he had fallen from the shot. But I knew he had been hit.

A dark, ugly, vicious need to kill Mitch for shooting Gabe roared up from deep inside of me. I grasped the long board and scrambled up off the floor. The board was about a half inch thick, two feet wide, and four feet long. I felt a stream of blood from the nail I'd caught my hand on roll down my arm. All I cared about was Gabe. I had to get to Gabe, and that meant going through Mitch.

Mitch was rushing to the left, looking for Gabe and Angel. I ran after him.

A vicious growl rose up behind me. Ali! She must have followed Zoë out of the Jeep. I had left the driver's side door unlatched.

"I want that necklace!" Zoë screamed from somewhere behind me.

Two feet in front of me, Mitch skidded to a stop and started to turn around. He still had the gun he'd shot Gabe with.

Ali ran up even with my left leg and stopped, dropping to a crouch. Her growl was a deep rumbling noise that made the hair on my neck rise. "Down, Ali!" I yelled at her. I didn't want Mitch to shoot her.

At the same time, I turned to my right, lifted the board so that the flat part was parallel to the ceiling, and swung hard. I pivoted left on my foot, leaning everything I had into the board.

That bastard had shot Gabe.

The edge of the board caught Mitch in his side just below his left arm. It cracked hard into his ribs and sent him flying into the wall. I didn't see the gun.

The impact dug dozens of splinters into my hands. I dropped the board, desperate to get to Gabe.

Ali launched herself from her crouch right at Mitch. He had hit the wall and slid down. He wrapped his arms over his middle and doubled over. Ali bared her teeth at his throat.

"Hold him, Ali," Gabe yelled, rising up from between the second and third rows of the theater seats.

I blinked, wondering how he had gotten there. He had a dark river of blood running down his right arm, but he was alive. Where was Angel? That was my last thought as I was tackled from behind. A mass of weight hit me in the middle of my back, throwing me into Mitch and Ali.

"I want my necklace!" Zoë wrapped both her arms

around me and squeezed. She had powerful arms, and a closed pocketknife clenched in one fist. It flashed through my mind that the pocketknife was what she'd had in her skirt pocket. Stupid! I hadn't checked even after seeing her fishing around for something in that pocket back in the motel room. She'd been able to cut herself free of the tape.

Ali rolled out from the pile of people and barked in furious agitation. Mitch was trapped beneath me, and Zoë was on top of my back. She let go of my middle to grab hold of the necklace and started yanking it, trying to get it off my neck.

I ignored Zoë and her efforts to shred the skin around my throat with the necklace. Mitch was squirming beneath me and I didn't know if he still had his gun or not.

"Damn it, Zoë, let go!" I bellowed as she jerked the necklace, snapping my head back.

Mitch got both hands free and reached up to wrap them around my throat. But he was having trouble getting a strong grip with two women rolling around on top of him.

How the hell had I become a victim sandwich? I thrashed around, trying to throw Zoë off my back and at the same time get my right elbow into Mitch's injured left side. Finally, the necklace broke, and my head snapped down into Mitch's face. My elbow slammed into his side.

"Fuck!" Mitch screamed, his arms wrapping around me in spite of the pain he had to be in.

"Ali, here!" I heard Gabe roar the command. And then, Gabe said, "Let go of her *now*!"

I stopped fighting Mitch and looked up. Gabe knelt beside us with a gun shoved up against Mitch's temple, pointed in a direction away from me.

He didn't look at me. "Turn your head, babe. This will be messy."

The cold steel in his voice sent a shiver down my spine. I saw his face, his eyes. Black and feral, not a trace of the semitame man Gabe usually presented to the world. He would shoot Mitch through the head, and was calm enough to tell me to turn my head to avoid the gore.

Mitch let go of me.

"Move," Gabe said.

I crawled backward off Mitch. I wanted to yell at Gabe not to kill him if he didn't have to, but I couldn't get the words out. I was worried about his shoulder, too. He was losing a lot of blood. It had to hurt like a bitch.

A set of hands helped me to my feet.

I looked up. "Angel." She was OK. Her face was strained, and there was a raw red mark around her mouth from the tape that had been pulled off.

She hugged me. "Gabe couldn't get to his gun. Ali picked up Mitch's gun and brought it to him."

I loved my dog. I looked around to see where she was. I was shocked to see Zoë sitting with her back against the wall. Ali sat a foot or two from Zoë's left hip with the broken necklace in front of her right paw, along with the closed pocketknife. Zoë's intense brown eyes glared at Ali, then at the necklace on the floor. Every time Zoë made any kind of move toward the necklace or the knife, Ali pulled back her lip to reveal her wickedly large teeth.

I looked back at Gabe. He had Mitch on his stomach and was in the process of handcuffing him. Or trying to. It looked like Gabe was struggling to get his right arm to work properly. I let go of Angel, went to Gabe, and knelt beside him. "You hold the gun on him." I took the cuffs and snapped the bracelets around Mitch's wrists.

No one in the theater doubted for a second that Gabe

would shoot Mitch if he moved. When I was done, I turned to Gabe. "How bad is the wound?"

He met my gaze. "I'll live. I wasn't so sure about that when I saw Mitch turn the gun on you. My gun had flown out of my hand when Mitch shot me. I was dragging Angel under the seats with me and we couldn't find the damn gun." He closed his eyes, a raw and desperate expression passing over his face. "Then Zoë attacked you and I knew Mitch was going to kill you."

I put my hand on his forearm. I needed something to put pressure on his wound.

Gabe opened his eyes and looked at me. "I'd have found a way to free you from him, one way or another, but Ali brought me his gun."

I smiled. "And you brought me Ali. Remember?" Gabe had given Ali to the boys and me when we were in danger from some bad people my husband had cheated.

Angel handed me the blanket from the Jeep. "Put this on Gabe's wound. The police are here."

She had had the presence of mind to run out to the Jeep and get a blanket for Gabe even after her ordeal of being kidnapped. God, Angel was something. "OK. Thanks." I moved to Gabe's side to get a better look at his arm. Ugh. There was a big ugly jagged gash across the outside of his biceps. I didn't think the bullet was in the arm, but the wound was deep. To Angel, I said, "Tell the cops we need an ambulance."

"No." Gabe growled the word.

I carefully put the cleanest part of the blanket on the wound and pressed. Gabe jerked at the pressure, then held still. I looked at his face. Pale. The sheer adrenaline that had kept him going was draining away. "You're going to the hospital."

He shook his head.

God, he was just like the boys. "Interesting, considering all the times that you dropped me off at the hospital and left. There was always some pressing business that couldn't wait. I had thought I was pretty low on your priority list."

I saw a small smile twitch his mouth.

"But now I think I know the truth. You're afraid of hospitals."

He ignored me and looked toward the boarded-up door.

I looked over and saw Detective Vance come through with several uniforms. All of them had flashlights and their guns were drawn. "Vance," I said, "over here. Mitch St. Claire is in handcuffs. Gabe's been shot. And Ali is watching Zoë."

"Who is this?" Vance's voice snapped out the question.

I glanced back again and saw him standing in front of the first row of seats, staring down. An involuntary shudder quivered from my gut outward. "Zack. He's not missing anymore."

Vance looked up over the rows of seats to me. "What the hell happened in here? Why didn't you call the police?"

I looked up at Angel. "Can you hold this for me? Don't let Gabe bully you either."

Angel knelt down and took over.

I stood up and felt at least a dozen aches and pains. I had to stop getting knocked around by criminals and crazies. A surge of adrenaline pushed it aside, and I stalked by Ali and Zoë, pausing to say, "Good job, Ali." Then I went up to Vance. "We did call the police, Vance. The first time, when Zack broke into Angel's house, the second time, when he threatened her with a gun, then when I found the diamond necklace in the sex-toy kit, then when Mitch firebombed Angel's car, and finally, when we found Zack dead on her bed, remember?" I took a breath. "Oh wait, you didn't believe us." That had felt like a betrayal. Sure,

Vance and I had a complicated relationship, but did he really think I'd steal a diamond necklace?

His eyes zeroed in on me. "You weren't exactly credible, Shaw. Angel's kidnapped, then she's not. There's a man with a gun in her house but no sign of forced entry. Your friend's in financial trouble and her car's conveniently firebombed and totaled. You call in a body on the bed and then the body's gone. Bodies don't get up and walk out."

I looked down at Zack. "This one did, didn't it?"

"Evidently," Vance muttered. Then he sighed. "Hugh Crimson called us and spilled his guts. What a mope. He told us all about Mitch, giving him the key to Angel's house and putting the tracking device on Angel's car. I did manage to get out of Hugh that Mitch had mentioned this theater, which is what led me here." Vance looked around the old theater and shook his head. "No wonder Angel told the background investigators that her ex is a lying sack of shit."

Vance had once been furious at me for not believing in him. Now the tables were turned. "You should have believed me, Vance."

His gaze did a slow search down my face, to the battered tank top and lower, then back up. "I never know with you, Shaw," he said, his voice dropping to a throb that was unique to him. "I can't pin you down. You're so fiercely loyal, I thought maybe you just couldn't see . . ." he trailed off.

"That my best friend was desperate?" Guilt slammed into me. "You'd be right. But Angel's not a thief or that desperate for money." God, I had failed Angel. It hurt me to face it. She had been torn up and worried about her mom, draining away most of her money in desperation to help her. I did believe Angel that she had money coming in and would be OK financially. But money wouldn't fix her old guilt.

That's what friends were for—to ease the pains we carry around inside of us.

And Hugh had twisted that knife in her. Where I had failed Angel was letting her feel alone and guilty. "Gabe thought the same thing you did, too. At least he did for a while."

Vance narrowed his eyes. "Yeah, well, you gotta admit that whole story about a romance fan stealing a sex-toy kit with the necklace inside of it was crazy. But we were running down recently rented green Ford Focus cars . . . just in case you were telling the truth."

In case I was telling the truth? That was supposed to make me feel better? I turned around and saw that two uniformed cops had Zoë on her feet and handcuffed. Another uniform had a first-aid kit that he was using on Gabe, while Angel and Ali watched.

I turned back to Vance and said, "Come here." I walked to Zoë.

Vance followed.

I stopped in front of her.

Vance came up behind me and said to the two uniformed cops, "Go watch the body. The ambulance will be here any second. Keep them as far away from the body as possible."

One of the cops handed Vance two bags. One had the diamond necklace, the other one the small pocketknife that Zoë had cut herself free with. Then the two cops walked away on their squeaky shoes.

I said, "Zoë, I'm keeping my promise. This is R. V. Logan."

I turned to Vance and caught the frozen look on his face. "And this," I gestured to Zoë, "is your biggest fan."

I turned around just as Zoë screamed her joy and flung herself at Vance.

Now all I had to do was convince Gabe he was going to the hospital.

Blaine picked Gabe, Angel, and me up from the hospital in his Hyundai. Gabe was very cooperative, even though he was scrunched up in the backseat next to me. He had his head resting against the window, asleep.

I'd lost count of the stitches it took to close his shoulder.

When we got to Gabe's house, I was stunned to find Grandpa and the boys there. Joel ran up and flung himself at me as I got out of the car. It hurt like hell, but I didn't care. I hugged him. "Hey, Joel," I eased him away. My stomach hurt from Zoë's kick in the motel room, followed by her tackle in the theater, but I was more worried about my son. "I'm OK, you know that, right?"

His face was strained and white. "Is Gabe OK?"

I nodded. "The bullet grazed his arm. He had stitches, but he'll be fine." I looked back over my shoulder. Blaine was helping him out.

I looked over at TJ. He had opened Angel's door and was helping her out.

My throat closed up. With my arm around Joel, I watched TJ help ease her out of the car, then say, "Angel, you really scared us." When she was standing, he gently hugged her.

Affection like that didn't come easy for TJ. But he seemed to understand how badly Angel needed it.

Angel looked over TJ's shoulder at me. Her eyes filled with tears, but she smiled and hugged him back. She let go and said to both TJ and Joel, "Your mom and Gabe saved me."

"Boys," Grandpa called from the door. "Bring Angel, Gabe, and your mom inside."

We all went into the house and gathered into the family

room/kitchen. It smelled like chicken noodle soup and cheese. Ali walked over to us. She was stiff but seemed OK. Grandpa followed her. "She's fine, Sam. Bruised shoulder. Vet said she will be fine."

I let go of Joel and hugged Grandpa. "What are you all doing here?"

He hugged me back, then let go. "Best place for Gabe to rest."

Then he went over to Angel and hugged her. "We didn't want you to go home yet. So the boys and I will camp out here in the family room. Angel has the guest room." He turned back to look at me. "You can take care of Gabe in his room."

Gabe came up beside me. "Your family invaded my house."

I looked up at him. His gaze was still a little hazy and he didn't look all that steady. "Yes, they've made themselves at home." I couldn't tell if he was annoyed or not.

He moved his head up and down slightly. "Good."

My gut eased. "Are you hungry?"

"I'd be more hungry if I wasn't drugged." His gaze sharpened slightly on my face.

"Probably." I took his good arm and led him to a kitchen chair. Because I was a frequent patient at the emergency room, I'd managed to get a doctor to inject Gabe with a tranquilizer right away. It had taken a few minutes for Gabe to realize it hadn't been a pain shot, but by then, it was too late. He was pissed.

Too bad.

Grandpa came to the table with a big mug of soup. "Thought it'd be easier for you this way." He set it down in front of Gabe. "Grilled cheese sandwiches coming right up."

TJ and Joel brought more mugs of soup. Angel and

Blaine sat down with us. Ali came up and put her head in my lap. I petted her head and wondered for the zillionth time how she could be so smart.

Grandpa and the boys crowded in and the seven of us, plus a dog, packed in around Gabe's kitchen table. I wondered how he really felt about it, but he'd have to live with it tonight. I wasn't leaving him alone. I wasn't sending Angel home alone, and I wasn't going to send away Grandpa and the boys.

I loved them all.

Blaine would probably go home, but he was part of my family as well.

Joel was on the other side of Gabe and said, "Gabe, how did you get shot?"

He turned to answer, but Angel jumped in from where she sat on my left. "He shoved me back in my seat and jumped in front of me. If he hadn't done that, I'd be dead." She picked up her mug of soup and sipped it.

I had seen it, and knew it was true. But hearing it made my entire stomach roll over. I could have lost both Gabe and Angel that night. I pushed my food away. I felt Gabe's eyes on me, but I didn't look at him. I focused on Joel. "Both of them are heroes. Gabe saved Angel. He had her untied and got her away. Angel figured out who was feeding Mitch information. I pretty much screwed up the whole thing."

Joel stared at me, his blue eyes wide. "Grandpa said you took that guy down with a board."

I shook my head. "That was desperation and fear. I knew Mitch had shot Gabe. It made me crazy."

Gabe took hold of my hand. "Your mom didn't screw anything up."

Angel added, "The reason Mitch was able to get the

drop on me to kidnap me was my fury at Hugh. Your mom had warned me not to let my feelings for Hugh distract me. That's exactly what I did."

I turned to look at her. "But when I said that, I hadn't realized how deeply he was involved."

She settled her green eyes on me. "But you were still right. If I had stepped back from my feelings, I'd have been more rational. We could have put it together faster, and gotten Vance a lead he could run with. Sam," she said as she reached out to take my other hand, "this wasn't your fault." She looked into my eyes. "And I knew I wasn't going to die alone without anyone fighting to save me."

Gabe let go of my hand and I reached over to hug Angel. "God, Angel, I hope you will always know that."

She hugged me back. "TJ and Joel said they'd watch a movie with me until I fall asleep. I want to sleep out here with them. Barney can take the guest room."

I was sure that she was looking out for my grandpa. He was getting older, and sleeping on the floor or couch wouldn't be easy for him. But she loved Grandpa, so that was her right to look out for him. I nodded. And she did love my boys. I believed that she wanted to watch movies with them.

Blaine looked around the table. "I'm going home." He looked over at me. "Boss, I'll be in the office early. We have a lot to do before the open house."

Regret snaked though my upset stomach. "Blaine, we have to cancel that." I loved Heart Mates, but I cared more about Gabe and Angel. They both needed time to recover, and I was going to take care of them.

But I also longed to get back to work on finding people the heart mates they dreamed of.

"No!" Gabe and Blaine said at the same time.

"I agree," Grandpa offered, then he stood. "Sam, help Gabe to bed. The boys and I will get the dishes. And we'll take care of Angel. I'll come get you if we need anything."

Gabe's room was simple. Rustic pine dresser, twin nightstands, and headboard for a large king-size bed. From the hallway entrance, the bed took up a good portion of the right side of the room. Straight ahead, then to the left, was the bathroom. I went to the dresser and started looking for a pair of sweatpants or shorts.

Gabe didn't protest as I helped him out of his jeans and into the shorts. I pulled the sheets back. "Sit here." Then I got out a pain pill and an antibiotic for him. I filled a glass of water in the bathroom, and I came back into the room and handed them to him.

He took them.

I was worried. Gabe hadn't said much. I took the glass and asked, "Are you in a lot of pain?"

"No. Come to bed, babe." He looked up at me and frowned. "Get a T-shirt out of my dresser."

I looked down at my clothes. The pink tank was toast. That happened to a lot of my clothes. I went to the drawer and found a folded blue T-shirt. Gabe was neater than I was. I pulled off my shirt and tried not to make a face at the aching pain in my back and stomach. My hands were sore, too, so I was careful when I peeled down my jeans. I slid the shirt on over my head.

"Take a pain pill."

I looked at Gabe. "I don't need one. And I'm not taking your prescription."

He stood.

I backed up and hit his dresser. "Gabe, I'm fine. I took some Tylenol—"

He reached out with his left hand, catching the light

blue shirt I had just pulled on. He was surprisingly strong for someone who had been shot. "Take a pain pill or I swear to God I'll force it down your throat. I've taken a few kicks and tackles like you did from Zoë. I didn't miss the cuts on your hands either. I heard you refuse pain medication at the hospital. If you hadn't had me tranquilized, you'd have damned well taken the pain medication."

I saw it in his face. The raw determination. I reached over and took out a pain pill. If Gabe needed something, I'd wake up. But the truth was, my family was there. Someone would hear Gabe if I didn't. "Fine, but I'm not sorry I had them give you the tranquilizer."

He let go of my shirt and watched me take the pill. I set the glass down. "Now will you get in bed?"

He turned and went back to the bed. I helped him lie back and got in on his left side.

"Sam."

I reached over and turned off the light, then lay back. "What?"

He reached out his left hand to wrap his warm fingers around mine. "Thank you."

I wasn't sure what he meant. "For being here?"

His voice was thin and raw. "For understanding. About the hospital, I mean."

I closed my eyes in the dark night. I knew Gabe had a problem with emergency rooms. He had once raced to one hoping that by some miracle the rescue squad, and then the emergency room personnel, had saved his wife and baby.

But they had been dead on arrival. His world had died that day.

And Gabe had blamed himself. Emergency rooms reminded him. I knew it, and he accepted that I knew it. I squeezed his hand back. "Thank you for understanding."

I felt his small smile in the darkness. "That you love me?"

My mouth was dry. "That I love you."

19

Word was out that Gabe and I had cracked the Casino Jewel Thief case. That drew even more people than I had expected to the Heart Mates open house. The office had been filled with a sea of people all evening. I stood in the reception area chatting with a few people.

"Boss, ten minutes to the last showing of the promotional video in the interview room."

I turned around and looked at Blaine. For the open house, he had worn a pair of black slacks and a short-sleeved button-down shirt hanging loose over his pants. His brown eyes glittered. Much of the credit for our success that night belonged to Blaine. We had signed on seven new clients, and at least a half dozen others had expressed interest. "I'll be there, Blaine."

Blaine moved off to mingle. Gabe broke away from several women. He was dressed in black on black, complete with a black sling. He looked hot. Dangerous and hot. Women had noticed and surrounded him all evening. Now his gaze locked onto me. "Excellent turnout, babe."

I smiled. "I'm sure the mention of the open house in

the newspaper helped." It had been mentioned in the article about the Casino Jewel Thief.

His eyes smoldered. "I can't believe I had you in my bed last night and didn't get you naked and panting. Now that I see you in that dress, I'm going to have to remedy that."

My breath caught. I had on a red halter dress. It was cocktail length with an uneven hem. I looked around, but no one had heard Gabe. A few women had their eyes on him though. Let 'em look. "Listen up, hunk. You are on injury leave. Now behave yourself."

He arched an eyebrow. "Sorry, sugar, but I made you a promise."

"What promise?" He was making me forget we were in a public place.

He leaned into my ear and whispered. "Handcuffs and sex toys."

His words and scent stirred up a fiery heat in me. "Back off, stud. I have work to do." I took a step back from him to keep from melting into a puddle at his feet. "I told Blaine I'd watch the promotional video he made."

A loud voice cut in. "Sam! Yoo-hoo!" Linda Simpkins called out as she came in the door.

Gabe caressed my bare shoulder. "I always keep my promises, babe." Then he turned to go chat with some drooling women.

I turned to Linda and saw that she was wearing her black blazer. Uh-oh, she wore that blazer in her role as the PTA president. Which meant that she probably had just left a PTA meeting and was here on a mission. I swallowed a groan and managed to say, "Hi."

Linda was flushed and excited. "Sam, now that you have solved the Casino Jewel Thief case, I have an idea."

I had to head her off. "But you see, because I was away from work, I'm more busy than ever—"

"Sure, but it's only a few nights. Besides, people would pay money to dunk you. We're getting community leaders to volunteer for the dunking booth. And you are a community leader now." She pasted on a big, huge smile.

Dunking booth? Oh no, I was not going in a dunking booth! *Think! What's my excuse?* Wait, I was a grown woman, a professional woman. I didn't need an excuse, I just had to say no. "I'm—"

I stopped talking when Fireman Bob sauntered up. He was carrying two glasses of wine. "Samantha, I thought you and your friend might like some wine."

Perfect! "Thanks." I took a glass. "This is Linda, Bob. Sorry to rush off, but I have to find Blaine." I turned and hurried toward the interview room. Whew! It was wrong of me to pawn Linda off on Bob, but I was pretty sure Bob could handle Linda. Who knew, maybe *he* would want to be in the dunking booth.

A man stepped in front of me.

Stopping, I put my businesswoman smile on and looked up. Right into Vance's brown eyes. "Vance!" I took a breath. "Uh, I'm surprised to see you here."

"I would think so, after you dumped Zoë Cash on me." His glare was menacing.

I tilted my head, watching Vance. "You deserved it." Mild hurt curled in my chest. As much as I tried to dislike Vance, there was a part of me that did like him. He looked good. From his tailored suit right down to his expensive shoes. "So is Zoë outing you?" I had to admit to a flash of regret about that. Maybe I liked keeping Vance's secret of being a romance writer. *Bad girl, Sam.*

He dropped his gaze into his wine for a second, then sighed. "Zoë and I came to an understanding. I didn't file any charges against her, and I promised her an entire set of signed first edition R. V. Logan books. And a signed copy of every future book released. Provided she doesn't reveal my secret or pop up anywhere that I am."

She was that easy to get rid of? "Uh-huh. Did you sleep with her?" *Very bad girl, Sam.*

He sipped his wine and said nothing.

Damn. "I take it she's not going to press kidnapping charges against me?"

He flashed his dimples. "No. Given that she stole the necklace from your house, she was in a precarious position."

I figured as much. "Congratulations, Vance, you get credit for breaking a major case." In the cop world, the work Gabe and I had done didn't count as much as Vance's arrest of the Casino Jewel Thief. "Did Mitch talk?"

"His real name is Scott Smith." He smirked. "It really is Smith. And he's talking. Got himself a good lawyer. He'll be cutting a deal and turning over some real interesting characters."

"Mob connections?" I still couldn't believe it.

"On both coasts." The arrogance melted from his face. For several long seconds, I saw the man behind the cop. "But that wouldn't have been worth finding your dead body in that theater."

My stomach clenched. "I had to go in there." I met his gaze. "You would have done it if you'd been in my shoes."

For a second, Vance looked at me in understanding, and then he shrugged it off. "I would never have taken a sex-toy kit from a stranger in a casino in the first place."

Angel walked up wearing a stunning emerald green gown with a killer slit up the back. "What about Hugh?"

Vance's face tightened in disgust. "He could face some charges for putting the tracking device on your car leading to the car being firebombed, but his defense lawyer daddy will get him off. I doubt he'll have his job left at the security company when we're through investigating, though."

Angel nodded, then said, "Hugh's dad called me. He wants to pay my mom's medical bills."

Vance's voice went cop-hard, "In exchange for getting charges against Hugh dropped?"

She smiled at him. "No. Because he's always been a decent man. Sorry for the moron that is his son, but he loves his son. He would have given me the money if I had asked before any of this happened. I forgot that."

I took Angel's hand, understanding. She had people who loved her and would help her. "Don't forget again."

She smiled. "I won't."

I turned back to Vance. "So we're done?"

He slammed his gold-speckled brown gaze into me. "Done? You and me? I doubt it." He turned and left.

"That cop's walking around with a boner for you."

I damn near choked on my wine. "Angel!" Then I burst out laughing. Angel was Angel and I loved her for that. "I have to go watch Blaine's video. Are you coming?"

She grinned. "I'm going to go hang around Fireman Bob. I think I have a fire I need him to put out." She sashayed off.

I watched her for a second and thought, *Go get him, Angel.* It was time for her to let go of Hugh. If Bob could help her do that, I hoped he would unroll his fire hose and go to work.

The interview room door behind me opened. "Boss?"

"I'm coming, Blaine." I turned and went inside. We had set up twelve folding chairs for people who wanted to watch the video. The oak table was pushed into a corner and had wine, cheese, and coffee on it. Blaine indicated a seat up front next to him. I passed several people I knew, including Linda, Dom, Grandpa, TJ, and Joel. Blaine turned on the tape.

I sat back and watched. Blaine had done a fabulous job.

I was in some shots, but mostly he showed clients and couples happy with Heart Mates. It was a fast-moving six-minute video, complete with music. As the music faded, I felt so proud I nearly cried. Blaine and me, we were a hell of a team. We were going to succeed with Heart Mates. I had to look down to regain my composure. Then I looked back up to the TV screen.

Omigod! My heart tripped so that a second of air locked in my lungs.

There I was in full color—the picture that Dee had taken of me. Caught snooping in Gabe's office, holding that envelope, and my clothes rumpled and stained from the fight with Zack in Angel's house. My face was a frozen shot of guilt.

The caption read: *Samantha Shaw caught red-handed while pursuing her beloved hobby of snooping.*

Laughter broke out. Hard, gut-rolling, can't-breathe laughter.

I looked over to my *ex*-assistant sitting smugly on my right. "You are so dead." I stood up and had to fight back a smile. OK, damn it, it was funny. Gabe had gotten his revenge.

And where was Gabe?

I didn't care how injured he was, that man was going down. I looked at Blaine. "Where is he?"

Blaine stopped laughing and reached into the breast pocket of his shirt. "He's next door." He held out a key.

I frowned at the key. "Next door where?" I took the key. "What's this?" I already had Gabe's house key.

Blaine looked bored. "He's in the office that was just leased."

I looked down at the key, then to the picture of me on the TV screen. The one where I was holding that envelope. There was supposed to be a lease agreement inside that envelope. Then I looked at Blaine. "Gabe leased that suite. And you knew it."

A pleased smile cracked his face.

"Men." I stalked out of the interview room, passing a few stragglers who hadn't left yet, and went out the front door. Turning left, I stopped at the door of the suite next to mine, stuck the key in, and opened it.

Inside, it smelled of musty air scented with warm vanilla. "Gabe?" Fear tickled the back of my neck. I'd just walked into a dark building the night before and nearly lost both Gabe and Angel.

"In here, babe."

The fear left at the sound of his deep voice. I went in. There were two candles burning on top of a card table, and a bottle of wine and two filled glasses. Underneath the card table was a lantern set on low. Next to the card table was a brown leather couch—just like Angel's. Gabe sat on the couch. He had his right arm in the sling cradled in his lap. His left arm was stretched out on the back of the couch. I stopped a few feet from him. "That looks like Angel's couch."

"Angel had it repaired for you. We figured it would be too crowded in Heart Mates to bring it in for the open house so we left it here for now."

I fought down a smile. That sounded like Angel. But I was here to yell at Gabe for publicly humiliating me at my open house. And leasing the suite next to mine in secret. "Really? Then get off my couch, Pulizzi." If he thought that the sling was going to save his butt, he didn't know me very well.

Gabe rolled up to his feet and towered over me. "What's the matter, Sam? You look upset."

I narrowed my eyes. "I look better than I did in that picture."

He did a slow search with his eyes, down and back up my red halter dress.

"Stop that." It pissed me off that he could turn me on when I was trying to be mad. And maybe I was a little scared. What was Gabe up to? "Let's talk about why you leased this suite without talking to me."

He quirked up his eyebrow. "You saw the envelope with the lease agreement inside it."

"I didn't open it."

He grinned. "Only because my assistant showed up before you could figure out how to open it without me finding out. Then you ran off my assistant."

"You fired her," I pointed out.

Gabe's eyes hardened, his nose flared, and his mouth thinned. He reached out, picked up a glass of wine, and polished off half of it. Then he looked at me. "No one gets between me and you when you are in danger. Dee knew the rules."

I shivered. For a flash, I saw the primitive man in Gabe, the street fighter with his own brand of justice. I stuck my hand out and snagged the remaining glass of wine. Taking a sip, I knew I wasn't afraid of Gabe. It wasn't fear of him that trembled through me, but fear of the depth of our feelings for each other. It wasn't supposed to be like this— the soccer mom and the dangerous ex-cop.

But it was. And I knew what he meant. I'd felt the exact same thing when I realized Mitch had shot him and was going to finish him off. My brain had slid into a kill-or-be-killed gear that I thought only existed for my two sons.

Gabe settled his gaze on me. "The end result is the same—I need an assistant."

I looked over my wineglass. "You're not making sense, Pulizzi."

"You have an excellent assistant."

Outrage reared up in my head. "You leased the suite next to me to steal Blaine? That's low!" A stab of guilt tore into my stomach. I couldn't afford to pay Blaine what he was worth. Gabe could.

"Jesus, babe, you are looking a little bloodthirsty. I'm not going to steal Blaine." He set his wineglass down, then reached out to cup my cheek. "He wouldn't leave you, you know."

I did know that. "Then how would you get my assistant? Do you think he's going to work for both of us? Run back and forth between suites? Use call forwarding?"

He caressed my cheek. "It'd be easier if we removed the wall separating the offices. Put Blaine in the middle and hire him help when the time comes that he needs it. I'll match what you pay him."

Stunned, I stood there trying to make sense of it.

Gabe took the glass from my hand and set it down. Then he reached out and pulled me to him with his good arm. "Is it that hard to trust me, babe? Take the leap—I swear I'll catch you if you stumble."

Oh, hell. My mouth was dry. I was taking a bigger step into Gabe's world, a world that fascinated me as much as the world of romance. I loved Heart Mates, but I wanted more. "You want me to train for my PI license."

He said softly, "It's not a matter of what I want. It's what you want. We already know you are going to make a success of Heart Mates, but is that enough for you?"

I reached up, touching his face. He had shaved before the open house. His face was smooth and taut. I could feel the tension in him. He was asking me to take a risk, but he was taking just as big a risk. "I want to do it."

The tension drained from him. He kissed me, a soft and gentle kiss. He broke the kiss and stepped back. "We'll start right now with some basic training." He reached to the small of his back.

And brought out a pair of silver handcuffs.

I backed up. "You wouldn't dare! Besides your arm is hurt. You have stitches." But he would, and I damn well knew it. I had to think fast.

Gabe kept my stare while dropping the cuffs on the table. Then he used his good arm and he pulled me into his hard body. "I won't have to fight with you, sweetheart. We're going home, and you are going to be very cooperative when I cuff you to my bed." He slid his hand over my hip. "Then show you my surprise."

I blinked, the heat of his hand making me hot enough to want to be at his sexual mercy. "What surprise?"

Against my mouth, he whispered, "Sex toys. And I have extra batteries."

His kiss didn't need batteries.